THE 8 BALL MAGIC OF SUZIE Q.

THE 8 BALL MAGIC OF SUZIE Q.

JODY J. SPERLING

ebook ISBN: [978-1-959613-02-2]

Paperback ISBN: [978-1-959613-09-1]

Audiobook ISBN: [978-1-959613-07-7]

Cover design by Ashley J.

Edited by Hilda Manard, Gissele Weaver, and Barbara Rosenthul

Printed in the United States of America

cre8 collabor8 Press, 309 N. Thomas Ave. Oakland, NE 68045

For David Paul Sperling
to whom every cat is Boaze Kitty

1 March 1937 - 28 February 2023

1

Since Lyle left, I hated breakfast, hated food, which couldn't explain why I spent the first two hours of every morning at Leo's Diner, down the block from my office, staring at the perfect egg, sunny side up, yolk so yellow it popped like a bullet to the brain. I think I always meant to eat, but I just couldn't get around to it. Nicotine and bourbon seemed to be my only companions as I pieced together what some would call a workaholic's existence and others would call an endless bender.

I recently wrapped a case for a gynecologist who lost—of all things —her cockatiel. As she was cutting the final check for services rendered, she told me if I didn't plan to ixnay the cancer sticks at least, breakfast was all that stood between me and an early grave. I didn't have the heart to tell her I've died ten times already, not that anyone believes me anyway.

Just as I was spiking my coffee with the last Magdalene from my flask, the bell jingled over the front door, and the neighborhood psychic walked in. If Janis Joplin and a 1950s Pan Am flight attendant had fallen into a taffy puller, the rope of candy shooting out the ass end would've looked nearly about how the woman who approached my table did. Her eyes popped behind glasses like librarians in a Tarantino flick might wear, and she had the sort of looks newly pubescent boys learn to avert their eyes from, lest they discover the meaning of blue balls.

Listen to me, getting all poetic. I beg your pardon. Perhaps I'd hit the bourbon too enthusiastically for eight in the morning. She caught me off guard when she—the psychic—helped herself to the empty chair opposite me at the table. "Let's pretend we don't know each other." She smelled like strawberry jam and hemp—the kind you smoke.

I flicked my lighter, not like I needed the practice. "Shouldn't be hard." Other than the occasional unsolved case where a client fired me and tried her hand at prognostication to learn if her husband was the cheating bastard she knew he was, the psychic and I had no reason to associate. She paid her rent, mine got paid too, when the landlord cornered me. Okay, that's not entirely true. Lyle paid up through the end of the year after he took the new job, as if that excused his betrayal. I twitched my hand in the general direction of her aura. "Crystal ball stopped working?"

The only thing more annoying than pious religious people are woo-woo peddlers, the ones who believe their bullshit and sell a future so vague it could apply to anyone. And in case you're curious, that includes politicians. Campaign promises can go fuck themselves.

Ms. Fortune Teller reached into her coat pocket and came out with two shooters of Magdalene. Would've cost her all of three bucks at Big Bear across the road. "For you."

No one ever butters you up for nothing. I sipped my coffee and made a point of not touching the offered liquor. "I don't break laws, and I don't give friends-and-family-discounts." You might think I was behaving presumptuously, assuming the lady meant to engage me for an investigation, but what kind of detective would I be if I couldn't smell desperation? "And I don't accept bribes." On second thought, I made like Houdini and disappeared the bourbon because thirst is elusive, and I'm a hunter.

"Suzie Q." She offered her hand. It was soft and white the way swans are supposed to be but never are. I held her grip a beat too long. When we broke she reached again into her pea coat, and I thought if she offered any more bourbon, I'd stick her with my breakfast ticket and make tracks, because that much booze would be a stand-in for guilt.

Instead, she produced a Magic 8 Ball. It had the heft of an antique. "This Eight-Ball says you're the one for the case."

These days, toys are made to break: flimsy plastic components, hasty designs, half-assed stickers. When I was a kid, you could shake the Magic 8 Ball, ask it if the sucker across the table from you ever had a concussion and brain her on the temple hard enough to make her see whole constellations before the thing said, *Chances are good.* Her 8 Ball was that kind—three pounds I'd bet. "Did it tell you my rate's four hundred a day, plus expenses?"

"I'll give you six hundred for exclusive rights."

Sandra came by with the coffee pot, asked Suzie if she needed a cup. Suzie shook her head. Sandra crossed her arms and narrowed her eyes. I told Sandra Suzie was picking up the tab so I'd take one of those fancy hot cocoas with the whipped topping and Hershey's chocolate syrup. That earned me a wink, and Sandra's winks are something I covet. If I haven't mentioned, Sandra's one of the few people I think of as a friend these days, and she may be the only person on this planet who can outsmoke me. She can squeeze a pack into an eight-hour shift and still serve twenty tables without anyone having to wait for refills. It's more magic than a stupid 8 Ball. That's for sure.

When she left to get my drink, I shot a sidelong glance at Suzie so she understood who was boss. "I've already got contracts with clients I can't break just to go exclusive, but I'll shelve the cold cases for seven-fifty." It was an egregious overreach, but Suzie'd done it to herself. Never offer someone more money before you start the negotiation.

My jaw almost came unhinged when she agreed to the fee. No haggling? Who has that kind of money? I needed a moment to collect myself. "It's a deal."

She stared at her hands for a moment so I thought my easy acceptance had given her a case of buyer's remorse. Was she having second thoughts? I knew she wasn't when she flicked her eyes back up. Desperation's more unmistakable than a smile. "Don't you wanna know what I'm hiring you for?"

The urge for one of those shooters began to crowd my thinking. At least that's what I'll blame it on. "Lady, for that kind of fee, you could ask me to quit smoking and I'd give it my best effort."

I was aiming for a chuckle, but her eyes held that bitter sadness. She fished a locket out of her purse. I wondered how some women carried such big bags all around. Probably it was a trend started by the chiropractic lobby. She slid the locket across the table. I took it between thumb and forefinger. With gentle pressure, I popped it open. Inside a picture of a firepoint Siamese stared cross-eyed into the middle distance. "His name's Boaze Kitty, but everyone calls him just Boaze."

Seven hundred and fifty big ones a day to find a cat? I didn't know whether to be insulted or flattered. Either my reputation proceeded me, or this was a new low—probably both. I didn't want to say something I'd regret, somewhat more challenging when your vocal cords are constantly lubricated with bourbon. "Excuse me for asking, but what makes Just Boaze so valuable to you?"

She swept her hair with the back of her hand the way people will at customer service employees to show impatience. "I guess you've never loved anyone?"

Suzie was sneaky good to look at, those soft angled features, sharp cat eyes, hair that teased a curl with shots of gray and gave her a distinguished air. I thought of Princess Buttercup, *You mock my pain,* but played it casual. "Loving animals never made sense to me, I guess. With them, you never have to earn it. Now, people on the other hand."

"The only thing that separates humans from animals is your state of mind."

I broke the egg yolk on my plate. It spread like so much blood. "Hannibal Lecter might agree." Something felt tangled to me. I swiped a wedge of toast through the yolk and took a big bite. Sometimes regret tastes like butter and egg. My stomach had all but given up on solids. "There's gotta be a better reason than some toy telling you to hire me to find your cat."

Suzie examined the 8 Ball. I swear it was respect I saw in her eyes. "For everything it is, it isn't a toy. Farthest thing from it." She shook it and told me to ask it a question.

It was the kind of thing you'd argue against longer than just giving in and playing along. "Why did my partner leave me for the governor's office?"

Suzie stopped shaking. She waited for the answer to appear. When it did, she smiled. "You must love her."

Before I could temper a reply my anger lashed out. "*Him.* Why does everyone always assume—"

"I'm sorry. You said partner, and I associate that word with same-sex relationships."

"We ran the agency together."

"Did he have feelings for you too?"

I'd spent the better part of the last months denying my feelings to anyone who came within throwing distance of such an observation, and maybe I was tired of lying. "Maybe. Once. On the second Tuesday of every month. I don't know. I think I thought he did. Fuck it. Your stupid toy." The little white triangle read *Reply hazy, try again.* "Why don't we cut the bullshit and talk business? I'm perfectly happy being miserable all by myself in the mornings, and I don't need you to remind me what I lost."

Suzie reached across the table, plucked up my coffee cup and drained it. It had to have been equal parts Magdalene and coffee. She drew her lips back and sucked air through her teeth. "Paint thinner." She replaced the cup. "The Eight-Ball doesn't answer questions about love, and it won't give you winning lotto numbers. Whether it knows the picks is a whole other question."

I weighed my options. Tease the psychic and risk losing the easiest money of my career, play along and know I'm the fool, or buy myself some time to get a little drunker so the answer would be more apparent. "I need a smoke."

Before I could move to stand, Suzie shot her hand across the table and took my wrist. "I need your help, detective Mia."

It should be universally obvious, touching me is an act of aggression, comes with the profession, but her hand vibrated at some primal level that made me feel sympathy for her. "A, call me Luke, and B, why do you need me if you've got that Eight-Ball you swear ain't a toy?"

Suzie released her grip. "Might be tough for a person like you to understand, but I love my cat. He's been with me over ten years."

I thought about the logo over Suzie's shop, had always thought it was a cat staring into a crystal ball, but zooming in on my memory of the silhouette, I spotted the upright glint of infinity—a cat and a Magic 8 Ball. "A person like me." I wanted to tell her I knew more about love than the Romance Poets, and don't act all surprised I know a thing or two about poetry. Anyways, I snagged a smoke and plucked it between my fingers for comfort, and perhaps a sense of urgency. "All right. Let's step outside. My lungs are burning."

You never hear anyone talk about the dying breath of winter the way they do about summer. There's no Indian winter, but whatever it was, the air had a crisp bite to it for being a leg and hip into spring. Smoke alerted my brain to the situation at hand. "So you feel too good for lost cat flyers or what?"

Suzie stood far enough away I knew she hated cigarettes. Too bad for her. She glanced down the street like she feared being watched. "He was abducted. Flyers won't help."

I flicked ash. "Someone break into your office? Forced entry?"

"Nothing like that."

"Family members got a grudge?"

"They don't know where I am."

"Fat chance." I rolled my eyes because people always think they can hide. Be me for a day, and you'll get why nobody is invisible. "If you had to pick, who'd wanna hurt you this way?"

"It's not my family."

She pushed the bridge of her glasses square to her nose. "Yeah, look, I'm an only child, my mom has emphysema so bad she's tied to a built-in oxygen line, and my dad is legally blind."

Where defenses are concerned, hers were pretty decent. "Maybe they hired someone?"

"I legally changed my last name to Q. twelve years ago, on my eighteenth birthday. Pardon me, but I just don't think they'd look that hard."

You can hang on to a pet theory just so long—pardon the pun—and it's time to move on. I finished my smoke and waved Suzie on. "Boyfriend?"

Suzie smiled. It was the unmistakable smile of sexual bliss. Right, right, significant others are more than a tingling in the G-spot, I get it, but I'm just the messenger. That smile said she was nesting with a patient Casanova type. She even twirled a lock of hair behind her ear. "He's run himself ragged helping me look for Boaze."

And case closed. He was guilty as a priest at a bar mitzvah. I'd explain how I knew, but you'll want the drawn-out story regardless, so let's cut to the chase. Just remember, guilty people work the hardest.

We stepped inside the entrance to our building, rounded the lobby to the stairs, and climbed to the second floor all while Suzie gushed about the man who finally appreciated her for who she was. I wanted to tell her she was missing the marquee for the back alley.

I stopped in front of my office door. It was time to scrape the glass pane and rename the agency. There was no more K in the M&K Detective Agency, but I couldn't bring myself to accept it. Love and denial must be bedmates in every life. "Hey, if that Eight-Ball is everything you say it is, let me ask it a question."

Suzie lit up like a penny slot, and I wondered if I'd regret asking. She thrust the thing at me. It was every bit as I'd guessed. I shook it and wondered at the smooth action. You couldn't feel liquid sloshing at all. "Did Ransom DeLonghi stop by my office two weeks ago?"

I held the 8 Ball out before my face and waited for the plastic cube to report *My sources say no*, but the thing surprised me. Maybe Suzie had a special button she could press, causing the 8 Ball to give a more personalized reply as a digital readout, because the response was not given on the white die floating in purple liquid. Instead, letters in the shape of an old-fashioned alarm clock printed across the display window, and as unnerving as the manner of the display was what it said: *With a sharp tool and pep in his step no less. Haha.*

2

Don't ask me how a person who cries over nothing and believes sweater vests are still a stylish choice can be trusted to counsel anyone, but ever since Judge Burnurd sentenced me to court-mandated therapy for my third DUI, I'd been visiting the sobbing shrink weekly.

He dabbed at his eyes with a tissue from the box perched in the most prominent spot on his desk as if drying your tears or blowing your nose could solve the most complex human grief. More often than not, he'd offer me a tissue a half dozen times in our forty-five-minute session, even when my eyes were so dry they practically scaled over. He motioned to the chaise lounge. "Have a seat...you look...unsettled on your feet...are you drunk already?" He always spoke like he had to translate his words from a foreign language on the spot, but when he assumed I'd bristle at his commentary he got double-choppy.

I sat. "You know, I just got a pretty big case, and I've been kicking around some leads. Might've skipped a wink or two. Maybe I've had a few nips this morning. So sue me." I studied the philodendron on the pedestal by the window. Some people have a green thumb, but this vine was in a whole other league, like an ad for Miracle Grow or something. Maybe he watered it with his tears.

He jotted chicken-scratch in his notebook. "And...any progress...in your dealings with Governor...DeLonghi?"

I scraped my index fingernail across an eyetooth. "Progress. Sure. I progressively hate her more every day." I think he expected elaboration, but I filled the room with silence because hate is fairly two-dimensional in that way.

He noted something else. The scribble of his pen enraged me. He studied me over his bifocals. "And...have you been...working on your visualizations...regarding Mr. Kulupchik?"

The visualizations in question...so listen, I can accept blame where it's due, because I'd been the one to bring the story of my pocketknife into therapy, and it's true I feel more deeply when drunk so I cried when telling how I'd lost it, but what really interested the therapist was my mentioning sometimes lying awake at night missing my knife.

Strictly speaking, the lying awake part is true, and not metaphorical. At least, I don't think it's metaphorical. The space between dream and reality can be slick. But so the therapist said I was projecting my feelings about Lyle onto the pocketknife, to which I asked how I could be projecting feelings when I'm actively speaking about Lyle whenever anyone asks, but he says the things I'm saying about Lyle are all the surface details I'm able to process, while the deeper feelings of abandonment and sorrow and loss, I'm embedding on the knife.

Until you've loved a knife the way I loved mine, I guess I can understand how you'd think my feelings about it were metaphorical.

I once even visited Bruce, the man whose leg I'd buried the knife in, in prison. He landed there of all things for murdering Nelly Strahpawn, the owner of the dance club where he'd worked. Shortly after, the club closed, and Omaha is a better place for it. Likewise, I sleep better at night choosing to believe justice doesn't, regarding the gravest of its violators, you know, sleep better. There's a story about Nelly I've told elsewhere, if you want to look, but I'd caution against it. She ruined lives, or did her damnedest to, and that should cover it.

But about Bruce, I was saying I'd visited him in prison to ask if he happened to know where my knife was. He vowed he'd no memory of it. I let him off on a technicality.

"Pardon me...miss Mia." The therapist tapped my knee with the end of his pen. I go places in my mind that are almost impenetrable. The therapist calls it PTSD aggravated by self-medication. I don't have a name for it yet. "Detective Mia!" He tapped again, more urgently. "I was asking...if you feel you have room...to appreciate how your former partner has taken an admirable promotion...as a reward for his saving the life...of our governor."

"Not my governor."

The therapist inked another note, offered me a tissue, and sighed. "You do know I'm required to provide...updates on our therapeutic progress...to your probation officer?"

"I'm not refusing to talk."

He waved his hand in my direction and blew at the air. "I might've called that progress...two months ago." He used the tissue I'd refused to dab his own eye. Perhaps he had a plumbing disorder causing all those tears. "Mr. Kushpuntik is...in a uniquely privileged position. There are career police officers...decorated Marines...and trained secret servicemen who—"

"Service*people*, thank you very much." Men are always trying to dismiss women. I ashed an imaginary cigarette. "We've been over this, all right. And can you tell me what kind of therapy it is where you tell me how to think over and over again until I agree I'm wrong and you're right?"

I think his cheeks flushed a bit at that. He cleared his throat. "I've never once told you...how to think...much less accused you of being wrong...but it is my job...to ensure you are confronting facts...and learning to process them in healthy ways...so you don't continue to self-medicate...and put others in harm's way."

The laugh caught me off guard, and I'll admit, it didn't help my case, but some accusations are so foolish they hurt. "What's really so wrong with having a few drinks while driving? I've never hit anyone, never been in a crash, never so much as failed to slow at a yield sign."

"It only takes...one time." He jotted while he spoke. "And I think... you're being too generous...with your self-evaluation."

"Would you say you think I'm wrong with my self-evaluation?"

"I'd...I'd say you want to trap me...in an irrelevant discussion about right and wrong...and I'd say that people don't get DUI's...for obeying the laws of traffic."

I stood just long enough to let my indignation ground and closed my eyes to keep my mood in check. "I haven't been pulled over while driving for almost twenty years, and that bastard cop used a bullshit excuse to make me take that sobriety test. It just so happens the handicapped spot was the best one for watching my mark that day, and I had my detective shield."

The therapist rose, presumably to mirror me in an effort to maintain an air of trust, though I'd never trusted him to begin with. He squared his shoulder to mine, a sign confrontation was the intent. "You were three times...the legal limit...in a running automobile with no paying client to justify your location."

"Details shmetails! I wasn't driving."

"You had to have driven...to get there in the first place."

"But they can't prove when I started drinking. Maybe I was stone so—"

"How many times...do we have to have this argument, Lucia?"

I refrained from yelling. "Until you admit the police have it out for me." I punched at the air. "No matter what you or anyone says, I know Marva DeLonghi's as dirty as a bucket of pig slop. Whatever spell she's got on everyone, I'm going to expose her."

The therapist raised his timbre to match, and I admired him for it. For being such a diminutive man, he had the skill to go bold with vigor. "You only say those things...because Mr. Kasparchuxic chose Governor DeLonghi...over you."

The dam broke and my anger poured through. "She stole him to make me miserable, and he was only ever there at the fucking mall because I told him where to go and who to look for, but no one ever gives me credit. I mean, the god damn guy escaped. Lyle didn't even catch him, but he's the hero, and I'm nobody!" My arms conducted a mad kind of symphony. "I'm called the drunken loose cannon who barely managed to catch fucking Magnus fucking Adderpaine before he slit his own throat to avoid taking responsibility for hiring Marva's would-be assassin. No thank you. He was the patsy. Marva set them all up then walks away, looking brave and heroic. I don't think so. She's filthy!"

My therapist sat, offering a sad smile. "What will it take...to move past this delusion?"

Look. The thing is, you get used to people thinking you're crazy. I'm not so detached from the everyday I forget I'd call me crazy if I hadn't gone through what I'd gone through, and the truth was, if I didn't pull it together, I'd never be released from mandatory therapy. If for no other reason, I needed to gather myself. "You're right. It's time for me to move on."

"You've said this before."

"Sometimes I relapse."

He offered me a tissue. "You've also said that...but...until you seek help...for your drinking...how can I believe you?"

I waved away the offered tissue. "AA's not for everyone."

"There's always Antabuse."

"That shit'll liquify your guts."

"No more than the bourbon...you're currently liquifying it with."

I didn't say at least the alcohol felt good doing it. "Look, I won't drink and drive anymore."

"And do you admit your feelings...toward your knife...symbolize your feelings...toward Mr. Ketchupnock?"

Why can't someone have a beloved knife? What's so different about a teddy bear and a pocketknife? "I'll openly admit I love Lyle."

"Then...I can admit...we're seeing progress."

3

I drank two long pulls off the flask before lighting a cigarette. The Lyft driver pulled to the curb. I glanced over my shoulder. The shrink watched from his third-floor window. I smiled and waved, *Fuck you very much*, motioned with my cigarette, to indicate I had to finish before the driver could whisk me away. The miserable bastard dabbed his eyes with a tissue, waved, and turned away, but I knew he'd keep an eye out.

"Lady, I'm not waiting around." The driver was burly as a turnip with pug dog eyes. I think the eye thing is tied to blood pressure but I'm no doctor. "Change of heart. Get out of here. I flicked him a ten-spot for his trouble then doubled back to the building where the third-floor windows had no vantage. As he drove off, I put in a *67 to the therapist's office. When his assistant answered, I said I was a mother and my son was actively suicidal.

When the call connected, I lowered my voice and sobbed incoherently. As the assisstant began to manage the situation, I muted my phone, jogged to my van, and fired her up, grateful she didn't backfire for once. Our Chevy Savana—I still think of it as Lyle's and mine— might not be the only one on its final life, but it was showing signs of cussed stubbornness I could relate to. As I pulled onto the interstate, the assistant told me the therapist would receive my call. When he greeted me, I gave him my best ditzy blond-mom routine. "Hey, like, just wanted to let you know, um, like, my son isn't feeling super down anymore, so like, I guess we're all better here, um, yeah. Buh-bye!"

A minute later my phone vibrated. I figured it was Dr. Weepy calling to tell me my trick hadn't fooled him, but it was a text message. Squinting, I brought the text into focus. Suzie Q. wanted updates on Mr. Pusspuss. I hit the microphone button and dictated a quick reply. "We'll find Just Boaze safe and well. Still on the trail."

Truth was, I'd done precious little for the fifteen hundred Suzie had so far racked up in charges. At the rate I was going, I might even need to offer her a moderate discount to keep my conscience from pestering me.

I cruised down Maple toward the office, smoking and leveling my chemical balance. It was unseasonably warm, and the open window reminded me of childhood summers watching Cubs Spring Training at HoHoKam Park, though I'll try to avoid boring you with tales of my youth.

There's a golden ratio of Magdalene to brain matter where everything seems manageable. As I rolled through downtown Benson, I decided to stop at Big Bear for smokes, planning to relax for the rest of the day in the office. Therapy is hard work.

Kendra was behind the counter. She asked about Lyle. I hadn't told her he'd left. She wanted to have his babies, and gave me free shit because of it. I said he was as rich and famous as ever. She giggled, which got me down, because I knew how it felt to feel warmed by the possibility of him. I hated how pathetically sentimental I'd become.

I got an extra handle of bourbon and a carton of smokes. She tossed in a few chocolate raspberry pies for Lyle.

Indiana Bob was over at the corner where Radial Highway and Maple Street intersect. He held his cardboard sign: *Jesus thinks you should buy me beer*. I gave him the chocolate pies and a pack of smokes. When he smiled, it swallowed half his forehead in skin folds. "You know, Lulu, you might be the only good person in this damn state. Hell, the whole world."

Why argue semantics? What's good anyway? "Would you still think of me as good if I killed an important person?"

He nibbled a chocolate pie and made a low rumbling sound in his chest. "Why they go ruining a perfectly good thing by putting fruit in it?"

I shrugged. He said a good person would call Rotella's and let them know chocolate was better without raspberry. I told him chocolate raspberry was Lyle's favorite. Indybob studied his last bite of pie like it had the answers to his deepest curiosity. "That's what makes you good and him not."

I passed him my flask. "I think you're biased cause I feed your addictions."

He drank a nip. "Lady Alcohol *is* a powerful persuader."

I mock-socked him in the chin. "Stay warm, Indybob."

He patted my back. "Stay good."

I gave him the kind of smile that said good was the last thing in my plans, which at some point had shifted from having a lazy day in the office to weighing the pros and cons of an assassination attempt.

I fired up the Savana like so much buckshot during duck hunting season. A leisurely cruise was just the thing to cool my head. An hour west on Interstate 80 with a bottle of Magdalene, a steady stream of smoke and an open window was just the thing to cure what ailed.

The sun illuminated quartz and mica in the blacktop, and if I squinted, I could almost believe the road was diamond crusted. Just beyond the Platte River a boar hurtled across the Interstate. Wild pigs are supposed to be a bad omen. My life had turned into a bad omen.

It almost seemed the van drove itself that hour west down Interstate 80, because when I pulled into the handicapped spot out front of the capitol in Lincoln, I hardly remembered how I'd arrived. I fished the binoculars out of the glovebox and glassed the main entrance. It was easy to imagine myself walking across that open lawn, up the granite stairs, through the giant oak doors, past security, up two flights of stairs, down a wide hallway, and into the governor's office. And then what, Luke? Guns weren't in my code of conduct and I wouldn't insult my true knife by replacing it. I was a detective without a weapon—nothing but the wit of my tongue and a decent haymaker if push came to shove.

Just idling there, though, relieved some of the pressure. I opened Twitter on my phone and asked the world what the ideal flavor pairing for chocolate was. You don't realize until you've missed a few days, how important sleep is. As I alternated between glassing the capitol, replying to the chocolate trivia, and sipping on bourbon, my eyes fluttered and I knew it was a bad idea to...

4

I rouse from the dream of a voice deep as the sizzle of tobacco and hot as molten rock. It says I'd died enough for this life. The voice booms from a figure both terrible and beautiful, an essence wrapped in smoke and bright as sunlight shadowed by cloud. It says death is final.

I thought it was the sudden cold that had lifted me from sleep, but the THUD, THUD! on my window mutilated that idea. Wiping drool from my chin, I hard blinked, in an effort to force out the drunken pins and needles in my brain. If you've never lived out of your car before, you might not know how a warm body will make the inside of the glass glaze with frost on a frigid day, and Nebraska is famous for having all 23 seasons in the time it takes to drink a can of Dr. Pepper.

Trying to start the car to roll down the window, I realized why it'd gotten cold. I'd left the engine running and used up all my fuel. I balled my hand into a fist and circled it on my window, expecting the cleared spot to show the face of a police officer. The public defender who'd represented me after my last DUI told me the next one would be life in prison. On the bright side, the cop wouldn't care too bad that I was driving on a suspended license given the worse charge.

What can I say? I've always enjoyed the bottle, but that doesn't make my decisions savory or even understandable. Maybe I should take my therapy more seriously.

The form on the other side of the door emerged as ice melted in rivulets. A sob caught in the back of my throat. I hadn't seen him in too long. And god he looked good. I'll say this about his job, the governor's office had led him to pack on a good twenty pounds of muscle, and it showed from his neck down to his elbows—less lanky and more ropey. He wore a black button-up and a slim fitting jacket unzipped. The fedora sat casual on his head. My Lyle.

As I opened the door he bit into a thick cheese burger. The grease and char felt something like a hug. I focused all my energy on not smiling, because I knew he wasn't down here to chum it up with me, and it took all of five seconds to set the stage for how he felt.

"Marv says this is it, Lu." He shook a box of Boston Baked Beans into his cupped hand, offered me some.

I declined, choosing instead a fresh cigarette. He reoriented himself downwind of me and nibbled on a string-cut French fry. I drew the smoke into my lungs, pulling it down to my toes. Not quite what I really wanted, but the best I could ask for. "It for what? She's admitted you're too good for her and need to come back to M&K?"

He bit into a bosc pear. "I make more in a day than we did in a month, huh." Juice ran down his chin, and he swiped it away with the cuff of his shirtsleeve.

What was the point in saying something like that? "Yeah, and you won't let me forget it every time you have Hy-Vee deliver a fucking load of groceries to the office."

"Telling me you don't need it." He made quick work of an apple, core and all.

My nourishment, much as it was, was cold bacon and eggs from Leos, usually snarfed between midnight and when I passed out, so the perishables usually did before I got around to them. "I'd rather have my partner back."

He swatted at the air like I'd said the most brainless of things. "Look, I was always trash there, and you know it." I went to hit the flask, but he caught me by the wrist. "I can smell you're drunk. Let's not make bad worse, huh?"

I ripped my arm away. On top of everything, Marva had reduced him to a respectable man. This was not how I'd imagined talking with Lyle after so many months. If I'd known he'd deal personally with me, I'd have maybe prepared some words.

He patted my elbow in a way I can only describe as brotherly. "See, Marv's ordered I take the camera down, so if you show up here drunk again, I'll have no idea, and that means you'll be the Lincoln PD's problem."

"Don't you realize that manipulating bitch is using you?" I meant to sound more composed, aggressive not defensive. Add it to my list of failures. I said some things about trying to look out for my friend, but they fell flatter than a newly minted dollar bill.

He popped a whole, hardboiled egg in his mouth. Flecks of egg white projected from his lips as he spoke. "Thing is, if you hadn't been a big part of saving her life, she'd already've cut you loose. From where I'm standing, she's already turned a blind eye to a heap of taxpayer dollars spent on your drunken antics."

I imagined slapping the face off that whore. She knew I'd been the only reason she wasn't killed at Regency Mall, but between her brainwashing and Lyle's appetite for approval, you'd be hard-pressed to find a person who even knew my name. "Hey, if she'd left well-enough alone, she'd've already forgotten my name."

Lyle made like he was doing me a favor not pushing back and ate a lemon drop. "Wanna hear something crazy?"

I shrugged. Nothing seemed crazy anymore. "Tell me the moon's made of cheese why don't you."

"Ask me before I took this job if there was a living soul who was more attached to a pocketknife than you, and I'd put money on no, huh?" He spat a cherry pit. A bit of red juice caught in the five-o'clock shadow on his chin. "But the other night, I was working late, catching up on paperwork and such, and I hear Ransom, the first man of Nebraska himself, on the phone going on and on about some knife, how he'd put it in safe keeping, but then, Marv comes storming in, and he fell silent as an empty grave. Swear to god, he's got a fixation he doesn't want her knowing about—but they hate each other so what's new, huh."

He wanted me to laugh, release the pressure valve, but a fish on a hook got itself in trouble. "Maybe Marva doesn't understand what loving someone or something is like, because she's a coldhearted bitch."

Lyle finished a fried roll and licked his lips. "What's your real problem with Marv, huh?"

Of all people, he doubted me, and I wasn't going to stoop to telling the whole story again so I gave him the second-best truth. "You did more good with me on one night, than you've done in all the time you've been with the governor's office." I couldn't say her name. Not then.

Lyle picked a few candied cashews from something resembling trail mix. His patience with me was spiking my blood pressure. *Get mad!* I wanted to know I could make him feel something. He explored his hands, empty for a change. "Debbie says she'd come back if you asked."

Debbie Lenvil once held my hand as I overdosed on sleeping medication, but she didn't remember any of it. She's, sugarcane kind. I believe she lived by her own permutation of an old Chinese proverb, *Save a life and you're responsible for that life.* She'd flipped it on its head. It was as if she decided since a judge had seen fit to convict her to life in prison for the murder of her husband she'd transferred her life to me when I discovered the evidence exonerating her.

I was ready to confess my undying love just to give Lyle everything he needed to put the knife through my heart, when a mass of seething bodies emerged around us. They raised oversized signs taped to broomstick handles, all written in the same chunky block-letter script. Whoever had put those signs together had determination, and a naked mole rat's eyesight. I pictured the hardware store that'd sold gallons of black paint and construction staples.

Lyle finished off a chicken wing and cursed under his breath.

In the near distance someone was piping Tom Petty into the crowd, and if you don't think he's a voice for social change, you aren't listening closely. True enough, they were all standing down the street in a line, and their faces were painted, obscuring the children they probably were. And they were dancing in the zoo that was the street south of the capitol.

As Lyle retreated, he told me to stay put. He'd send a detail to get me home so I didn't drive drunk. I meant to decline his offer, but the Savana had no gas, and my legs were weak with rejection.

From a break in the crowd Lyle called back to me. His voice inflicted equal parts pain and pleasure. "Call ahead next time, huh? We'll grab Leadbelly and talk like old times."

It was hard to imitate a smile and harder to wave back at him. I was starting to think we'd never work together again, and the thought made me a last-place racehorse at the Kentucky Derby.

5

GOATEE GUY AND MR. WHITE TEETH CONVERGED ON THE van a half hour after the cops and capitol security cleared out the flash mob protest. Mr. White Teeth smiled falsely at me as he dumped a gallon of unleaded from a red gas can into the Savana. Under Lyle's instruction he went to fill it—said he'd meet me at the office. Goatee Guy couldn't stop trash-talking the protestors. I kept my mouth shut to avoid trouble, which was an accomplishment given my blood alcohol levels. Goatee Guy drove us toward the interstate in a black Toyota Prius with tinted windows and a scanner radio that occasionally beeped and honked in its own private language.

When Marva's staff wasn't zipping around in battery-powered golf carts on nearby business, they drove their hybrid fleet around like Ms. America's solution to world peace. The Governor fit the capitol with solar panels and took every opportunity to boast about how she'd worked with local contractors from underprivileged communities to repurpose gray water for the lawns and gardens on all government properties. It didn't matter that every conservative in a 500-mile radius lamented the solar panels as eyesores on the architecture or that local businesses complained about the city smelling like hot shit during the summer. Marva DeLonghi meant to be so progressive even Greta Thunberg would squirm, and yet I suspected beneath the bravado and pomp, Marva's true plan was to enrage anyone who opposed her. The values she pretended to embrace were good values, but all she wanted was to laugh behind the backs of the people dumb enough to praise her. She'd just as soon betray an ally as buy off an opponent.

Oh, and did I mention state employees were "strongly urged" to participate in meatless Mondays, under threat of losing funding for beloved service programs if they refused to participate? Somehow that made people love her more.

If you kept your gaze superficial enough, Marva's cabinet looked like a CNN wet dream, but if you spent ten minutes around her people you could feel the rage and mockery oozing from it all. It's not jealousy that makes me say this. She'd built an elaborate fuck-you of values good people embraced, ones she claimed to support, and she enjoyed watching her opponent boil over at her. Though, miserable as all that was, I could've ignored all her two-facedness if she hadn't stolen everything I cared about, taken it from me and flaunted it, from the monthly letters she mailed to my office with lists of Lyle's accomplishments to the client referrals she sent my way. It was all done to boil my blood, and it worked. I despised her.

Goatee Guy hit the Interstate and treated traffic like a lawbreaker, flashers all the way. He set the cruise at one-twenty and bragged about it. Testosterone mystifies me at times, but when a man believes the speed of his car proves his testicular virility, I feel sorry for him.

We blazed past Sapp Brothers on the outskirts of town in under thirty minutes. As we approached the 72nd Street exit, light snow began falling. A day that began in the low 70s had devolved into frozen chaos.

Goatee Guy parked out front of my office. I managed a thanks for the lift, but before my hand gripped the handle, he asked if I wanted to grab a drink. It was a tough call. I weighed the pros and cons and decided he could get me warmed up with a double at Jake's.

As I sipped fancy bourbon and smoked my cigarette on the heated patio, dodging snowflakes and imagining a life where I wasn't the idiot, Goatee Guy told me about his ex-wife. I often wonder why divorced men think an ex-wife is a good topic to broach with a woman they hardly know, but he wasn't getting access to my pleasure cave no matter his tactics, so I humored him for a while—three drinks to be exact. That was when I feigned surprise and pretended my period had started. After keeping him waiting a quarter of an hour, I returned to the table and went on and on about the blood, how I thought I was probably broken because even supers couldn't contain my flow for more than twenty minutes. It seemed this got the point across, because he paid the tab and said he needed to get back to the capitol. I told him I understood. Work came first, and though I was looking forward to a good roll in the hay, as it were, I admired his dedication to the job.

He lingered on "a roll in the hay" a beat longer than I wanted, and I was already working out rebuttals if he decided fucking a menstruating woman was a turn on, when he took a phone call. Saved by Mr. White Teeth, who'd dropped off the Savana out back of the office. I wished him well and gave him the hotline for creepy men as my own phone number. I have it memorized. Call it if you want: (605) 475-6968.

As a cover for his reputation, probably because he'd recognized I wasn't into his big-dick-energy, he asked if I thought the bartender was lonely. I almost wanted to see him try it with her and find himself emotionally eviscerated. She did not suffer foolish men, and he was a true fool. Instead, I told him I thought Annie had standards. He opted to mop his wounded pride off the floor, tuck it in his pants pocket, and examine the backs of his thumbs.

His resolve seemed to sharpen, or his wounded ego needed honing. With a glow of challenge in his demeanor, he reminded me if I was found outside the capitol for any reason, I'd just as well punch my own ticket to three hots and a cot. His words not mine. I said we lived in a free country and I'd go where I wanted when I wanted. "So why don't you make like an egg and get the hell out of here before I beat the shit out of you."

A woman who will threaten a man with physical violence has the same chaotic power as a baboon in a cage, boundless rage forced into an orderly body. Mr. Goatee shook his head, gave his best chuckle with a casual breathiness, but he was ass in the air surrendered. I liked to think he'd run the odds of me getting in a couple good licks and having to explain to the dentist that a woman had dropped him with a 1950s haymaker.

He'd hardly scrammed when Annie rushed toward me. She was slim, endowed, pigtailed and drunk and didn't care who knew it. In short, I loved her like a sister. She said my date had stiffed her and felt I should know since we all knew what they say about men with small gratuities.

"What's that say about men who have no gratuity?"

She smiled, shrugging. "Can't imagine Lyle puts up with a shit guy like that." Her eyes went all computational as she considered something. "Look, I can set you up with a—"

"He wasn't my date, honey."

She folded her arms across her chest. Remember that part about well-endowed? Well I sometimes flushed with jealousy, because though my face had its charms, I pretty much lived in sports bras or nothing at all. Saved on the wardrobe expenses I suppose. But Annie's were perky and natural as a squirrel in a tree. I tried to sooth myself that where it counted, I had her beat, though. She tended bar, and I could still outdrink her, her sister, and her sister's mom combined, even on an empty stomach. She nudged my shoulder playfully. "A rabid bat? With a sex addiction?"

I rolled my eyes. "You get my point."

Annie moved in closer to get the conspiratorial atmosphere just right. "You know, Freud would say sex jokes are a one-to-one that you're carnally starved. Ever consider that?"

My problem was forced monogamy. Don't get me wrong. I wanted to fall for another man, get that carnal feast, but the heart wills, and the mind is no rival. "My date runs on one double-A battery, and I never have to fake pleasure, so I think I'm fine, thanks."

"Defensive humor. We're two for two on the Freudometer."

I wanted to diffuse the situation. "My not-date is personal security for Governor DeLonghi, and I was just trying to share a few bits of professional wisdom with him."

Annie's eyes got all dopey with infatuation. "You need to tell her! She deserves better than that asshole."

I've gotten used to people drooling over Marva. She deserved an

Academy Award for the way she'd enraptured the youth in our state, but hearing Annie rise to her support baffled me. I guess I assumed any woman who liked me would naturally hate my mortal enemy, and I know what you're thinking: it's sexist of me to give men a pass just because Marva's more than easy on the eyes, so I guess I'm currently failing that part of gender studies. I shrugged. "I'm sure she deserves exactly what she gets." I imagined wrapping my hands around Marva's neck and squeezing, blood vessels popping in her eyes, throttling until her tongue goes blue, and moaning with pleasure as her trachea snaps irreversibly, but the fantasy gave no relief.

Annie asked about Lyle. I'd somehow neglected, in the months since he'd hired on with everyone's darling, to mention I was flying solo. I guess when someone mentioned him, I always opted to pretend he was busy or sick or sleeping or with family or on vacation. Actually, I was running out of reasons for him failing to appear at the bar with me.

Her eyes got wide. "Paris? Why didn't you go with him?"

Why had I said he was in Paris? "The agency doesn't run itself, you know."

She bummed a smoke. Someone was waiting to cash out at the bar, but I didn't mention it, lighting her smoke for her. She inhaled. "Not like you have any major cases at the moment."

"Lost turtles don't find themselves."

She shrugged. "Don't tell me you're still taking Mrs. James's money for the turtle."

I had that feeling you get when the kidney stone first passes and you might as well have dropped your kidney into a smelting furnace. "Mrs. Burkley-James has more than enough to spare, and I've yet to get the sense the turtle is anyone's soup."

"Jesus, Luke. Do you ever feel anything? Like, I mean, emotionally."

I dug my wallet from my purse, if you can call the thing I carry a purse, plucked forty bucks from it, and stabbed it into Annie's hand. I folded my hands around hers and squeezed. "You got a customer, and there's your tip from the asshole not-date. Don't spend it all in one place."

She said something about bartenders drinking free. I asked if that was the owner's policy. She winked and thanked me for the money. I pulled my collar to my chin. Usually Annie made me happy, but even sharing some gossip had done nothing for my mood. I figured it was time to move on from Lyle. Shoot, maybe if I accepted the facts—he was gone—I could even forget about Marva eventually.

Annie stubbed her smoke and went inside. I used the back gate and walked up the block and across Maple to the office. Goatee Guy had told me Mr. White Teeth put the van key in my mailbox. I snagged it, meaning to go inside to mope, but I got a sudden hankering for a fish sandwich with American cheese and extra mayo so I turned back and hopped in the van. I lit a smoke and dug under the opening in the passenger seat, retrieving a mostly empty bottle of Magdalene. There was enough to sterilize my gut.

I made like a compass and went north. Half an hour later I was in Papillion. Someone must've paid a lot of money to whoever voted, because this beige town had won third in the country for best places to raise a family. Sure, it had its charms if you enjoyed chain restaurants, and perfectly useless split-level, three-bedroom houses.

I turned into a Burger King parking lot. The boy working the cash register needed braces and a clean hat. His hair was probably the culprit. I cleared my throat to get his attention. He looked up from his cellphone. I gave my best impression of a neutral friendliness. "Debbie in?"

His baritone left me speechless. "Deb?"

I shifted my weight to one leg and loaded my hip to seem slightly menacing. "The one and only."

He leaned into his microphone and bellowed her name. A few moments later she emerged from somewhere in the back, sweat on her brow, glasses slipped to the edge of her nose, branded ball cap flattening her lightning-storm curls. No sooner than she'd seen me, she removed her work uniform. Beneath the BK HAVE IT YOUR WAY polo, she wore a neon pink cami that barely contained her numerous contours. I was fond of her then, battle weary but ready for the call. She tossed shed gear at cellphone boy and told him to tell Prescot she was quitting, effective immediately.

It was probably the right thing to do to affirm her choice or her courage, but I said nothing. I just turned on my heels, made for the door, and held it for her to follow me. She asked for the keys, which I tossed to her, glad to resign the Savana to someone sober. "What about your car?"

It crossed my mind I was unlikable, but how often had I thought that before, and here I was changing nothing and overjoyed to accept myself, weaknesses and all. She started the van. "I'll figure it out later."

6

I dropped my cigarette butt in the Smoker's Genie because when Debbie was around, littering earned me a homicidal glare. If I haven't mentioned, but I'm sure I have, I got her off a life behind bars conviction for the murder of Denton Reginold, her abusive husband, and in almost every way, I'm certain it was both the correct exoneration, but regardless the right thing to do.

Given there are Marva DeLonghis in the world who can commit atrocities for breakfast and accept humanitarian awards for supper, there may also be people who can act in calculated self-defense and still suffer the full weight of the law. Okay, I'm being cagey. I've always, privately thought there was a ten percent chance Debbie offed her husband with a genius plan that was, in fact, too smart for the courts until lil' old me came along to scoop up the pieces. Some people are definitely too smart for their own good.

It's also possible I'm too high strung and Debbie is simply that sweet and that kind, and that wonderful that she can be wronged to any level and suffer with a smile on her face. If you believe the stories about Mama Theresa, I guess you can believe anything.

She handed me a perfume spritzer as we stepped inside the Stockyards apartments. It's a beautiful building with a blood-soaked history in South Omaha. I tried to refuse the perfume, but she said first impressions mattered. I said that was what I'd hired her back to deal with. She pursed her lips but dropped the perfume back in her shoulder bag.

"You know what's stupid?" I hit the up arrow for the elevators.

"Breakfast cereal."

I gave Debbie my best glare. "Hippy names. I mean, do they really think just by naming their baby Sunshine that the little tyke is going to have a happy life?"

We rocketed up the elevator shaft. "I think names with meaning are powerful."

I nipped off my flask. "Because both of us have pointless names, and you're jealous?"

The elevator doors opened. Debbie followed me out. "My name means 'the bee' and it suggests I'm industrious, a teacher and a great judge of character."

"Whatever. I guess I just think it's crazy that someone is willing to pay almost a thousand bucks a day for me to find her lost cat."

"You mean abducted, right?"

I double-checked my phone and stopped in front of apartment 1521. "Allegedly abducted."

Debbie raised her eyebrows at me. I mimed for her to knock. She did. A moment later the door popped open a couple inches with the chain engaged. I shouldered close. "We're looking for an...um..." I couldn't speak the name without feeling a giggle follow. "Um..."

Debbie leaned in. "Is Mr. Element home?"

The man on the other side of the door was our guy, and it surprised me not one bit that a psychic had chosen to date him. He tried to fulfill his role as if this was a movie and he was acting as its star. "Depends who's asking." He lingered on the "ing" with a bit of a mope.

I thumbed open my wallet to the badge. "Detectives Mia and Lenvil. Are you Fyre Element?"

"Oh my god! Is it really so hard to pronounce a simple name? It's *Fee*, as in Fee, Fie, Fo Fum. and *Ray*, as in Do, Ray, Me, Fa So, La, Te fucking Do!"

"Fee-Ray?" I repeated, with as much disdain as I could, which was a lot. "And your last name? Did I get that close enough?" He hadn't technically admitted to being the subject, but in my profession, assumptions this sure-fire—pun intended—are more than admissible.

Fyre nodded with a pout. "What do you need?"

Debbie opened her mouth to lead, but that was a role violation. I leaned in. "You're Suzie's boyfriend."

"We don't do gender roles."

"Her significant other."

"Sometimes I don't feel significant." He swung the door to within a centimeter of shutting, and I was about to go nuclear. A moment of quiet followed while I created a new extreme on the blood pressure chart. He squeaked the door open slightly. "But yes. She's my BAE and I can't remember life before her."

I side-eyed Debbie. "So you'd say you love her?"

"Duh."

Debbie pushed her glasses up the bridge of her nose. "Mind if we come in, ask a few questions?"

He swiveled his head like he'd been challenged, squinted at Debbie. "Pshhaw." The door closed with finality.

7

I turned on Debbie the way a bad hand in poker will clear you out right down to the car keys. In hushed yells I blamed her for freezing the suspect. She patted my elbow. Usually that kind of condescension sets me to a rolling boil, but she had no malice or ego to spark off of, and I calmed.

It was tough to admit I didn't deserve her. I shook my head. "You do know what it means when someone refuses to talk?"

She nodded, gave a little shrug. "Never feels good to be someone's second choice."

Now she was speaking my language. "You mean Fyre?"

"That the guy feels like he's less important to Suzie than her cat."

She was right, and that was it. Some eggs you break by cracking, others you heat from the inside until they explode. Debbie had cooled him because she'd allowed him to feel at ease enough to shut us down.

I raised my hand in a fist, pounding on the door. My voice was a bullhorn. I told Mr. Element we just had a few questions about his erectile dysfunction. Before my hand fell on the door for the third strike it swung all the way in. My momentum carried me through the threshold.

Fyre was red-faced. "People hear things."

Debbie strutted in behind me, scanning the place as if she meant to make a purchase offer on it. "Do you or don't you?"

Spittle framed his reply. "Do I what?"

Debbie squared him up stern as a boss. "Have a soft prick."

"Goddamn!" He stepped back. "I'm a hundred percent red blooded."

I think Debbie agreed his attitude conveyed guilt, because neither of us returned to the accusation for leverage. Sex difficulties were one of a few topics that worked opposite of the interrogation strategies. With things like accents, facial tics, even body weight, you could work a person by commenting on those insecurities, and the person would crack open like a chestnut at Christmastide. Sex, though put them under lock and key.

Thing was, I knew as soon as we stepped in Fyre's apartment he'd stolen Just Boaze, and from there it was all a matter of sewing the pieces together. I picked an easy clam knife to start the process. "What do you make of the whole cat burglar situation, Fyre?" I pronounced his name phonetically.

He snapped harder than I expected. "I told you, it's Fee-Ray!" Clearly he felt what he'd done was the right thing, and it wasn't a crime of passion. He really cared about Suzie. Debbie was righter than she knew. Mr. Element just wanted to have first place in his woman's heart. I couldn't fault him.

Debbie slipped up beside me. "Could you, perhaps, get me a glass of way-treh with ice, Fee-Ray?"

I cracked a smile and had to turn away to avoid a full laugh.

"Hey, I thought this was America." He stomped toward the kitchen and banged a cabinet open, snapping a pint glass from the shelf. There were tears in his eyes. "Innocent until proven otherwise."

I strode to the bar top bracing my hands on it with menace. "Sure, in court, you're innocent. But I don't see no judge and jury here." I turned toward Debbie. "How about you?"

She nodded. Kept her mouth shut. Debbie must've learned to be a detective from watching mothers of teenagers. She gave this stern expression that said she already knew your secrets so you might as well fess up for your talking-to.

Fyre considered her, found no comfort there and tried me—found worse. He handed Debbie her glass. "What do you want to know?"

This was good. He'd settled on a plan, and a person with plans is bound to slip up. I dug my flask from my jacket pocket and sanitized my sinuses. "Mind if I look around the place?"

He rolled his eyes. "Feel free."

Debbie worked him with some basic questions while I scanned the place for clues. I wasn't looking for a hidden cat carrier or a fluff mouse, not even premium catnip. Nobody was dumb enough to keep his girlfriend's abducted cat at his own home. Everybody was dumb enough to trust other people though, so when I found a framed picture of Fyre with a group of people who seemed friendly with him, I snapped a photo on my phone and lingered until he and Debbie came after me.

Either way I'd follow up with these folks, but I figured I might catch a lead, some kind of tell from his behavior toward them.

Debbie said they were just talking about a gal who had it out for Suzie, and Fyre thought maybe she'd have probable cause and a motive to steal Boaze Kitty. It was a clear red herring if I'd ever seen one, pointless misdirection, though I feigned interest. We danced around some story about the lady's accusations that Suzie's business was a hack—you think?—and how the woman had demanded a refund, but the policy... yada, yada.

We followed this with a heap of small talk. In the business we call it rapport-building, and it's meant to get a mark feeling comfortable to blunder, though the closer I watched Debbie, the more I picked up on signs she'd bought Fyre's story, which was okay because she didn't need to investigate. That was my job, but with all the info I wanted on the friends in the picture, the hobnobbery was wearing me down so I quickly shifted subjects and played the old is-that-a-brother card.

Fyre laughed. "That guy? I'm way better looking. Nah. He and I go way back, though." I managed to learn his name: Cort. I also learned he worked at Omaha Federal Credit Union. After a couple failed nudges, I gave up on getting the other two people's names from the photo. Cort would tell me all about it if he wasn't involved. That's the thing about friends and trust. They have no idea they have anything to keep quiet about, so you get a lot from them.

8

A foggy swirl of smoke danced on the ceiling with nowhere much to go but up. Between my fingers, a lit cigarette smoldered. In the other hand I gently swirled a snifter of Magdalene. The TV was nursing-home-loud because I do my best thinking when my stress rivals a concussion. Debbie sat behind the desk in the office chair, knitting a green stocking cap for a baby in Petroslov or some such place.

The news anchor stood bathed in yellow spotlight outside Lincoln City Hall. Earlier that night a flash mob five-hundred strong assembled around the building. They'd performed a choreographed line dance to "Whatever Happened to Peace on Earth?" by Willie Nelson. The TV broadcast cut away to film of the scene, showing those same blocky cardboard signs written by the same shaky hand as all the others I'd seen. I found the number of five-dollar words amusing, wondering how many of the protestors knew what the text on their sign meant.

As a brief diversion from pondering Just Boaze, I searched my phone for past Willie Nelson concerts in the Lincoln area and discovered he'd played there just over five years ago with none other than Tom Petty, may he rest in peace. The White Stripes and Vintage Ocelot had also taken the stage that day. I imagined it was a phenomenal concert.

Plucking the cigarette in my lips to read about the Nelson-headlined benefit for Peace and Indigenous People's Sovereignty, I nearly swallowed it coal and all when Suzie flung our office door wide. It slammed into the stop, rebounded, and rattled the fogged glass. She aimed her finger at me like a fifty-caliber rifle. "What were you—"

She trailed off into a fit of coughing. Just one more reason to enjoy cigarette smoke. It creates a human shield. I muted the TV and adjusted in my chair, watching as she stomped across the room to the closest window. She fiddled with the lock mechanism, failed and tensed. Panic built. I've often noticed pot smokers are the most opposed to tobacco smoke, as if pot leaves the lungs unscarred.

I stood. "Need some help with that?"

She nodded. Talk about letting the steam out of a tantrum. I had a more or less clear notion of why she'd burst into the office anyway, so a simple greeting with a request for an update would've been fine, but people do have emotions. I'm no different.

I opened the window by releasing the side lock and slid the screen up. The smoke was in no more rush to be out in the cold night than I was, but if it made Suzie feel better, what harm did it do?

When she gained her composure the finger pointing came out again, though noticeably less vehement. "I didn't hire you to go out and make my boyfriend feel like a convicted criminal, did I?"

I leaned back in my chair and drew on my cigarette. I let the smoke linger in my lungs, just the way I like it. "You hired me to find Just Boaze, and I'm working on it."

"Fyre loves my cat just as much as I do. He's been beside himself that she's been taken."

"Interesting." I examined my knuckles for no other reason than to break eye contact. "Because he didn't seem too broken up about it when I visited him."

Suzie mock-laughed. "Who could be when they're on back feet from word one?"

Debbie shifted in her chair. I knew her well enough to understand her body language meant she sympathized with Suzie, so I needed to go easy or I'd spark her defensiveness, but instead I doubled down because Luke E. Mia is nothing if not stubborn. I sipped my bourbon. "So how about this. If you've got bones with my methods, why not fire me? Or should I say why don't you 'fee-ray' me?"

"I should. Goddess Queen knows I should end our contract, but the Eight-Ball hasn't changed its mind about you."

It was a curious object, one I had a mind to mock even more than my usual appetite for mockery. I snuffed out my butt. "If the Magic Eight-Ball knows so much, why don't you ask it who stole your fucking cat?"

Suzie'd set that one up and I walked right into it. She even smirked. "I told you. It won't answer questions about love."

Debbie must've decided I looked sufficiently stupid because she rose from her knitting and clapped her hands. "I can honestly tell you, Ms. Q., Luke did some fine investigative work today, and while it can seem like she's putting someone on the hot seat, I know no one who more skillfully pursues truth than she does. And we have good reason to believe we've narrowed our search to a small number of suspects, but until we've spoken with all parties, it's too early to share more, as you could inadvertently spoil our elem...or I should say need for surprise."

Suzie puckered her lips and squinted slightly. It was an expression I'd come to recognize and appreciate. She made that face when someone won her over or was unexpectedly charming. Debbie had a way of charming. One I was, however, strangely immune to. "All right, then. But please, show my boyfriend the respect he deserves."

I promised her I would, which, given he was behind the abduction and lying to his girlfriend, wouldn't be much, but I needed the T-crosses and the I-dots before I could do anything, so I decided to play nice. "Can I get you anything to drink?" I raised my glass to endorse the power of intoxication.

Suzie leaned into the window, looking out onto the street where some late-night rowdiness was afoot. "You know, I can actually feel my lungs getting second-hand cancer right now, so I think I'm going to go, but thanks."

Debbie rose and showed Suzie to the door. Closing it behind our client, Debbie turned back toward me. I'd only ever seen her angry on two occasions and both were on my behalf, so this one struck me hard. I shrugged raising my arms in the characteristic way that wordlessly asks *what?*

The ends of her words were clipped she was so upset. "I don't like lying for you, and if I'm honest, I believe you're stealing that woman's money the way you're handling this case."

I lit another cigarette, studied it a bit. "Well tell me how you really feel."

"There's nothing funny about this."

"What did you lie for me about?" I leaned forward and speared the ash tray so I could rest it on my knee. "Far as I could tell you gave a fully adequate summary of our work so far."

Debbie stomped one foot, madder, then, than I'd ever seen her. "Adequate? We have no clue who took her cat, but I saw no other response to your behavior than to pretend we were all but closed on this."

Paint me baffled. I long-blinked to calm my sudden nerves. Lyle never questioned my investigative vigor. "Honey, I don't know if you maybe hit your head but I'm bet-it-on-red positive Mr. Fyre Element is the guilty party. I knew the minute we met him."

Debbie cut in. "That's impossible."

I stood, pointing toward the door. "I'll remind you you said that. Now get the fuck out of my office."

Debbie froze. Her jaw hung slack. After a moment, she sucked in a heavy breath, gathered her knitting, and fled. I turned my back on the door and wished I hadn't. Marva DeLonghi was on the television screen. The ribbon racing along the bottom of the screen detailed a new crackdown on the protestors making Lincoln's streets unsafe. There was a reward being offered for the identity of the Flash Mob Organizer. I cocked my arm and hurled the snifter at the TV. The screen webbed as glass and ice erupted, splattering against the wall.

9

THE IRON BARS SLID OPEN, SLAMMING INTO A CRADLE AS A guard accompanied me out of the prison block. Wind whipped rain across my face. I'd never felt more grateful for weather. Lyle stood by the passenger side of a Lincoln Continental parked out front, holding a black umbrella, gnawing on a red vine, wearing his fedora and a tan tweed jacket. He made the jacket look sexy though it wasn't his style.

I think I should've felt ashamed under the circumstances, but my thrill at being with Lyle overwhelmed everything else. I held my breath as I neared. Lyle smirked at me. It meant so much to me. He could have scowled. I'd been a fool. He tipped his hat and opened the passenger door for me. Being near him, I felt at home.

He came around to the driver seat, tossing a banana peel on the pavement as he sat behind the wheel. I nodded at the peel. "That's littering."

He fired the engine and unwrapped a packaged s'more. "Biodegradable."

This was a routine of ours. I hassled him about his red-bloodedness, and he fired a comeback at everything.

As we pulled out toward the road he crammed the last half of a cheeseburger in his mouth and handed me a pack of Sphere menthol. "You can have one in the car, huh."

I depressed the coil lighter. When it popped and I slipped it from the holder, my hand trembled guiding it to the cigarette, my first in two weeks. It wasn't so long ago, prisons had a spot on the yard for smoking and a ration for tobacco. Since the virus, our freedoms were being stripped from us, and we were surrendering them with a smile. I looked around for a flask, but it seemed the latest DUI was enough to keep Lyle from fueling that specific behavior. I refused to ask and be lectured. Instead, I focused on gratitude. "Thanks for coming down."

He bit into a fried Twinkie. Its aroma filled the air. "This is the last time." He sized me up. "Marv let me use her stamp to wipe this one off the books, but she told me it was a bad choice. Said you're incurable and hopeless, huh."

I contained my rage. The woman hated me, just on principle it seemed. But trashing her to Lyle was a quick way to ruin our time. "She's wrong about me."

Lyle steered with his knees while he buttered a slice of steaming Texas Toast. "I don't want you to feel guilty, huh, but this one came out of my own paycheck, and it wasn't cheap."

Was that Marva's touch? I could see her being petty that way. Had she forced him to deliver that message as a condition of her pardon? "You already pay my rent and half my smokes—"

"Half?" He nibbled on a ripe quickle.

"It's been a stressful few months."

"Well." He eyed my cigarette, almost burned to the filter already. My hand was steadying. He patted my leg. Those fingers were five bolts of lightning and I a grounding rod. "Maybe, at least, you can use the two weeks sobriety to quit boozing, huh."

That word stung. He'd never cared before. My hate for Governor DeLonghi intensified with each mile of the interstate. "Hey, I guess you're going to tell me she made you use PTO to drive me around too." I expected a rebuttal, but she had made him, and I saw it so clearly. She was using leverage. The bar was in place. And I was doing all the lifting for her. Every time he saw me looking out of control, he added a bit more doubt to our history. I had to keep it together. "I'll pay you back."

He squeezed Sriracha on a Polish sausage. "You can't afford that."

"I forgive you for not knowing my personal finances, since you don't work cases with me anymore, but I've got a client that's paying a middle, four-figure daily for my services."

He bit through a Tootsie Pop, crunching with vigor. "You sure about that, huh? Something tells me it's a bit of a downer to have a PI on payroll whose out of commission for fourteen days."

He had a point. I lit a second cigarette, daring him to tell me to toss it. "I think she'll understand." There was no reason to believe that.

As Lyle worked through a bag of boiled peanuts, I watched the fields of corn and soy roll past. Once upon a time, these moments of quiet between us would've been comfy as a warm bath, but I wanted to break it now with anything. Lyle spared me, though what he said reminded me more of the adage be careful what you wish for.

He said my behavior was bad PR for the governor—like she was so important. My struggles reflected nothing on Lyle.

"The media are sharks, huh." He peeled a pork rib from a half rack, knee-driving so much I considered asking if his driving was any safer than mine with Magdalene. I somehow held back, stepping so far out of character I felt like I was in someone else's book. He crumpled a barbeque-sauce-soaked strip of tin foil and tossed it in the backseat. "Marv's fighting for every millimeter, and when the head of her security is tied to a loose-and-free alcoholic, it's just one more thing."

I laughed. "That sounds like a line if I've ever heard one."

He tore open a bag of cheese crackers. "She got your DUI dropped, Lu." He pronounced DUI like the little guy from *Duck Tales*, Dewey. "But you treat her like she's—"

"A politician?" Tears threatened, and I refused to let it happen. I smoked so hard my brainstem fogged. "Of all the private eyes in all the state in this whole damn world, she had to steal you."

Lyle dipped a flank steak sandwich in a chipotle aioli. "I called Debbie. Told her you'll be needing her, huh." He dribbled some of the meat juice on his suit jacket. "She's expecting you today."

Absurd that it came to me this way, but I thought about telling him getting Debbie would require me driving, but I realized he'd know. Lyle was never a moralist. He was a friend. I saw through myself just enough to understand he meant well. "Who hired her this time?"

"She's making pizzas at Casey's in Blair."

"Blair?" That was a long haul.

"Try getting a job when you can't list any references because you keep having to quit—"

"I never asked her to walk off a job."

Lyle dug into a bag of caramel corn. "How many times have you fired her?"

He had a point. I ran my hand through my hair. If you're backed into a corner, change the subject. "How's the hunt for the Flash Mob Organizer going?"

Lyle sipped an XL vanilla milkshake. "Ha! If you don't get me fired, that bastard definitely will."

I lit a cigarette. "Know who you're looking for?"

He eyed me that way I used to love. It said, *No clue,* and so did he, "huh."

I pressed into my temples and smiled slightly. "You're looking for someone in academia, probably tenured, with extreme myopia."

He pulled into the parking lot at the office. "You and your pet theories." He crumpled his milkshake cup. "Remember how you thought the Cereal Burglar was some tiny little lady?"

I didn't mention I'd made the right bet on the Cereal Burglar, uncovered her play, and decided to let her go. It wouldn't change anything, and her reason for robbing all those pharmacies was justified, as far as I was concerned. "Everybody misses the mark sometimes." I opened the door and stepped out. "But I've got a good feeling on this Flash Mob character. Trust me."

Lyle told me to stay out of trouble and shifted into reverse. I thought about offering him everything, the whole world and more just to stay, but I couldn't imagine being that pathetic.

10

I parked out front of the gas pumps at Casey's with a straight shot to the door, polished off the last of my flask, and killed the engine. Rust outlined all the tender parts of the Savana. I dropped my cigarette on the pavement, ground it beneath my boot. Smoke chuffed in a halo beneath my heel. I snatched the butt to trash it.

Behind the cash register, Debbie spoke to a boy with enough acne to map a constellation. I cleared my throat. Debbie looked up. The boy was saying something about discounts. Debbie reached behind her neck and untied her apron. The boy didn't stop talking, even when Debbie started walking away. She slipped around the counter and I followed her outside.

As she asked for the keys, a man in a Casey's polo, black pants, and black tennis shoes jogged out. "Where you going?"

Debbie kept toward the van, opening the door and stepping behind the wheel. The man tossed his hands up. "What the hell, Deb?"

She either didn't hear or she ignored him. I turned. "Hey."

"What's she think she's doing?"

I looked between him and Debbie. "Looks like she's planning to drive that van."

The man pointed at me. His hand trembled. I felt slightly bad. "You could try talking some sense into her."

I tapped a cigarette from my pack and planted it between my lips. "You gotta have it to give it."

11

The sun weighed on us like a 4th of July picnic in New Orleans. Somewhere in the distance, a hurricane force tornado tore homes to toothpicks. On the horizon, a green tint suggested the storm had its eye on us. I stood on the stoop smoking. Suzie had just leveled her ultimatum. She agreed to return me to payroll for one day, but if I didn't deliver real progress on Just Boaze by night's end, my contract was up.

Debbie sidled up beside me. "We could start with the leads Fyre tipped us to."

I typed out a tweet about people feeling special, pocketed my phone, and flicked my cigarette into the gutter. It hit a puddle and sizzled. I gathered the butt and dropped it in the trash. "Oh I've got leads, honey. The Elemental had a picture in his apartment. We're going to squeeze milk out of those stones."

Debbie's shoulders slumped. "Why are you doing this?"

I started toward the back of the building, uncapping my flask as I walked. "I can't decide what pisses me off more, the fact that you question me after seeing how I work, or the fact that you can't see what a d-bag Fyre is."

Debbie dug in her purse for the van keys. It was on pace to be a hottest on-this-date-in-history record. I still pulled my jacket collar to my chin. Debbie fired the engine. "Where to?"

I typed the address for Omaha Federal Credit Union into my map app, and selected *GO*. The phone fit perfectly on the plastic lip of the clear window for the speedometer. I rested it there. She examined the destination. "If you need money—"

"Just drive."

She did. I smoked. When we arrived, I told her to ask for Cort Benedict. She wanted to know why. I told her to tell him she was a private detective and we needed to ask him important question about crimes regarding Fyre. She was nervous he'd be noncooperative. I said I'd handle that if it happened.

Several minutes later, she emerged again, followed by the nerdy smiling guy from Fyre's bedroom photo. And I could read Cort's body like a children's book. Innocent. Nevertheless, I chopped it up, went through the motions, ensured the guy understood he needed to keep his mouth shut during an active investigation—all that jazz.

We were wrapping up when I decided to hop off script. I had a couple good puffs of my smoke left so why not? "You ever seen Suzie's Magic Eight-Ball?" I classed it down with "seen" to make that social connection.

And the thing is, a PI's intuition rarely misses. His eyes got that attentive clear glass kind of complexion. "Keep it away from me. That's all I'm going to say about that. But I will say I don't get what Fee sees in her. She's ninety-nine percent woo-woo, and one hundred percent crazy."

I tried getting more about the Magic 8 Ball, but when he said that was all he was going to say about it, he meant it. We thanked him for his time, and I gave him my standard close, the afterthought that's actually the most important detail. You think if I went over to talk with Freaky Dean at Big John's Billiards, he'd let me bend his ear?"

"I don't know, man. With you asking after Fee, I just don't know. They're pretty tight."

I offered a confidential smile. "I get you. I hear you. Well thanks for your help." With a wave of my hand, I motioned for Debbie. "Take it easy."

Cort nodded, looking confused like he missed the point of this whole hand and glove. Back in the Savana, Debbie started in on her Doubting Thomas. I told her to save it. "We'll be cashing bank by the week's end and then our biggest question will go back to being where we find enough work to keep the lights on."

Debbie nodded. She said she'd been giving some thought to the caseload problem. We still had the turtle lady and a couple scoops scheduled to check in on travelling businessmen with eager dicks. Debbie thought if we put an ad on Facebook, we might get a steady drip of work. She said finding missing pets was a noble way to spend a life. Shoot, I didn't know about noble, but it beat fleeing creditors.

On the other hand, and I didn't know how to say this, I viewed Debbie as a seatwarmer, keeping Lyle's spot at the table well-conditioned for when he realized Marva was a parasite and worse. It had to happen eventually. He was too smart to linger under her spell much longer, and when he came back, well, our agency couldn't afford a team of three.

About halfway to Big John's, I got a hankering for French fries. Any time I feel hungry, I go for it, because food usually makes me sick to my stomach. That might be an early warning sign for cirrhosis or whatever, but I prefer to kick cans down roads. "Stop here." Debbie scanned for where here might be. I couldn't blame her for the confusion. "Bronco's."

She made the turn, but the tires squealed like a car chase, and I swore for an instant it felt the van might reorient its center of gravity, but it kept the road. "You're not hungry?"

I scrubbed out my smoke, nipped off the flask, and opened my door. "They have the best fries here."

Debbie shook her head, smirking. "I worked here, remember?"

"How could I forget?" I hopped out of the van. "I'm sure they understood. That was an important case." The case in question was a chimpanzee at the Woodmen tower. I might tell the story elsewhere, but it was touch and go for a few people during that rampage. I will say that. Touch. And go.

Inside it was clear the manager had not forgotten. I think his name was Bob, maybe Bobby. Perhaps Robert. He glared at Debbie, but she stood tall. His scowl would've melted me, so it was tough not to admire Debbie then. He crossed his arms. "You got a lotta nerve showing your face in here after what you did."

Debbie approached the counter. You would've needed a steak knife to cut the tension in the room. She rested her hand on the lip of the Formica, narrowed just one eye, and leaned in. "I saved lives that day."

Bob/Bobby/Rob matched her intensity, and they were all but nose-to-nose. I feared the man's breath, but Debbie held her ground. Bob/Bobby/Rob bared his teeth a little. "Not here you didn't. Fact is, Manuel nearly died trying to take orders and serve guests at the same time."

Anger sketched on her face, Debbie stayed in it, two quick draws in an old west duel, and it was anyone's guess who'd relent. I wondered if fries had been a wise idea. "Tell him I apologize." She spoke with such disdain.

Sweat broke on Bob/Bobby/Rob's forehead. "Tell him yourself."

Debbie brought her other hand to the counter, slow and heavy. The loose skin on her arms gently pendulumed. "I will. Where is he?"

"Where do you think?"

Then, sudden as it'd happened, it ended. They both stood, instinctively brushing imagined dirt from their pants. Debbie cupped her hands around her mouth and called back through the order window. "Manuel! It's Deb. I'm sorry I left you high and dry that day. Glad you got through it. I owe you."

From somewhere in the sizzling kitchen a man's voice erupted. "Pinche basura." The voice carried with a depth James Earl Jones would've appreciated, but the man who burst from behind the swinging red doors stood no taller than Danny DeVito.

The man came around the counter, smiling like a lightbulb in hell. Que onda, Diablo?" They embraced. He pulled back and studied her, looked at me. Eyes to kill as sudden as a switch. "Ella?"

Debbie nodded. "Sí."

Maybe I got bumped in the head, because I thought they slipped into a foreign language, and the only thing I caught was Bob/Bobby/Rob saying. "She's the one, you say." I gathered they were talking about me. A series of exchanges followed before Debbie motioned for me to follow her. She planted us at a curved booth in the corner of the restaurant. The sun pounding through the windows had superheated the vinyl fabric so when I sat, I might've just as well been in a volcano. Debbie couldn't stop glowing. She praised Manuel and his cooking, and it turned out Bob/Bobby/Rob was actually named Darrin so I was close.

Our fries came, slathered in cheese sauce. I didn't mention my preference for ketchup mixed with mayonnaise, because the fries were free-ninety-nine, and it's tough to complain about that. As Debbie plowed her way through the fries, she shared a detailed plan to turn M&K Detective Agency into the definitive "lost things" agency in Nebraska. I meant to tell Debbie there was no chance she was the future of my agency, but a brief wave of sentimentality got trapped in my throat.

12

"I THOUGHT YOU SAID YOU WERE HUNGRY."

My cigarette came to the same fiery end they all do. "That makes two of us." I stuffed the butt in the ashtray and closed the lid. Bourbon could fill the empty spaces.

Debbie parked behind Big John's Billiards. I asked if she wanted to be as far from the door as possible. She asked what the problem with exercise was. I said it was more about efficiency. She said she needed all the exercise she could get, and as an example jiggled the excess skin on her upper arms. I said fries and cheese sauce was a bigger problem than parking as far from the entry as possible.

The heat outside melted tar, but inside the poolhall the lights were dim enough everyone was James Dean and Marilyn Monroe. Everyone, in this case being me, Debbie, and the man behind the counter who eyed us like we'd fallen from the sky. Pool seemed not to have many enthusiasts at noon on a weekday.

Debbie raised her hand in greeting. "Which table is the truest?"

He considered her a while. "Five."

She turned. Each stained-glass lampshade over the tables had a number glazed into it. She squinted at the table with the 5. "Uh-uh." She scanned the floor. "Gimme seven."

"

"It's reserved."

Debbie checked her wrist where a watch would be. "What time?"

"Soon." The man turned his back to us. When he faced us again, he had the set of balls for table five. "Cash or card?"

Debbie gave me a long-eyed stare. I weighed the gain in taking her side. "She asked you a question, bud."

He set the rack on the counter. "What'd you say to me?"

I checked on Debbie. She glowed. I pulled my jacket tight. "You wouldn't happen to be Kyle Rackless?"

He crossed his arms and stiffened his spine. "Would you be about ready to tell me what the fuck two pussy lickers are doing in a pool hall when you should be at work polishing your boss's doorknobs?"

I mirrored his rigid posture. "You seem to be mixing your metaphors, as if I was a pussy licker—which there's nothing wrong with —I wouldn't be polishing any doorknobs. Oh, and while we're at it, clitoris is the preferred term, though I'm not surprised if you don't know where, much less what the clitoris is since it's abundantly clear your intimacy with women would be reserved for Pornhub." I rolled my shoulders back. "Oh, and most importantly, you don't own this place, Kyle."

He considered his response, and surprised me with only modest hostility. "What do you want?" I'd expected a fight, even felt cheated.

Debbie leaned in. "So you are Kyler?"

"Kyle."

I admired her technique. Use the just-barely-wrong name as a distraction for a deflecting reply. It worked and he knew it almost as soon as he'd corrected her. "Well Kyle, we're private detectives, and we've got just one question for you."

The confidence impressed me. I'd seen most sides of Debbie, but this breezy jousting persona worked for her. She was no Lyle, but in a pinch, she'd be good to have by your side.

Kyle rested his hand on the rack of pool balls. "You got a warrant?"

"This isn't Law and Order, dipshit." I hit my flask. It burned just right.

"I don't care what it is. No warrant, no questions."

My patience was thinner than a spring roll wrapper, and I was sharpening my tongue to do damage when Debbie cut in. "What if I win a bet?"

"I'd have to make a bet first, wouldn't I, toots?"

Debbie produced her wallet from her purse and opened the zipper. She thumbed out four hundred-dollar bills. "You beat me in a game of pool on Table Seven, and these are yours. I win, and you answer our question."

He licked his lips. I was suddenly treading water in a pool I hadn't realized we'd dived in. There was the fact of that cash and where it'd come from. Fast food didn't pay that way, and I knew I didn't. Then there was the bet. I was just guessing, but I had a fair idea Kyle didn't manage a pool hall because he liked the sound of billiards cracking so when he asked what if his answer was more costly than four hundred Benjis and Debbie sweetened the offer to eight, I had a real moment of vertigo.

Kyle snatched the money. "I'll even let you break." He put the bills on the cash register, replaced the Table 5 rack with the one for 7 and snagged a pool cue from a rack in the shadows by a rusty metal cabinet.

It was like a high-speed car crash you were helpless to dodge. "Debbie."

She patted my hand. "Chill."

We followed Kyle. He racked the balls, placed the cue, and told Debbie to pick her weapon. Seemed she'd run out of words because she kept her lips sealed as she browsed the sticks along the back wall. Kyle bellowed over at her that the sticks didn't bite. She turned and winked at him, took her time. When she'd selected a cue, she approached in a manner reminiscent of Sunday mass—solemn, somber, and sincere.

Kyle stood in the distance. His wolfish delight practically had an aroma. "You wanna hit the white ball pretty hard, hon. Can't bust it, and if you don't get a decent break, makes for a sloppy game. Not that it'll matter for me." He grinned. "Want me to show you how to hold the stick?"

What I thought was going to happen was Debbie would lose the game and play on Kyle's sympathies, and we'd be fifty bucks in the hole from

Suzie's day rate. I thought Debbie had probably considered the math herself, and I was readying to give her a talking to about how we don't spend our fee recklessly. I thought it was going to happen that way when she lined up her shot dead on and drove the cue so hard my ears rang. Both balls in the second row dropped into the middle pockets and three more balls besides, in corner pockets. She'd pocketed four stripes leaving her the nine, twelve and fourteen. Only after she'd cleared the table with her next four shots did she smile at Kyle and thank him for his thoughtful instruction.

He rested his cue on the side of the table and crossed his arms. "Props to you, toots. You sharked me."

"Hey—" Debbie started fishing her balls out of the pockets—"it's not my fault you didn't take a fat old lady serious, is it?"

He nodded at the table. "If you're so confident, let's make it double or nothing."

Debbie scoffed. "I only have one question I want to ask anyway. There's nothing in it for me."

"All right." Kyle put his hands in his pockets. "But seeing as you played on my reserved table, I'll have to charge you my reserved rate, and this table's going for a grand a game."

I coughed into my hand. "Bullshit."

He ground his toe on the carpet, making mock coy. "My table, my fees. So go ahead and ask your question. Then you can settle your bill. Sound good?"

I shook my head. "No it—"

Debbie stepped forward. "Best of three. Nine ball. First game counts." She dug a quarter from her pocket. "Flip for the break. Call it in the air."

Kyle nodded. "Heads."

The quarter landed on the carpet, George Washington's stoic mug facing us in profile. Kyle snagged the triangle. "Rack em virginal."

I hit my flask. "Haha. He's a funny guy. Tight like a virgin. Must've missed your calling to do standup."

Kyle did a passable job of pretending I wasn't there. Debbie racked. Kyle closed in as she retreated. There were shadows everywhere. Kyle positioned the cue ball nearly on the right bumper. On the break, he almost scratched. The three, four and nine balls all pocketed. Kyle gave a whoop. "That, my dear, is what we call—"

"A golden break." She rolled her eyes. "You still think I'm a good Mormon, I guess."

Kyle patted his belly. "Where's that quarter?"

Debbie retrieved it from her pocket. Kyle called heads. It landed heads. She racked the balls and eyed me. It was the first time since we'd stepped foot in the building Debbie seemed uncertain. We were one shot from parting ways with twenty-two hundred dollars, and look, before you go challenging my math, I was positive Kyle would gloat and expect us to pay the table fee in addition to his double or nothing.

He placed the cue ball, filled his lungs, and broke, sinking five balls, but the nine ball came to a stop with only the cue ball between it and the corner pocket. "Good luck there, chubs, or you can pay me now and spare the embarrassment."

I told him if he made one more negative comment about either of us, he'd be using any money he got from us on a dental bill. "Doesn't look too bad to me, anyway. She's got a clear shot from what I see."

Kyle practically danced as he mansplained how the cue ball could not touch any balls out of sequence or it resulted in a scratch. He also lingered on describing how a scratch on the nine ball resulted in an instant loss. That put matters in perspective. I saw no way Debbie would avoid hitting the nine.

She stepped up to the cue ball. "Whiffs are a ball in hand too, for the record." She went up on her toes, had her pool cue almost vertical, and tested a little back and forth joggle. Kyle glared. She readjusted the cue's angle. Sweat beaded on my upper lip. I hit my flask.

Debbie gave a sharp jab of her stick. Blink and you'd have missed it. The cue ball jumped the nine, smooched the one, and spun backwards, kissing the nine ball into the corner pocket. Debbie gave a hop that would've made a ballerina proud. She beamed.

Kyle snapped his cue stick over his knee. It sounded like an expensive tantrum. He drew a big breath and held it. He hadn't honored his first deal so I didn't expect him to honor his second. He fixed Debbie with a hard look. "Mad props." A storm passed over his face. "You must be nationally ranked."

Debbie smiled shyly. "I learned in prison. Wasn't much else to do. How about—"

The words almost got out, and if I knew one thing about Kyle, I knew he'd use any question as *the* question. "Stop." I seized Debbie's elbow. "That's not our question."

Debbie looked at me, realized what she'd almost done, and covered her mouth with her hand. I squeezed her arm reassuringly. The near miss returned me to myself. Anxiety is my safe place. I aimed a finger at Kyle. "Time to pay up."

He shook his head. "What's your question?"

I considered my approach. Whatever I asked, it couldn't elicit a yes or no reply, but if it was too vague or needed too much detail, he could squirm out. What Debbie could do with a pool cue, I meant to do with words. "Who helped Fyre steal Suzie's cat, Boaze?"

People will always have an obvious reaction to shock. Some flush, others gasp. People will grab at their chest or even cover their mouth. Kyle pinched his temples between thumb and middle finger, burying his face in his hand. He collected himself. In a small voice he said, "Wasn't me."

I stepped forward. "That's not an answer, Kyle, and we both know it. But here's the deal." I glanced at Debbie. The anger on her face thrilled me because she was responding to what Kyle's reply confirmed —something I'd known, but about which no one had believed me— Fyre was behind the cat knapping. "At this point this isn't a legal matter, and we prefer to keep it that way so if you'll cooperate nobody needs to know you helped. Suzie loves her cat, and you can help her get it back." Morality has never been top of mind for me, but I had the hunch a moral shove might tip this guy in our favor. "You can go to sleep tonight knowing you did the right thing. Think about that."

He remained silent long enough, I feared he'd decided not to coop- erate. Then he lifted his head, wiped his lips and told the story. Fyre, Kyle and their friend Tanya had been out drinking on a night Suzie was working. After a few cocktails, Fyre opened up about feeling inferior to —of all things—Suzie's cat. Neither Kyle nor Tanya felt Suzie was a match for Fyre, but they wanted him to be happy so they hatched a silly plan to abduct the cat.

In the days following, though Kyle and Tanya had sobered and thought better of the cat thing, Fyre grew adamant they help. Kyle distanced himself because he didn't feel Fyre was being fair. But when the cat went missing, he more or less connected the dots. He was positive Tanya had gone through with the plan, but he never spoke to her about it because if she confirmed having done it, he'd be guilty by association.

He said the retarded thing was, they'd all been really close before the cat incident, but afterward, they rarely spent time together. "That fucking whackjob cunt bucket. I wish she'd never come around. We had a good thing without her."

I turned away to vent my anger about his using the R and C words, because I didn't want to distract the confession. To hide my anger, I cleaned up the pool balls and returned Debbie's cue from her. "Look at the bright side. I think it's safe to say, Miss Whackjob won't be a problem for you anymore, because even if she's the forgiving sort, she really loves her cat, and Fyre made a bad choice."

We talked a bit more about what would happen next and what Kyle should expect. He said, in a strange way, letting the cat out of the bag, so to speak, left him a ton lighter. We laughed. If I were in a generous mood, I'd point out how it was clear Kyle had fierce loyalty and genuine concern for the people he loved.

Debbie thanked him for the best challenge at billiards she'd had in years, and he told her she was a hell of a shot. We almost walked out with her money still on the cash register, but Kyle saw it, and called out before the door shut. He brought it over. "Hotter than hell out."

"That's Omaha for you." Debbie tipped an imaginary hat at him.

As we drove off, Debbie's warmth vanished. I was smoking like an industrial chemical factory, feeling the thrill of a case on the tipping point. I reached for my pocketknife to look at my reflection in a sharp weapon, but the knife was gone. Had been. That soured the moment some.

Debbie punched the steering wheel at a stoplight. "What the hell is wrong with that asshole? How can you be that insecure?"

I thought about how my therapist had suggested Lyle didn't have to be my partner to be my friend. "Sometimes there's just not room in someone's heart to be shared."

The light turned green. Debbie hit the gas. "How are you going to break it to Suzie?"

"I'm not." I ashed my cigarette out the window. "Until it's all buttoned up. We know who, but that's only the most important part."

13

White fat had congealed on my cold bacon. The
bourbon in my coffee steamed. I typed a tweet into my phone about
heartbreak but deleted it. I swiped over to my text messages and opened
my conversation with Lyle. What did I want to say? *Hi.* I deleted it an
put the phone face down on the table. Sipped from my mug. Alcohol
vapors are their own special experience. They intoxicate your lungs.

I snatched my phone again, opened the texts, typed *Hello* and sent
it, staring at the screen like it'd betrayed me. A minute passed. The text
remained in delivered status. Several minutes passed. Heat radiated from
my cheeks. I hated myself for being an idiot.

I poured the coffee down my throat. It scorched all the way to the
chest-plate on its descent. Pain as a form of wholeness. I raised my hand
to get Sandra's attention just as the bell above the entrance jingled and
Suzie entered. I'd sent her confirmation she'd be reunited with Just
Boaze within hours. She'd replied with a question mark. I didn't
respond. Seems she found my silence unacceptable, and I can't say I
blame her given the bill she'd already paid.

She sat. The vinyl booth sighed. So did Suzie. She was hot the way a
dry drunk will get when she finds a half empty bottle of wine in the
toilet tank she forgot she'd stored there. I braced for a tongue lashing.
She drummed fingers on the table, looking at me over the rims of her

cat-eye glasses. It was easy to forget her kind of beauty, but when it snuck up on you, you really felt it. She leaned in. "So?"

"Ask your Magic Eight-Ball, why don't you?" I spun my pack of smokes on the tabletop. Sphere is about the only brand still making soft packs, and I wonder why. Few things are as gratifying as tapping a filter from the square slit of a soft pack.

She turned her head askance. "You know it won't answer love questions."

I guess she really thought it was some kind of mystical object and not just a toy. "Well I guess me and it are of a mind at the moment, then."

She reached for my empty coffee cup, raised it to her nose. "You'll be lucky to make it to forty."

On this we agreed, and I said so. "Look, I have one more stop to make and you'll be reunited with Just Boaze, like I said. Give me three hours."

She leaned back. Sandra stopped by. "Coffee?"

Suzie shook her head. I nodded. My phone vibrated on the table, but by pure will-power and embarrassment, I let it be. Kind of like that philosopher said—what's his face?—until I confirmed what the notification was, it was both a reply from Lyle and not one at the same time; that's the gist anyway.

Suzie dug an envelope from her purse. "Sign this."

I raised my hand palm splayed. "I'm not signing anything."

She urged it toward me. "You don't seriously expect me to pay you after I made it abundantly clear yesterday was your last shot. And don't tell me that text message was some kind of proof of anything, because all you want to do is delay."

There were a half dozen ways to skin this...situation, each of which had its drawbacks. I tried the easiest of the bunch. "You said the Eight-Ball recommended me."

She sighed. "I've been known to misunderstand its replies."

"And now you think this is one of those times?"

She took my coffee and sipped it. "Maybe. Could be."

Her strange impulse to manage me with my mug intrigued me. "Well, here's the deal, Suzie Q. I'm going to wrap this case up today, and

I'm going to reunite you with your cat, and I'm going do it gratis, one hundred percent free. How's that sound?"

She returned the envelope to her purse. "Sounds to me like you're trying to avoid getting fired."

"Looks like it worked."

She smirked. "For now." Suzie moved to stand.

I adjusted my cigarettes so they nudged the plate of untouched bacon and eggs. "Let me ask you something."

She smoothed her shirt. It was long and flowing and needed no smoothing. "Shoot."

"If that Magic Eight-Ball of yours is so useful, how come it refuses to answer so many questions? Seems to me the Eight-Ball thinks everything is all about love."

Suzie inflated one cheek and puckered her lips slightly. "You know. I'd say it's the opposite. I'm surprised how many things people do in this life that have absolutely nothing to do with love." She grabbed her chin between thumb and forefinger. "Which, speaking of love, I want you to know that if Boaze is dead, you can expect I won't let it go unpunished."

She wasn't my favorite client, but I figured she'd be an even worse enemy. "That's not fair. You'd have no way of knowing when he was killed."

She adjusted her glasses on the bridge of her nose. "He's alive until you prove otherwise."

A chill ran up my spine, and with it a shock of remembrance. My only D in college: philosophy. "Schrödinger's Box is a bullshit way to see the world. The cat is either dead or it's not. End of story."

Suzie shrugged. She dug in her purse and grabbed the envelope again. "If that's the case, then why don't you tell me are you fired or not?"

I had to give it to her. She'd outmaneuvered me there. "I guess I'll have to ask the Magic Eight-Ball, won't I?"

She again tucked the envelope away. "Sorry. That's not going to happen."

14

If you're not from Omaha, you don't understand what it means to live in District 66, but it's like this: they play by their own rules. District 66 is an island near midtown, surrounded by undifferentiated Omaha. The borders of the district are almost visible in how one side of Blondo Street between 90th and 72nd has thick green grass, while the other side has weed-choked lawns dead from drought after the first hot spell.

Tanya worked as a life guard at the Hillside Public Pool, a neighborhood on the far corner of the district. All the other pools in the city opened after Memorial Day, but Hillside, being a neighborhood in District 66, opened its gently heated, saline pool and bar on April 15th, kicking off the season with a special event for accountants who'd just finished tax season and needed to let loose.

Debbie parked the van with its nose facing Cole Creek. "This is kind of effed up, but the more I think about it, the more I think there's something badass about caring for someone so much you'd do something illegal for them."

I lit another cigarette, scoping the pool for Tanya. The lifeguard chairs were vacant. "I used to have a friend like that."

Without hesitation, Debbie said she'd do something illegal for me. I considered her through a wave of smoke. Probably the correct response was to say thanks or even that I'd do the same for her, but I couldn't and mean it, so I didn't. The Savana's engine ticked and pinged. It seemed so loud. Debbie slapped her knees. "Welp. There's no time like the present."

We walked the length of the parking lot. I kept the pace slow enough to finish my cigarette. It tasted a bit sour the way tobacco will when you're teetering on the edge of overdoing it. I said something about swimming in my childhood, but it felt insincere.

We opened the gate to the pool. I aimed for the bar, sneaking a last slug off the flask. Magdalene is a razorblade to reason and a comfort to self-doubt. The man behind the counter polished giant glass goblets, the kind made for drinks with umbrellas and tropical fruit slices. His tongue ran laps around his teeth as he scrutinized us. "Ladies."

I nodded. "What's on tap?"

"Memberships?"

"Never heard of it. Must be local."

Debbie laughed. She looked between the barman and I. One thing I've always had a knack for is a straight face. I don't joke often, but when I do, I like it to hurt. The barman considered my response. His thoughts were on the verge of vocal, or so I imagined, because his eyes asked if I was incredibly stupid or annoyingly snarky. Neither was my desired effect.

The barman draped his towel over a shoulder. "Do you have membership cards, ladies?"

Any place requiring memberships for participation is trying to swindle people, and I don't care how cheap a slice of Costco food court pizza is. Though once I'd considered an icy draught on a chilly afternoon, I had it in mind the standoff would end with a pint glass or a right hook. "We're here on business." I showed him my badge. "Is Tanya in?"

The barman narrowed his eyes. "That thing looks like you got it off Amazon."

I flipped the badge closed. "Ebay, actually. I prefer to argue about things. It gives them more value."

"If you say so." He placed a newly dry goblet in a wood rack overhead. "Well, I hate to say this, but I can't serve drinks to nonmembers, and my boss would have my head if I let two hobby detectives at one of his employees."

Few things get me off balance so much as having my work belittled. "For your information, I'm the reason your governor isn't a blood smear on a rack of fur coats at Regency."

The barman dried another goblet. I could've sworn he'd dried them all already. "You don't look like a man."

It took me a moment. "That was my partner, Lyle. I tipped him where to go."

"Never send a woman to do a man's job."

Two strikes for the barman, and if there was a third, it was going to be my fist. "I pack twice the punch of most guys. Try me."

"If by punch, you mean a loud bark, I'll buy it."

He was two seconds away from having a dental realignment. "I don't know what your problem is b—"

"My problem is—" he leaned in, and I could smell his stink of self-superiority—"you come here acting like somebody invited you, when the truth is, everywhere you go, people wish you'd leave."

His comment hit a little closer to home than I'd have preferred. That's the life of a PI. But I'm not sure how I'd have responded had Debbie not melted like a Hershey's in a hot car. Her whole body swooned as an hourglass with an ass bought in Brazil, and Barbie's boobies emerged from the office door beside the bar. The lady wore a one-piece bathing suit that contained her Fans Only regions to the legal limit, and not an atom's-breadth more. Across her chest in yellow block letters, stretching for miles, was the word *Lifeguard*. On her backside, a big yellow plus sign.

Debbie's jaw didn't just drop to the ground, it rolled into the pool and slurped down the drain. I had to shake her shoulder to keep her from frying like an egg and rocketing into space. Madame Brazil was recognizably Tanya from the photo on Fyre's dresser top, but with an extra half million under the hood. As I drifted from the barman—who was buzzing nonsense in my ear—I wondered how much it payed being a members-only lifeguard.

Debbie and I moved in lockstep toward Tanya, or more like, Debbie levitated an inch above the textured cement poolside, dragging me behind her. We caught up with Tanya at the lifeguard chair. I'll blame what came next on plastic surgery, or hypnosis, or both. Someone tapped my shoulder to which I had an instant, and merciless reaction. Call it strike three.

The barman rode my fist like a passenger train into the pool. Those in attendance numbered two, not including Tanya, Debbie or myself—elderly men sleeping in pool chairs. I shook my hand. A tooth poked from my pinky knuckle. The finger had broken too, if that matters. Alcohol is both an antiseptic, and an anesthetic. I splashed some on my hand, and drank the flask empty.

Tanya assumed a boxing stance. I admired her pluck. Debbie, beside me, uttered just above a whisper, "Duh, duh, duh." Her body flushed. I can't claim to know intent, but I think Debbie was trying to justify my behavior, but failed to find her speech in the overflow of nerves.

I stepped back and slightly spread my arms to indicate deference. "You might want to do your job."

She looked from me to the barman, floating face down in the water. I had the sense she'd never needed to haul someone from the pool before.

Debbie saved Tanya the displeasure of wet hair, diving into the pool. It was probably for the best. Debbie must've been on the verge of cooking her brain, and would've benefitted from the cool down. She made like Lassie and guided the man to dry ground. Only then did Tanya recognize she had some role to perform. She walked over—not especially hurried—and knelt beside the barman. Placing two fingers in the hollow of his throat she closed her eyes. A moment later, she leaned her ear to his nose and at last declared he was breathing.

Debbie had returned to my side, sopping wet and considerably less stupefied. I performed the sign of the cross—a mockery of the moment, for those who know me well, but an appearance of solemnity to all else. "He wouldn't take no for an answer. I'm sure you can relate."

Tanya offered a glowing smile, caught herself, and tried to resume a neutral expression. "Should we call the police?"

I shook my head, dug in my hip pocket and produced my badge, which I flashed and replaced. "He's only sleeping."

"Oh." Tanya folded her arms under her chest, as it was too girthy to cross them over top.

Tanya had broken Debbie, who dripping wet, could only stare at the woman before us. I patted her back. "This is my partner Debbie—"

"Business partner." Debbie gulped.

Things had taken a pleasant turn. I snagged my cigarettes, leaning into my assumed authority. "Business before pleasure, they always say." I raised a cigarette to my lips. "You mind?"

The request seemed to confuse Tanya. She scanned the area for someone to give orders, but the only person who'd gladly do so had begun to gently snore. Debbie though, slapped my elbow. "You can wait."

I saw no point in debating, and tucked the smoke behind my ear. "So here's the deal. You fit the description of a woman named Tanya Wilkerson."

Her eyes made like hoot owls. "I did it for love."

Among the ways I'd pictured eliciting a confession, clarifying the suspect's name wasn't in the cards. "Did what, Tanya?"

Her eyes filled with tears. They fell down her face. "Don't make me say it."

Debbie raised a hand but held it short of Tanya's shoulder. "Oh! ... Oh, honey."

Tanya's brows furrowed. Her cheeks hollowed. "No matter what I did, how hard I tried, what lengths I went to, he never noticed me." She puffed her cheeks and blew a jet of air. "I'm walking around with fucking balloons in my chest and all he can talk about is Suzie, Suzie, Suzie." A story came spilling out so unlikely I nearly laughed and almost wept. Debbie did both.

Tanya met Fyre in 2018. At the time, people pronounced his name like the stuff that burns wood. She, Cort, Kyle and Fyre had taken a trip to Banff for a music festival, which is where the picture on Fyre's dresser had been taken.

From then, they'd been inseparable until Suzie. At first Suzie was just another friend in the circle, but soon Fyre was cancelling plans to be alone with her, and it didn't take a detective to see they were fucking.

Tanya tried one time to tell Fyre about her feelings, but Fyre refused to hear it, saying she was his best friend.

Then, in 2020, Fyre was laid off from waiting tables because of COVID. Suzie said it was the universe telling him to take a leap of faith so he began his own business as a TikTok influencer and demanded people call him Fee-Ray. His iPhone was filming from the moment he woke, it seemed. He sent all the footage to some chick in the Philippines to edit. In thirty days, he hit a thousand subs on YouTube, then 10k in sixty. By Christmas he hit a quarter-million, sharing what he called "the truth rich a-holes don't want you to know."

Tanya had been working at the University of Omaha Medical Center as a Physicians Assistant for years at that point, and she'd only seen Fyre a handful of times since he started his channel. When they bumped into each other, he'd filmed their interactions, calling her employer JP Mammon Chase and asking her if it felt good pumping innocent victims full of toxic sludge while promising to save their lives.

YouTube fame had changed him, but when he asked her—after New Years—to "come aboard", she thought she had a real chance to win his heart.

Plus, he was doing multiple six-figures in sales a month and promising to pay almost double her already very good salary. Looking back, she couldn't believe he'd convinced her to quit. His whole business was built on this conspiracy COVID was a hoax perpetrated by billionaires to oppress the masses. He said plenty of natural remedies obliterated COVID.

The thing was, and it still hadn't changed in Tanya's heart, she believed in Fyre's goodness, and it perhaps nudged her along that she was skeptical of the pandemic protocols for her own reasons, so she jumped aboard.

Later, she'd wonder, if it'd not been for her, would his wobbly empire have collapsed sooner, maybe causing Suzie to flee, but why ask the unknowable?

Especially because Tanya dove all-in, like head-first, into Fyre's business. Having seen strong data to prove its impact, she urged Fyre to include vitamin D to his subs. She helped him find a reputable supplier and argued with him until he was red-faced-spitting-mad that he needed to buy as much vitamin D as he could afford. Didn't he remember the toilet paper crisis?

Leading up to that, Fyre had scaled to a staff of six, and Cort led a team of 1040s who took inbound calls from ads. They sold Fyre's COVID Proof Course, his Vitamin Kick Ass, which he called a proprietary blend but was just repackaged D, and Blue Earth Crystals Suzie swore by.

So much money poured in that even when YouTube banned Fyre's channel and TikTok's algorithm suppressed him and his only outlet was Twitter, nobody even whispered about potential problems. Instead, Fyre started dumping all his cash into Reddit and Discord where the youths were flocking for truth online anyway. He bled cash at alarming rates, but said it was a matter of time before his fans demanded justice and he was reinstated and vindicated.

It was around then, partying at Fyre's 200-acre ranch near Calhoun that a domino effect of catastrophes began. Tanya wanted to make sure neither Debbie nor I would judge her. I said we were a judgement-free zone.

Tanya said Fyre'd been drunk, and Suzie'd already returned to her stupid office in Benson. Fyre was griping about Suzie's obsession with self-reliance. Why couldn't she just let him take care of her. See his wealth! See it? And he said he didn't know why he loved her because she wasn't even his type. He liked women with—he gestured at his chest with slightly cupped hands—something to grab onto.

Tanya decided that night to get work done. Fyre never even noticed. She couldn't even catch him sneaking a peak, no matter how lowcut her top.

Later Fyre got booted from all the major Reddit forums on COVID for aggressive language and threatening comments. Then suppliers restocked vitamin D back and the toilet paper effect evaporated. As if that wasn't bad enough, a customer sued him for medical claims in one of his videos. He won the case but had to sell his acreage to afford legal fees. Tanya was the last one he fired, or terminated, if you will. By then, she'd developed a little bit of an addiction of sorts. Lip injections, Botox, butt implants, a waist reduction. The money had poured in, and she kept thinking, *after this next one, he'll love me*. After she had her eyes done, but before she'd had her rhinoplasty, Fyre said she looked different. She asked different good or different bad, and he'd hesitated long enough she'd had time to imagine murder. He said different good.

Weeks after it'd all come crashing down, Fyre'd called Tanya to meet him for beers, and he'd snapped, saying he could've taken it all in stride, but that he couldn't suffer the insult of his own girlfriend choosing to go home every night so her dumbshit cat wouldn't be lonely when he himself was in a blaze of agony.

Tanya said Suzie had everything and yet she'd rather cuddle a cat. She punched her thigh in frustration just recalling it. "I hate that woman worse than fat free cottage cheese."

I fidgeted with my hands, waiting for Tanya to go on. When she didn't, I urged her. "So..."

"So what?"

I examined my empty flask. The barman was beginning to rouse. "You stole the cat in hopes of Fyre seeing how loyal and caring you were. He didn't—obviously—but you still haven't given the cat back."

Tanya laughed. "I couldn't."

Debbie patted Tanya's shoulder and pulled Tanya in for a hug. "I understand." Tanya stiffened at the embrace. Debbie hugged tighter.

I moved my head so I was in Tanya's direct sightline. "It's not *your* cat."

A tear came down her cheek. "I couldn't do it to my dad."

And there it was. "Your biological father?"

She sniffed, pulling away from Debbie, and doing so with a bit of a wince, as if she found Debbie repulsive. "He's never bonded with an animal like he has with Boazy."

The irony of that statement was lost on this audience. "Seems it has more to do with the cat than the person." I tapped a cigarette into my hand. Debbie cleared her throat and darted her eyes toward my ear where I'd tucked the last unlit cigarette. I replaced the new one in its pack and plucked the former between my lips, lighting it. "Fact remains, you stole a cat, and that's prosecutable, my dear."

Tanya pleaded for mercy, saying she'd already sacrificed her body and her social life for Fyre, that most days she hurt in every conceivable place and that her former medical colleagues would pretend she didn't even exist rather than look at her. I felt badly for her. The level of commit-ment to Fyre earned my admiration, even if it had all the trappings of mental illness behind it. Debbie, though, was the one to assure Tanya we'd not report anything to the police.

Tanya looked confused. "You aren't the police?"

The barman was blinking awake.

In Chicago Cubs fandom, that's called a quick 0-2 count. For the rest of the world it's simply a good prompt to make like a dog with tape-worms and scoot. I hooked my arm under Debbie's and jerked her toward the exit. If I'd ever doubted her feelings, for me, it ended there. Despite the sobby love-at-first-sight she'd felt for Tanya, when I told her to run, she ran. And if you were to assume her size suggested she'd be closer to lumbering than loping, I'd not hold that against you, but I'd say you were dead wrong. She left me in the dust, and had the Savana fired up and in gear when I made the passenger seat.

15

I had Debbie park in the back of an apartment complex on Maple while I ran a quick search on Tanya. Her father was named Murton, and he was a man with great pride in his lawn. More than half his posts on Facebook had to do with the grass, and many of them showed his address number in the background. A quick crosscheck on whitepages.com confirmed the street he lived on, and so the moment had come.

Debbie voiced concern the police might pursue us, what with how we'd treated the barman, but I reminded her the van traced to Lyle, and Lyle would cover for us, even if he hated doing it. I texted Suzie the father's address and told her to meet us there ASAP. Debbie said I used Lyle and should be ashamed. I told Debbie to pull the van over. She asked why. I drank from my refilled flask. I told her because I said so.

She signaled and turned into the parking lot of a shop called Dee-sign Landscaping & Garden. Someone had painted it purple. It was the stuff of nightmares. I lit a cigarette. "Get out."

Debbie put the van in park. "Don't do this to yourself."

What difference did it make in the long run, but her saying "yourself" made the difference then. I pulled a great volume of smoke into my lungs and closed my eyes and let myself bathe in the haze of nicotine perfume. "Keep Lyle's name out of your fucking mouth."

Debbie's knuckle's paled on the steering wheel. "You're the boss."

"That's right. I am." I nodded. "Now let's get going."

16

The man who answered the door could've made commercials as any-dad. I'd have profiled him somewhere between fifty and seventy years of age, between sixty-seven and seventy-two inches tall, between one fifty or one eighty on the scale, clean white hair, good teeth and a winning smile, even reserved as it was. "May I help you ladies?

I'd told Suzie where to meet us for a positive ID, though I'd have rather gone without her. Emotions make people unpredictable, and Suzie beating us there suggested she was lit-match angry. We'd approached the door shoulder to shoulder, Suzie sandwiched between Debbie and I, and her invisible energy had me almost sparking. I moved slightly forward. Used to be Lyle who led in the emotional moments, because I made the tin woodsman in The Wizard of Oz look like Oprah Winfrey, and even if the cat burgling was wrong, there was more than one victim in this scenario. "Sir, I've been told your daughter, Tanya, gifted you an adult cat named Boaze."

Suzie trembled at her cat's name. Her lip quivered. "He's pale as milk, all but his paws and face, which look like he dipped them in the darkest night and the moonless sky stuck."

Murton crossed his arms over his chest, his pleasant expression fading. "What about it?"

Suzie seemed to grow an inch. "He's my cat. He was stolen from me."

As if on cue, Boaze came running. He gave a series of trills as he approached. Suzie knelt and Boaze leapt into her arms. It was nothing short of *Homeward Bound*, a part of my childhood I'd just as soon forget. Sentiment digests poorly in my stomach.

Murton, witnessing the scene, fell back several paces as if he'd been shot. The pained look on his face added to the injured effect. "Not my Boaze."

Suzie turned and carried the cat to her car. She drove away.

Her leaving captivated us all. Only the robin song of a cool spring day pierced the silence, then the engine sounds and the tires on gravel. A musky hay scent carried on the breeze. Murton's whole demeanor had crumbled into the form of a defeated man. I couldn't bear to see his suffering. "I know there's no replacing someone you love, but I want to take you to the Humane Society. There's a cat there that needs you."

He considered me. I considered my flask. As I've mentioned, emotion costs me a lot. He considered my flask. Debbie asked if he'd like a hug. He considered her, nodded. She moved in. He looked smaller still, in her arms. When they separated, he considered me again. "My daughter gave me that cat."

I glanced over my shoulder. My own past was out there somewhere. "She's made some bad choices." I turned back to Murton. "But I just spoke to her, and if anything was clear, it was that she loves you, and wanted to make you happy."

He shook his head. "You're telling me she stole that cat from the other woman."

Debbie nodded. I did too. "It's a long story, but what it comes down to is love." If you'd asked me a year ago what I loved, I'd have listed Magdalene bourbon, Sphere menthol, and a baseball game at Wrigley Field. That list had grown by one, and the addition of that one had opened me up to a whole mess of confusing mental intrusions. Even to just say love to another human being and not be talking about something silly like a double-play wouldn't have crossed my mind. Time changes us.

"Oh, hogwash!" Murton was like the four seasons, each distinct from the former. This indignation burned like the summer. "I let that girl in again despite my better judgement. She's always been a sorrow to me. Skipped her own mother's funeral, went and quit a perfectly respectable job to chase a fool of a boy, and now she's made a fool of me again. I'll not have it."

"Sir—" this was going to cost me self-respect to say—"the boy is a fool, but when you love someone, you can't see around it. That Tanya loves proves she's worth loving. Don't write her off."

He turned half way around, peered back into his house where no lights were on. "She's a liar and a thief, and no daughter of mine."

I raised a hand to protest, but he stepped aside and closed the door in our faces. Debbie and I were left looking at a bright red face of a lost opportunity. Debbie said she could never understand people who couldn't forgive. I suppose it's true to say, I can understand a lot, but Murton's choice left me cold. But it's easier looking from the outside in. "We'd better go."

The sun peaked out from the clouds for a moment, and a wind gusted. Most of the time, a case closed and a victim justified feels great, but celebration was the last thing on my mind. Debbie started the engine, lumbered the van onto the road and drove us away.

17

Two women had been arrested in a flash mob protest near the capitol that afternoon. Makynna Gray of KETV News At Nine introduced a clip of the moment. It looked like a thousand bodies imitating time-lapse sunflowers in repeat: heavy lettered signs, big words, swaying to and fro, and one of the arrested women was shown telling the officer who guided her into the police cruiser he wasn't half the man their organizer was. Her expression suggested carnal hunger. I considered how more often than not women are drawn to romantic partners close to their own age—a generalization, but founded.

A knock at the office door diverted my attention. Debbie put down her knitting. A pair of green, brown, and yellow mittens sized for a large squirrel maybe. "Come in."

The door opened, first a few inches, then the rest of the way. Suzie stepped in. She had a bag over her shoulders. It had a square mesh cage, and inside it, Just Boaze sat, calm as a Thomas Kinkade portrait. I extinguished my cigarette, because cats are more vulnerable to tobacco, or so it seemed to me.

Debbie stood. I already was. Suzie cleared her throat. "I'm sorry about earlier. I was overwhelmed." She coughed. Either the smoke or just the rawness of it all. She squared me up. If it'd been another person or a different place, I'd call it a provocative gesture, a fight-me-if-you-dare kind of thing. "Look. You were right. I was wrong. But I couldn't see it. The Eight-Ball was right about you, though. One in a million people won't back down to me. I'm not sure why, but people have a hard time saying no to me. The Eight-Ball knew you wouldn't."

There's never a time when it doesn't feel great to be told you were right. I opened the nearby window. "Since I'm apparently a one-in-a-million asshole, can I ask you a serious question?"

Suzie unshouldered her cat pack and set it on the ground. "Fire away."

"Do you really believe what you're saying about the Eight-Ball? Because, from where I'm standing, you sound a little woo-woo wackadoo."

Suzie smirked. "Sugarcoat it, why don't you?" I started to respond, but she spoke over me. "No, I understand. Most people believe the world is limited to the scientific, and those who don't tend to lump everything else into religion. Magic is, for most, nothing more than an illusion. Sure, we'll read horoscopes and fortune cookies, and we might even hope they're true, but only a small portion of the population has seen real magic, and seeks it out. But it is real, and not just for those who want it to be."

I'd seen magic, fled it, been nearly killed by it, and I understood how she felt. It gave me pause, because I knew how it felt to have people always calling you crazy because you'd experienced a corner of reality they hadn't. Life was like that. People tended to hold to the version of the world they knew and judge anyone who fell outside their scope of reality. "Call me a skeptical believer."

Suzie's face did something unique. She hadn't expected me to affirm her. "Okay."

I leaned against the window sill. "If your magic is real, why aren't your rich and famous?"

Suzie fluttered her eyes, looked at her feet shyly. "Who said I wasn't?"

I considered her daily rate, the way she hadn't argued my price. It seemed stupid of me to ask for so little if that was the case. "Maybe you're famous in the community of mystics or whatever."

"Surely someone told you about Fyre's business." She pronounced his name phonetically, which suggested she'd moved on from him, or was committed to doing so.

"Yes."

"Then you understand." She knelt, unzipping the cat pack. "It was because of the Eight-Ball, because of me that Fyre's little YouTube experiment succeeded. I just fed him the plans the Eight-Ball gave me, but as it always is, the Eight-Ball prefers chaos and has its own agenda."

"The bans and the lawsuit." It hit differently with her filling in the why when someone had already told me the how. Made it more real.

"Playing with magic is never a good idea." I'd forgotten Debbie was in the room. "Now that you've got your cat back, maybe it's time to get rid of the Eight-Ball."

Suzie shifted glancing at Debbie. "That's exactly what I'm going to do." She lifted Just Boaze out of the cat pack and he scaled her arm, draping his body over her shoulder. "Funny thing is, I rented the stupid thing on a whim. I'm going to email the owner, and tell them to give me the return address. My business is doing fine, and I've already lost more that I care about, than I care to admit."

Maybe I felt responsible for her hurting, and maybe I hated feeling guilty. "At least you got your cat back."

"There is that." She sighed. "It cost me the only man I ever loved."

I wanted to justify it so much, but some lows were too low to stoop to. Shrugging the guilt would be as easy as mentioning how loving a liar is no kind of love, but then, the heart wills, or something like that. "I'm sorry." If I couldn't shake the guilt, I could at least relate to her hurting. "You know, the man I love left me because of magic too."

"Lyle."

It was so bare, so unexpected. Suzie'd had the shop for years. He'd probably even stopped in on her from time to time. That was his way, the social one between us, but somehow I'd expected my feelings for him were private, and my heart hidden.

Debbie had returned to her knitting. "You speak of him as if he's gone, but he'd get together any time you called, honey."

I raised my hand as a loaded gun aimed at Debbie. "Don't."

She looked away. A tension thick enough to drive cars on settled over the room. Suzie broke it. "You take Venmo?"

All the apps that let people pay other people seemed crazy. I nodded. "Yeah sure. It's my phone number. I thought we were settled though." That was me just being honest.

She grabbed her phone from some fold in her flowing blue stole. As she tapped and swiped at the screen, I grew weary and wanted to be alone. "You showed me a truth I would've refused to see without you. That's worth more than money can buy, no matter how much it hurts."

I wanted to debate that, to say I'd had my painful truth, and life had lost its shine, so I hit the flask, and decided, fuck it, I'd tell her. Debbie'd heard it all before anyway, and said she believed me. She said she'd known me in past lives, but not the kind I was talking about. According to her, I was once King Halberdon of a Germanic tribe. Why not? Magic this, magic that. who's to decide?

Starting with the day Marva walked into M&K Detective Agency looking to hire two naïve PIs to find the person who was threatening her life and lasting all the way through nine deaths that started at in the basement of 20's Showgirl before I discovered Marva had hired her own hitman—Larry "Laser" Surlman—I told it all. I'd wanted to let him kill her and be done with it, in the aftermath, but that particular magic refused to let me live if Marva died. To the best of my knowledge, we were still inside that magic even now. If Lyle were to fail at his job and Marva was killed, boop, beep, bop, and back to the start, though—and I hadn't told anyone this before that moment when something about Suzie made it all pour out—for me, there was no going back. I'd met a fiery being in my dreams, a pillar of smoke and light that told me I'd come to the last stop on the turnstile. The smoke had a voice like a drift-wood fire on the beach near crashing waves.

I told Suzie how Debbie had helped me plan a way to save Lyle's life, which had always before that final try been the one elusive detail I couldn't bring off. And I told how after saving his life, he chose Marva over me—Marva, the architect of our misery. "If there was any way I could, I'd kill her, I swear to god, just so you know. So call the cops, report a psycho, have them lock me up, because I swear it. She'd be dead for all time if I could only find a way."

Debbie brought my cigarettes. "Need one?"

I scowled at her.

"If there's a way." Suzie's gaze darted around the room like she expected monsters. "This will know it." She was holding the Magic 8 Ball, arm extended toward me.

I longed for it to be real. Yearned to have it. "It's not yours?"

Debbie shook her head. "You don't want that, Luke. You want nothing to do—"

"Shut up."

Debbie retreated like she'd been hit. "Don't."

I shook my flask. It was low on fuel. "Why would you give it to me?"

Suzie's arm remained outstretched. "You can borrow it as long as you want it."

"But you did hear me? I want to *kill* the governor."

Suzie stepped forward. As she did, Just Boaze leapt off her shoulder and volunteered his body into the cat pack. And you might think I was a fool for what I did, that with all the ominous signs, all the warnings not to, that not taking the Magic 8 Ball was the obvious choice, but I'm guessing you've ignored obvious concerns before. "It sounds like she's not all that innocent herself."

I reached for the 8 Ball. "What if I just humiliate her? Just show Lyle who she really is?"

Suzie stepped forward. My fingertips grazed the solid obsidian body of the 8 Ball. "If there's a way it can be done."

I dropped my hand and shook my head. "I'll think about it."

Debbie gave a little hop. I smiled. This could be fun. "I'm kidding. If you'll let me borrow it, I'd be grateful."

Suzie handed me the 8 Ball. "Be careful. It does cause trouble. Sometimes more than it solves."

Maybe I'd expected a transfer of electricity or eerie warmth when the 8 Ball dropped in my hand, but there was none of that. Other than being heavy, it was just a thing, like any other thing. I shook it. "Is this a good idea?"

Suzie was zipping Just Boaze into his cat pack. She glanced back at me. It wasn't my imagination, and I believed it foretold danger, but she smirked nervously.

The 8 Ball said, *Always.*

Suzie said her goodbyes and let herself out, Debbie tried again to convince me I wanted nothing to do with the 8 Ball. I told her I wanted nothing to do with her, and asked her to leave.

18

More pets than you'd expect are stolen as a form of retaliation. The turtle we'd been hunting was with a man named Arnold Montaigne. Stonewall Jaxon, the Irish Wolf Hound had been abducted by a lady at a dog park who hated confederates, but before she could kill the dog and make an example of its owner, she fell in love with Stoney, as she came to call him. Even a parrot I'd long since cold-cased turned up with a family of Seventh Day Adventists who'd cooperated in extracting the animal from a church member's house because it took the lord's name in vain. They never were able to teach it reverence for god, but in each of these cases, the thieves were arrested, booked, charged, and sentenced to varying levels, and the rightful owners restored to their pets.

I was cornered and interviewed on KETV at the end of April for my string of solved cases. The reporter who interviewed me closed the conversation about M&K Detective Agency by saying, "Luke E. Mia, PI, the woman for the job, until the cows come home." If it hadn't felt good to be liked for a change, I'd not have let such a silly closer go unpunished.

Between the payouts on my lost and founds and the check Suzie had written—one zero more than I'd expected, or proof the Magic 8 Ball had made her wealthy—I had spending money for the first time in years.

I stocked up on the essentials: Magdalene, cigarettes, a Zippo and lighter fluid, and two new pairs of combat boots. Calls started coming in so heavy I had to turn business away. All the warnings about the 8 Ball's malicious side seemed like a scare tactic. I'd even started using it to see which cases were going to be the best buck for my time.

An incoming call might go like this.

Me: M&K. Luke speaking.

Caller: Hi. Um, my husband has been way too affectionate lately, and I'm afraid he's hiding something.

Me: What's your full name?

Caller: Sarah, with an H. Waynerite. That's W-A-Y—

Me: Hold please.

Me: (Shake shake.) How long will it take to get evidence that Sarah's husband is cheating on her?

8 Ball: Sarah's husband has cancer and he's afraid to tell her, tee-hee.

Me: You're an asshole.

Me: (Click, click.) Sarah, you there?

Sarah: Yuh.

Me: Sarah, I'm a little busy to take your case at the moment, but I have a strong instinct you should ask your husband if he's been to the doctor for any reason lately.

Or sometimes I'd get a call from someone that would be newsworthy but too involved, like the one with Sharma Swards.

Me: M&K. Luke speaking.

Sharma: My boss is stealing from the employees, and I have proof, but I need someone outside the company to break the case.

Me: Full name please.

Sharma: Sharma Kelen Swards.

Me: Please hold.

Me: (Shake, shake.) Who is Sharma Sward's boss?

8 Ball: Allen Lightfeote, haha!

Me: Oh, hell no!

Me: (Click, click.) Sharma?

Sharma: Yes.

Me: I'm the wrong person for a political case. You need a lawyer. I'm happy to recommend if you'd like.

She hung up. That does happen. Allan Lightfeote is the CEO of CHI Health in the Midwest, and as much as it would be great to have that kind of prestige for taking a person down, I'm happier working smalltime crime. Perhaps fewer lost pets and cheating spouses would have been nice, but not suits, ties, and vetoes either.

Now, just for the sake of clarity, the 8 Ball didn't outright offer solutions. It wanted me to work for the reward, but it would put me on the path of the people who knew the things I needed to know to find the answers I sought. If you've ever had to solve a mystery, you know how much time it saves when you don't have to find the people of interest, but they just fall into your lap. When you have to piece the puzzle together from scratch, you're going to spend a lot, lot longer, than if an outline is narrated to you by an all-knowing toy.

Where the purpose of my having it was concerned though, I'd found countless excuses to put off asking questions. It was somewhere in the third week since I'd had the Magic 8 Ball when I first worked up the courage to ask it about Marva DeLonghi—just one simple question. I shook the ball harder than usual, as if to convey a threat if the 8 Ball offered an answer I wasn't prepared to consider. "Is Marva vulnerable to anything?"

Maybe it was just me, or maybe the 8 Ball really did consider how to answer my question more carefully because it seemed to take longer in forming a reply. Either way, the result was both succinct and tantalizingly useless. *Yes, she is, tee-hee!*

I stared at those words until the blue letters blurred and my eyes burned, stared with a question burning in my mind I dared not ask—was the Magic 8 Ball of the same magic as the thread binding my life and Lyle's to Marva? In other words, when it reported she was vulnerable, did it do so with the knowledge of her connection to me, or ignorant of it?

19

I HOPPED ON TWITTER AND ASKED MY FOLLOWERS HOW many times they'd text or call a person without reply before they got the hint. Standing, I swayed. My flask was empty. I tripped on an empty bottle on my way to the pantry for more bourbon. My toe caught in a loose loop of carpet that had started with a cigarette ember burning through the backing. I tried to catch my fall, but my arms were three days sleepless and slow as Ativan. My face caught the floor at terminal velocity.

Waking sometime later, I felt around for my phone. I'd slept on the floor.

No.

Passed out.

Quite a feat for me.

I'd once entered a drinking contest with a Viking named Bjonchondreth and his horse Thunderbringer. I outlasted them both. My headache felt like Thunderbringer's revenge. I managed to rise to all fours, then slowly, ever so slowly to my feet.

The room swam. I counted my fingers and toes, recounted, and settled on twenty, which seemed to bode well for mathematicians everywhere. I negotiated a few wobbly steps and fell into my office chair. My desktop was covered in sticky notes with micro chicken scratch scribbles, my handwriting, but absent my memory. If I focused hard on any individual note, a kind of logic arose from the words written there.

I convinced myself to brew coffee. The digital readout on the Bunn machine startled me—not that it should've. Perhaps if I saw the date, then I might have just cause for concern, but I planned to avoid calendars. I made nine cups of coffee and dug a lite beer from the fridge. Lyle used to drink them—me, only in cases of emergency.

While I waited for the coffee to brew, I called Leo's. Sandra told me my bacon and eggs would be ready in five minutes.

It was yet full-dark out, the street quiet. Sandra unlocked the door for me and had the box in her hand. "You actually going to eat it this time?"

I took the box. "Have I been down in the last couple days?"

Sandra shook her head slightly. "Honey."

"I'm sorry."

She patted my elbow. "Ever tried AA? Saved my life."

"Thanks. I'll keep it in mind."

Upstairs, I did eat—scarfed, more like it. Keeping it down was another story. After that and the shower following, I returned to my desk with something resembling a clear head. I took one judicious pull on the last bottle of Magdalene in the place, and that got me fully centered. The notes on my desk locked into place. Other than an apparent brief obsession with asking the 8 Ball in varying ways if the Cubs would win the World Series, I'd grilled it for a strategy to topple Marva, and the outline had all the trappings of a primetime adventure.

The only thing I couldn't find were details on how to get Lyle back. That got me looking for the Magic 8 Ball. I scoured the office, finding it, at last, in the trashcan beneath my feet at the desk. I shook it. "Why did I throw you in the trash?"

The answer swam into the viewing area. *First, apologize.*

I wondered if it had eyes and hoped not, because my scowl of disbelief was no kindness. "I'm sorry."

Without my shaking it, a new answer materialized. *Just kidding. Haha!*

Before I started in on my grand plan, I needed to know the most important thing. "Will I put Lyle in danger if I do this?"

The window showed a series of answers, a trick I didn't know it could perform. *Roses are red / Violence is too / Love questions / are off limits / know that you do.*

I raised my hand, with the ball, meaning to hurl it against the wall. The wave of anger passed. I lowered my hand. Perhaps if I asked in another way. "Will anyone die if I go against Marva?"

One word swam to the surface: *Duh!*

20

I F I KEPT ONE EYE CLOSED WHILE I DROVE, I COULD FOLLOW the yellow dashes in the road and stay in my lane. Wind cut through my hair as smoke cycloned around the roof. Over the speakers, Eddie Vedder belted about going hungry and Chris Cornell echoed the sentiment. Grunge music is like vindication on tap. As I passed the UNO campus a shock of memory rattled me. Lyle and I had busted a cocaine dealer by the obelisk some years ago. The kid begged us not to tell his parents, and Lyle said if the kid could keep his jail time a secret, we'd do our part. It was a kindness I overlooked at the time. I wonder what happened to that boy.

Perhaps the Magic 8 Ball would know. I decided not to ask, that way I could imagine things ended up fine for him.

I turned off Dodge at Farnam, driving past Warren's house. That's Warren Buffet for those of you living beneath a rock. Irony was, I was driving past the house he owned in the Dundee neighborhood, headed for the building he's rumored to live in more often than not. As a majority owner of Kiewit, Warren has the top floor of their midtown office building as his own penthouse, or so the story goes.

East of Saddlecreek Boulevard, Farnam becomes a one-way westbound and the eastbound road snakes into Harney. I drove past midtown and flipped around, came back and parked out front of Crescent Moon. If I was ever hungry—a rarity—a Rueben sandwich from Crescent Moon was sure to top my list of cravings. Their sauerkraut had no equal, and the rye bread was homemade.

I glassed the Kiewit building, counting floors until my lenses stopped on the thirteenth window up. The corner office belonged to Galina Pandrez. I knew this because the Magic 8 Ball knew this. Her office was bathed in late-day sunlight. Oh to be a cat in that window.

My plan was to make trouble. I put my binoculars away, opened the car door and stepped out onto the street. A mild breeze blew. I pulled my collar close to my chin. It was warm, but I'm cold blooded.

Someone was exiting just as I arrived at the entrance. He held the door for me. I appreciate simple kindness, but I swear, as I thanked him, his face made a microexpression of disgust. Perhaps my sweat was equal parts exertion and debauchery.

Cream-colored granite shot through with black and silver veins coated every surface beneath the ceiling. The ceiling was of sound-dampening cork tile. A few vacant chairs surrounded a glass-topped coffee table. On the table, outdated magazines were fanned. The lobby was empty save a woman behind a desk. I approached her.

Her black hair was in a tight bun. She wore reading glasses on a chain. They were perched at the tip of her nose. At some time in her life, she'd loved the sun, a story her skin told in full. She sat still as an animal in highway headlights. I waited for her to address me. When the time drawn by her silence formed a disrespectful shape, I took my cue. "I'm here to see Ms. Pandrez."

The woman typed something on her keyboard. "She has no appointments I can see."

I shifted my weight from one hip to the other. "Ms. Pandrez isn't expecting me. I'm a detective, and I have a few questions for her."

The woman adjusted her readers. "Do you have a badge?"

I showed her. She laughed. "That's not a badge. That's a toy."

"It's a badge, and I'm a detective."

"Are you licensed and bonded?"

I had a mind to slap her across the face and tell it like it was. "My partner carried the license."

The woman straightened in her chair. "So you're playing detective with a fake badge, and you expect me to phone the Chair of Ecological Development and ask her to stop everything she's doing to speak with you?"

I visualized violence. "I'm not playing anything, and if you don't phone Ms. Pandrez, A-S-A-fucking-P, don't blame me for what happens next."

The woman smirked. My fire was lit. She tapped a fingernail on her granite desktop. "I'm sorry. I simply can't justify disrupting Ms. Pand—"

I lunged over the desk and took the snide little bitch's blazer in my fists and pulled her to her feet so our noses were sharing bacterial colonies. "You're going to call Ms. Pandrez right now, or I'm going to take your telephone here and break it over your head." I released her lapels. "Are we clear?"

For having been ambushed violently, the woman maintained an enviable degree of composure. She straightened her blazer, nodded to herself, and lifted the phone receiver. She looked at me with her finger hovering over the nine key. "You have a choice, Lucia." She pronounced my name lew-shuh. "You can turn around and walk out that door, or you can wait for security to arrive, because if I dial nine-one-one, a guard will be here in a moment and they will ensure you're detained until we can have you arrested."

This was not the kind of trouble I'd aimed to create, and I wondered if I was losing control. One thing was certain: I couldn't risk arrest. I turned without comment and retreated. Needing the last word is a sign of weakness, and I refused to cede that.

Outside I lit a cigarette and returned to the van. I smoked and brooded, sitting behind the steering wheel. My flask was dangerously close to empty. I conserved as I was able, but my brain showed signs of critical sobriety fatigue. Once I'd settled from my poor showing, I nabbed the 8 Ball and shook it. It didn't need shaking, but my superstitious side thought it might create more favorable answers if shaken. "How'd I do?"

Just fine...JK. ROTFL. Get it? I'm a ball. Rolling on the floor? Haha!

Imagine being teased by a Magic 8 Ball. "What should I have done differently?"

I'd more voiced that question in the rhetorical, but the 8 Ball answered anyway. *Diplomacy.*

When this whole thing was said and done, I'd be giving Suzie a piece of my mind. The 8 Ball was less malicious, and more condescending. "Next time you lead, then."

It showed no answer to that.

I grabbed the binoculars from the glove box and glassed Galina's office window. In the waning daylight, she'd illuminated her office lamps. An amber hue spilled from the windows. Of course, the woman was a workaholic. I killed time smoking, thinking about bourbon, and scrolling Twitter. I drafted a tweet asking for broken heart stories, but chose not to send it. Later, I opened a text to Lyle, and asked if he wanted to grab dinner some night but deleted the message unsent. At the rate I was going, I'd need to change my middle name to Pathetic.

Just past eight, Galina's light extinguished. I fired the engine, and shifted the Savana into drive. An employee garage exited into the alley on the south side of the building. I needed a vantage point of cars exiting the alley, without slowing for the cameras to record. Watching the digital clock, I waited two minutes then nosed onto the road. If my timing was off, Galina might not be driving out of the garage, and I'd be forced to circle, making it possible to miss her entirely.

But I've always been a good judge of time. It's one of my natural gifts, all the more heightened in sobriety. Galina's BMW pulled onto the road and made for Harney. She stayed east across the interstate. We were approaching downtown when flashers filled my rearview mirror. I startled, but the moderate shock of seeing the lights turned into deep fear when I realized the lights were directly behind me. Compared to the average person, I was sober, but the average person and I would blow the same blood alcohol, and I'd be punching a ticket to decades in prison, if not longer. Fleeing seemed a reasonable option, but I decided to trust my charm—a risk, for sure, but better odds than trying to shake a police cruiser in a broken-down passenger van.

I pulled to the side of the road and shifted into park. Galina drove away, ignorant of her tail. She'd be around another day. I had to focus on me. Lighting a fresh cigarette to mask the scent of alcohol, I rolled my window down. The officer aimed the cruiser's spotlight at my side-view mirror. I had to prevent him from looking at my license.

The scrape of footsteps on gravel drew near. A police radio chirped and muffled voices traded comments there. I imagined the inside of a prison cell—not a difficult feat, as I'd spent years in prison before. Going back had never been in the plans. And, listen, just in case you don't know the system inside and out, prison and jail are two wholly separate things. As a PI, you expect to spend time in jail if you're doing your job right, but lockup, the slammer, capital P prison, is...well, just trust me that you want to steer clear. I asked myself what I was willing to sacrifice to keep me from a fourth DUI.

21

The officer knelt by my door. His face came into focus. I sighed and gasped at once. When my wits had returned, I smiled. "Mike, what are you doing here?"

He withheld a smile. "Don't be too happy. You smell like a bar mat the day after Saint Paddy's."

I tried to seem serious, but this was an officer who owed his freedom and job to me. It's a long story, and sufficient to say his debt was such that it'd never dry up in this life. "Smells can be deceiving." I showed him my flask, tipping it upside down. A few drops dribbled out, but nothing to cry over. "See? Empty."

"Sure, but that's because you poured it down your throat."

I nodded. "No denying that, but it wasn't much."

He rose, ordering me to step out of the van. I couldn't place his mood—not the typical friendliness I'd come to expect from him. I asked him if the chief had finally let him work the busy beats again. He said he'd never be a downtown officer with his past. I asked how, if that was the case, he'd been on a route to catch me.

There must've been something fascinating on the backs of his knuckles, because he examined them a good while. "That's the thing, Lu." He shook his head. "I'm so far off my beat, if dispatch sends me a ten-thirty-nine I'm fucking fired."

I gathered something, but couldn't place it. "What do you mean?"

He looked away. "It's you, Lu. Someone put in a call on you. I recognized it by the description. Intoxicated, woman, around seventy-inches tall, blonde hair, blue eyes, easy to look at but tough to smell—"

"Bullshit, they said that."

He raised his hands like don't-shoot-the-messenger. "Swear to god. Plus driving an old, beat-up van helped narrow the possibilities."

I rolled my eyes, "Maybe the registration gave me away."

He puffed out his cheeks. "I'd've known even without that."

"Sure." Mike Shotz was never going to be in line for detective, but what he lacked in raw brain power, he more than made up for in usefulness. Having someone to call on the force who would pull records was a lifesaver. "So what's so important that you had to pull me off my tail?"

He flushed, and I could see I'd offended him, but it was too late. Words spoken can't be unsaid. "If I hadn't risked my neck to take the call on you, you'd be in cuffs right now, that's what."

"Last I checked, I'm a private detective and investigating is my job. I have it on good authority Galina Pandrez is involved in illegal activity. If following a lead is against the law, then send me to jail."

Mike clapped his hands together. "Let's pretend you didn't smell like an alley dumpster behind a dive bar. If I'm anybody else, you're coming in for questions just on the report that you assaulted a woman inside the Kiewit building."

My shoulders slumped. "They reported that?"

"What do you think, Lu?"

Few people could get away with calling me Lu. "All right, you saved my ass, but don't think that makes us even. Until you help me cover up a murder, you owe me."

He pursed his lips. It made him look tired. "You'll never let me forget it."

"Maybe because you keep needing reminders."

That little jab put color back in Mike's cheeks. "So who's paying, if I might ask?"

"Top secret."

He crossed his arms. "Do they know you're going around assaulting government employees?"

There are some benefits to working for yourself. "I'm pretty sure she knows everything I'm up to, yeah."

"And she's okay with it?"

That was a tougher question. "She probably wishes I'd've chosen a more...diplomatic strategy."

Shotz nodded. "This client of yours, she wouldn't happen to have a drinking problem would she?"

I shrugged. "She has no problem drinking that I'm aware of."

"Maybe you need to pay closer attention."

When did I become the butt of everyone's jokes? "How's the wife and kids, Shotz?"

He tipped his cap. "Ah! She's resorted to a kick in the balls."

"Maybe." I lit a cigarette. "When's the divorce final?"

He smiled, shyly. "We're getting back together, as a matter of fact."

His nickname should've been On-Again-Off-Again. "What'd you buy her flowers or something?"

"Har, har." He rolled his eyes. "Actually, I promised to quit streaming on Twitch, if she'd give me one last chance."

Adults playing video games is a strange phenomenon, but adults recording themselves live while playing video games and broadcasting it online for other adults to watch is depressing. "Weren't you making decent money on that, though?"

"More than decent."

"How's she going to afford her next pair of calfskin boots?"

"You know, not going to pretend I haven't thought about that. Way I see it, if she asks me to start livestreaming again, I can't get in the doghouse for it."

"You don't seriously believe that, do you?"

"Which part?"

I scrubbed out my cigarette coal and threaded the butt back into the pack. "The part about not getting in the doghouse. I'm no therapist, mind you, but I think it's safe to say, she wants you to afford life's pleasures by climbing the ladder at OPD."

"Then she should've married Sherlock Holmes."

"I think he's a little old for her."

Mike's radio beeped. He raised it to his ear, backed away, and listened for a beat. When he was done his mood had shifted. You could feel it like they say animals feel a shift in barometric pressure. He leaned in. "Speaking of old geezers, how's Lyle?"

There's a place around your sternum where if you get hit just right it stops your heart. His question felt like that—not because I minded talking about Lyle with him, but because his asking was agenda-driven, and all of a sudden I had the sense this is half of what'd brought Mike so far east. "You probably talk to him more than I do."

Mike shrugged. "Here and there. I doubt it."

He was too casual, and we both knew it. "Look. You got something to say, get on with it."

He sighed. "All right, but don't shoot the messenger."

"You know I hate guns."

"Cut it out, smart ass."

I was trying to make things easier on him, don't ask why. "Go on."

"Word on the street is you're kind of stalking your boy, and there's no secret you've got it out for the gov."

He was fumbling to seem casual to keep from pissing me off, but tough luck for him, because I hate the abbreviations and acronyms shtick. LOL makes me want to vomit. I have no FOMO on any acronyms, and YOLO is wrong by nine and counting, as far as I'm concerned. "I might've sat outside the capital once or twice. So what's the big deal?"

Mike kneaded his chin. "Pretty sure you've been cited six times, for parking in a handicapped spot, in Lincoln." He mock-counted them off on his fingers. "And maybe you'd like to tell me what your business with Galina Pandrez was tonight."

"Just the messenger, huh?" I tapped out a cigarette and lit it. "Is there anything wrong with being concerned for a friend?"

Shotz nodded at my pack. I had a mind to refuse him, but if karma's a real thing, I didn't want to withhold a future cigarette from myself. I gave him the one I'd just lit and sparked another for myself. He inhaled, and studied the glowing orange coal. "The governor's office has a folder on you, Lu."

"That makes two of us." I considered how nonsensical my comment sounded since I didn't have a folder on myself. "Keeping files...on stuff." How pathetic could I be? "On each other." I felt at my pockets but the flask was in the van's cupholder, and empty to boot. "Come on, Shotz. You of all people should know. When something stinks, we have a responsibility to dig up the truth."

Mike flicked ash. "Like the truth that Lyle landed one of the most prestigious jobs in state law enforcement? Like the fact that you've never congratulated him for his success? Like the truth that your behaviors basically telegraph aggression toward an elected official? What about the truth that despite a docket two miles long, Lyle has covered for you every time?"

"Jesus, Mikey! Whose side are you on, here?"

Mike dropped his cigarette, only half finished, and pulverized it beneath his boot heal. "I'm not taking sides, but I am saying to the untrained eye, your behavior's starting to look a little more than neurotic, if you know what I mean?"

You can try to dance around a subject, but that's never been me. "You think I'm out of line?"

He stalled, mentally rehearsing his reply. I think it's clear you have strong feelings about Lyle, and sometimes I wonder if that's muddled your usual levelheaded perspective."

There was no convincing him I had some inside track—anytime you want to pursue the "I alone" narrative bright red flashing light and a blaring horn materialize over your head as a voice from on high blares, "This is how cults begin". My hands felt useless, and I plunged them into my jacket pockets. "I can't believe no one else sees what a two-faced, lying, cheating, scheming asshole Marva DeLonghi is." I was approaching volatile territory and knew it, but I couldn't stop myself. "Do you actually think she hired Lyle because he was the most qualified for the job, or do you think she hates me that bad and knew what it'd do to take him from me?"

Shotz puffed up at this and I knew I'd as good as walked into a trap. "I think he saved her life, and she showed him the appropriate gratitude for that."

My own volume startled me. "I told him where to be!" With a deep breath, I settled myself. "And you're telling me, she didn't have any place for me on her staff?"

"Lu, don't get me wrong. We all think you're a helluva detective, but last I checked, you were recorded on live TV that night calling Marva DeLonghi censored names. You're the one who said, and I quote, 'She's a scourge, but we had no other choice than to save her.'"

I threw my hands in the air. "Jesus! I was drunk, and half in shock from dealing with Magnus Adderpaine."

"When aren't your drunk?"

I shot a scowl at the Savana, like it was to blame for the empty flask it contained. "Now."

Mike shrugged. "You sure smell like it."

Apparently my hygiene had gotten away from me, because everyone and their pet had something to say about my aroma. "Marva hired Magnus to kill her, and I proved it in court, but...never mind. It's not like you've heard this a thousand times. And you clearly don't believe me."

Mike shifted his weight and threaded his thumbs through his utility beltloops. "I don't believe you, and the jury didn't either. The defense provided ample evidence Marva had hired Magnus in a consultative role to help her preserve the migratory flyways of snow geese and Sandhill Cranes in Nebraska. There was clear and compelling evidence Magnus acted alone in hiring a hitman. And—"

"Larry Surlman."

"Whatever you say." Mike posted his hands on his hips, having settled into full lecture mode. No one believed my resurrection stories— two lives or nine lives didn't make any difference—and it hadn't helped, in the final math, Laser, known publicly as Larry Surlman escaped Lyle and remained at large. "Point is, you made enemies by preaching whacko conspiracies, and despite seeing the governor unite both parties to increase police funding while also helping pass wildlife protection acts you yourself used to rant and rave about, you maintain that she's some kind of secret force of evil."

I folded my arms across my chest. Mike and I had had this very conversation before. Shift the words, adjust the focus, but it'd all been said before. It was on me to accept I was alone on this, and unless the Magic 8 Ball's plan worked, I would die lonely and discredited. "Are we done here?"

Mike rolled his eyes. "You're welcome for saving your ass."

"Sure. Thanks."

22

I preferred the slight tacky cling of Leo's wooden chairs to the stale, claustrophobic air of our office. It'd been a little over a week since I'd come down for breakfast, but I'd emerged from a slight depression—okay, major—and showered. You know things are looking up when you have the energy to shave your pits and legs. When I arrived at my usual table, I felt ready to find some lost pets. I'd even managed to eat a toast wedge with half an egg over easy, but the bacon kept taunting me, and I couldn't make myself do it.

The bell over the door chimed just as I was dosing my coffee with a bit more Magdalene. A hand holding a Whatchamacallit was followed by a long, lean, strong body. Lyle sighted me instantly. I swept the Magic 8 Ball into my purse and tried to act casual.

Lyle sat. He wafted his hand in front of his nose. "Smells like a dishtub and a barback got in a fight with an overflowing ashtray, and I'm not sure who won, huh."

Maybe it was my new body wash. "Good to see you too."

He threw back a yogurt cup like a shot of tequila. "How's business?"

I could tell him the 8 Ball was doing wonders for my bank account, but I liked him spending the salary Marva gave him on my bare necessities. "I'm scraping by."

"Saw you on the news."

White lies had a time and place. "Doing a little pro bono work to manage the reputation your boss tried so hard to fuck over."

He made quick work of a corndog. "Who's trying to fuck who over, huh?"

I knew a bad alley when I saw one. "You bring me any smokes or what?"

He dug in his pocket, slapped a pack on the table. "Rest of the carton's in the car." I reached for the pack, but he kept his hand over it. "You ever gonna get an apartment again, so you don't have to live where you work?"

Thing was, he paid halfsies on the office, so I could still call it ours—not why he did it, since his was something far more chivalrous, something about guilt, sticking me with a bill I'd never agreed to pay, but anyways—I had a penny-pinchers mentality at heart. Never know when the cash'll dry up. "Shoot. I haven't thought about it lately."

He let his hand off the pack and turned his focus to a turkey and cheese footlong. Through a mouthful of sliced vegetables, bread, and animal murder, he grilled me on the Cubs. What did I think of their first month? How likely was it they'd turn it around? Was Dansby the heir to J-Hey? I volleyed off the replies with single-word answers: "Bad." "Un-," and "Yes." I grew up a fan of the lovable losers. The last few years represented a return to form. It took an attitude adjustment, but I could manage.

I finished my coffee. The buzz was headier in Lyle's company. "But you didn't come here to talk baseball, and you didn't drive all the way to Omaha to check on me."

He leaned back in his chair. "Fine, huh. I'm here to ask you, face-to-face, what's your long-game with Marv?"

At least he respected me enough to know I planned shit. "I'll put it this way: She makes Rod Blagojevich look like a boy scout, and I'm going to prove it."

Lyle bit into a baked apple. "I'll put it this way. You've got a friggin' screw loose if that's what you really think."

He couldn't know what he didn't know. "Just wait."

"No."

"No?"

He decapitated a cinnamon bear. "No."

"No what?"

"I'm not going to wait for you to fuck around and figure out on your own sweet time that Marv is one of the good ones."

There were a handful of ways I could slice this situation. I settled on avoidance. "Did you hear Sandra is quitting?" I'd just learned this myself when I arrived that morning.

"Quitting, huh?"

As if summoned, she appeared at our tableside. "Coffee?"

Lyle raised a hand to his brow and swiped at it. "Lu says you're quitting."

She nodded. "My last week."

"We'll miss you."

She smiled. "Where you been Putch?"

"Lu didn't tell you?"

Sandra's brow furrowed. Last she'd heard, he was on business in Spain. My reasons for his absence had grown increasingly absurd. "Tell me what?"

"I'm head of security for Governor DeLonghi."

"Hot damn!" She knocked on the tabletop. "Since when, honey?"

Lyle eyed me—catching on, I imagine. "Um...It's been eight months."

Sandra nodded. I wanted to see inside her thoughts. "So. No Spain then?"

"Spain?"

She nodded once, a tight little bob of her head. "Let me go grab your coffee."

I wanted to explain, but what could I say, *I never expected you to be gone this long?* or *People just like me better when you're around, and I have a hard time admitting I drove you off.* The last bit probably isn't even true. Maybe it was. I guess I could believe it was. "It's possible I didn't tell her you'd left.

Lyle shoved a cinnamon powdered donut into his mouth. He chewed it deliberately. "Look, Lu, you're going to get me fired. Marva sent me to tell you if I can't get you to stop harassing her and everyone she works with, she's gonna give me the ax."

Of course she'd light a fire and smoke me out. In a sea of acceptance, adoration, and love for the governor, I was the sole fish swimming against the current. Lyle couldn't even imagine she was playing him. "M&K is hiring."

"God damnit, Lu." He peeled the wrapper from a string cheese. "I like my job. I'm making a difference, and it challenges me."

I curled my lip. "You made more of a difference in one night working with me than you have in all the time with Marva."

He splayed his hands on the table. Sandra brought his coffee. He asked her what she'd do with all her free time. She said she'd probably travel. He asked where. She said Hawaii maybe, and Mexico, places with sun where it never snowed. He said he was jealous. She asked if he was eating. He said he'd take a Fantasy Island to go. She asked how he wanted his eggs. He asked for them beat within an inch of their lives. She laughed.

After she'd gone to enter his order, he wiped his palms down his face. "If you're hiring, Debbie could use the job. She's barely making ends meet at Taco Bell."

"I'll take that under consideration."

He peeled a banana. "Listen. I hate saying this, but I need you to hear me. I came to tell you it's time to stop harassing the governor. It's my ass on the line, and I believe you care about me, so if you can't do it for any other reason, leave her alone because it's what I want." I wanted to tell him he didn't know what he wanted. He scooted his chair back. "And if you don't listen and I catch wind of even one bit of funny business, just one sniff of BS...anything at all, and it'll be me personally who dumps gasoline on your head and strikes the match. We clear, huh?"

If there was any doubting my appearance to talk with Galina Pandrez had been a mistake, Marva sending Lyle eliminated it. I mimed zipping my lips, keying the lock and tossing it away. "You know I'd do anything for you, right?"

He nodded. Bit into a celery stick. "Yeah, well do this for me." He started to turn, then looked back. "And hey, don't forget Debbie, huh."

23

It was spiraling into the kind of day you'd rather chuck in a blender with ice cubes, bourbon, and gun powder. I parked outside the restaurant and stubbed out my cigarette. Taco Bell lobbies smell like humane society waiting rooms. Make your own judgements, but remember, I spend half my working life in and around animal shelters. Debbie peaked out from the drive thru nook and started in on her apron's knot.

I raised my hand. "Hold it."

She tossed the drive thru headset on the floor. "I forgive you, okay?"

"Who said I was asking?"

Debbie balled the apron by the cash register. "I'm good at reading intent."

I scoffed. "You're certainly good at ignoring evidence." I glanced at the menu. "Give me three Double Decker Tacos, two bean burritos, a Pintos and Cheese, and a Baja Blast."

Debbie stopped, mimicked a soldier's about face. She pulled up behind the register and started poking at the screen. After a moment, the register drawer popped open. She ripped the receipt from the printer, lifted the cash organizer and placed the receipt beneath it. "Someone waiting for us in the van?"

"Just me."

She called the order back, though I'm pretty sure modern fast-food joints don't need employees to do that anymore. After she tossed her apron on the floor, she turned her attention to me. "You actually hungry?"

I could say with all sincerity I was. "Starving." While we waited, I pocketed a fistful of Fire Sauce. Forget everything I've said about my appetite before. There was that moment and none before or since. That's all I can make of it.

When a big guy from the kitchen brought the food, he surveyed Debbie and asked what the hell was going on. She said something came up, and she had to go.

He shook his head. "Excuse me?"

Debbie grabbed the bag of food. "Tell Tom thanks for the opportunity. Things just weren't meant to be, you know."

"Deb?"

She turned, hoofing it for the door. The man looked at me. I had no idea how to respond. "Tell Tom I said sorry."

He raised one eyebrow. "Who are you?"

I looked at my wrist for the watch that had never been there. "I guess I'm Debbie's boss or something." I found the door and used it.

Clouds had rolled in, and the humidity had risen a hundred-fold. Debbie sat behind the wheel of the Savana. "You planning on sharing?"

I wasn't and said so. "But you can have a taco."

She opened it and swiped the lettuce from the top, balling it in the wrapper, which she held out for me to take. I wasn't too keen on her presumption but decided to let it slide. We were letting the argument play out in actions, not words.

I topped off the sodapop with what was left in my flask, and parked the cup in the cupholder to marinate. Contrary to popular belief, mixed drinks need to age and breathe. Debbie drove with one hand and her knee. I lost myself in the food. Sometimes nothing is more intoxicating than food, which didn't stop me from sampling my drink between the pintos and my second bean burrito.

Debbie said something really bad must've happened for me to be eating like I was. I ignored her. On 275, at the exit for Valley, I told

Debbie to pull off. She nodded. I asked her to stop on the shoulder. She studied me. "Are you feeling nauseous?"

"Nauseated."

"You are? Too much food?"

I shook my head. "It's not nauseous. If you say, 'I'm nauseous' it means you make others feel nauseated. The word you're looking for is nauseated."

She hmmphed, offered nothing more.

I dug in my purse and snagged the Magic 8 Ball. "You need to do me a favor."

Her eyes darted to and away from the 8 Ball. "I don't trust that thing."

"It's just a toy, right?"

She looked out the driver side window. "I never said that."

I held it out for her to take. She leaned away. I moved it closer. She'd crammed herself so close to the door, her body looked deformed. I raised the 8 Ball to hover before her eyes. "I need you to ask it one question."

"I don't want to."

I joggled the 8 Ball in my hand. "Are we going to work together or not?"

By degrees, she relaxed, her body loosening. "What am I supposed to ask it?"

I nodded. "Good. Now. Ask it why Lyle chose Marva over me."

Even before I'd begun to hand the Magic 8 Ball over, it began to formulate its standard reply to all things Lyle. *I cannot answer questions about love.*

Debbie straightened, assuming a posture of confidence. "I don't need a possessed toy to tell you that. She treated him like an equal. That appeals to people."

This was the first time I'd sensed Debbie's choice to be with me through all things was less about her devotion to me and more about her commitment to some promise she'd made herself. It stung to feel like I was an obligation. "Just ask it, would you?" She tested the Magic 8 Ball's weight balanced on her fingers, slowly let it settle into her hand.

Her uncertainty made a strange kind of sense to me, but I laughed. "It's not going to bite you."

"If biting was the worst it could do." She turned it over in her hand. Her mind was working at every level. She drew a long breath and held it. "Why did Lyle choose to work with Governor DeLonghi over Luke?" She watched as the answer swam onto the viewing window and read as it emerged. "For the money. Tee-hee, JK. ROTFL. It's good to feel wanted." Debbie dropped the ball and it fell to the floor board. "Get that thing away from me."

I was only too happy to and leaned across the seat, snatching it from beneath the brake pedal. As I did, I wondered if it had enough agency to stop on purpose, because it had come to rest in such a uniquely dangerous place. You could almost imagine it resisting momentum on a lane change to stay right where it rolled so you'd want to smash the brakes but instead plow into the back of a stopped car and die in a fiery crash. I dropped it in my purse and tried to forget what it had said.

24

I emerged from the dressing room in a prison orange, silk button-up with a notched collar, a pair of high-rise corduroy pants with flare bottoms, and cork wedges. Debbie, in jean overalls, a puffed sleeve blouse, and Chucks looked me over. I flipped my hair, hoping for casual-chic, but felt Halloween-flop. "Selection's kind of sparse, you think?"

A girl, seventeen tops, stood by in a V-neck t-shirt with the number fourteen emblazoned in sequins across her chest. She stepped forward. "This, like, huge group came by earlier. They bought everything in, like, the store. My manager's on her way, but she doesn't even know where to get more stuff." She rolled her eyes. "It's, like, a good problem to have, I guess, but between you and me, it's totally gonna take months of digging through the Goodwills to replenish her stock. It takes time to find actual, like, quality vintage. Right?"

One person's trash was another person's treasure, apparently, and if I had more time, after a comment like that, I'd skip the go-between and shop at the thrift stores. Though, who am I kidding? I hate clothes shopping. "Were you working when the group came in?"

"I basically live here, like..."

"What kind of people were they?" I tried to wring the poofs out of Debbie's sleeves.

The girl sighed, a huff of annoyance. "Look at you getting all salty." She flipped her hair. "They were, like, *people*, you know."

Patience is key, but some people make it hard. "Were they young, old, white, brown, black, fancy, frumpy? Did they have jewelry, piercings, tattoos? Anything that stood out?"

"They were mostly women." She dropped the emphasis on the second syllable of women like she'd offered a profound revelation. "I mean, like, ninety-nine percent, for real."

That observation was about as useful as a lawnmower without a blade. Flying Worm Vintage Clothing stocked exclusively women's clothing, so men in attendance would tend to be attached to a female shopper—not that there's anything wrong with men dressing as they please. Now, if the group had been 95% male..."What else."

The girl shrugged and sighed. "I don't know. They, like, looked like *you*."

Her cadence of speech suggested she felt her comments were equal parts insightful and dismissive. "Like me in what way?"

"Vibe check! I don't know—like, old and frumpy and totally basic."

Debbie snorted laughter. "I mean this in the most loving way possible, but you're selling this." She gestured to her outfit. "If you looked up extra in the dictionary, there'd be a picture of this outfit." She fixed me with a look I'd not seen on her before. "In all seriousness, is it absolutely necessary for us to dress like clowns?"

I shook my head, looked at the girl. "Looks like I'm gonna need to talk her off the ledge, if you want to give us a minute."

"KK." She spun on her heels and walked toward the registers. Under her breath, she said, "Clowns."

The orange top hugged all the worst places on me, and flowed where it had no business flowing. "I don't like this any more than you do, but we've got a job to do, you dig?" The girl's slang had dug its hooks in me.

Debbie tugged at her shirt collar. "We're going to stick out like chickens at a beef lobby."

"Funny you should say that." I tugged at my sleeve. "We're going to a benefit for Proposition Twenty-Nine, and this is how those clowns dress."

"Screw that! Are you calling me a clown? I signed the petition to get

Prop Twenty-Nine on ballots, and I don't own a single pair of overalls or shitty shoes."

I smirked. It was fun seeing Debbie get worked up. "You're the one who called them clowns."

"Did not."

I reminded her she said she was dressed like a clown. "And by the way, in case you think I'm some kind of backwater monster, I signed the petition too, but we're not the ones who started it."

"Then—" Debbie pinched the tip of her nose and held it a beat— "why are we dressing like we are? I mean look at me, I could be Starsky's mother, for godsakes!"

The girl cleared her throat. She must've decided we were taking too long, or getting too sus. "Do you, like, need anything *else*?"

Debbie jerked her thumb toward the exit. "To feel like all my self-respect hasn't blown away. For starters."

I shook my head, slow and exaggerated. "Just go ahead and ring us up and we'll be out of your hair."

The girl slithered her body sassy as a snake in sunshine. She made eyes at Debbie. "Nobody forced you to shop here."

She wasn't wrong. I swept my hand over my head in mock grandeur. "We need costumes for the soiree of soirees tonight. Retro's the theme, so here we are."

"Costumes?" The girl rolled her eyes. "You know, I never thought I'd be any more nonplussed about a customer than the old guy who bought all those women their clothes today. He talked to me like I was a four-year-old. But you're, like, totally worse."

She hadn't mentioned any old guys—worth a follow up, but it could wait. "What is it you think nonplussed means?"

The girl cocked her head, narrowing one eye. "Unhappy about something. Like, you know."

I shook my head. "Points for ambitious vocab, but it actually means total surprise, as in, 'You'd expected a boring shift at work but were nonplussed by the number of pain-in-the-ass customers who came in to shop today.'"

This got a smile from her, which for correcting someone's usage, is a no small win. "Are you going to buy the stuff, or just stand around sweating in it all afternoon?"

I said we'd buy what we were wearing if she could scare up a ten percent coupon. She said they didn't do coupons, and I said it was worth a try. We ducked into the changing room and as Debbie slipped out of her overalls, I flashed back to our time in prison together. Whenever my mind lands on memories from a failed life, I get a potent headache.

After we gathered our clothes and paid, I dashed for the outdoors, nicotine depleted and dizzy. Debbie came up beside me, standing shoulder-to-shoulder. I flicked my lighter closed. "Can you believe that place?"

She shifted her weight. Electric charge flowed through her. She leaned into me slightly. "I know how you feel."

Smoke lingered before my face. I drew on the filter, and the coal crackled. "How so?"

Debbie shifted so our shoulders formed a ninety-degree angle. "Somebody shit on you, so you want to shit on anything that person represents." She twisted her head and cracked her neck. "I've been...you know...I've been there too. Might not've killed Bobby, but I hated him enough, and I made his life hell the whole last year."

I flicked ash. Where Debbie was going, I didn't want to follow. "Fucker deserved it."

"No."

"He started it, and it would've gotten worse if he'd lived."

Debbie shrugged. "According to whom?"

"I read the reports. I've seen his kinda shit before."

"People change."

"Not people like him." I shook my head. "No. People like him think they deserve shit."

"Maybe." Debbie pulled back. "But maybe if I'd been able to be honest about who I was attracted to—"

"Life is a journey of self-discovery." This psychobabble was close to nauseous. "Anyway."

Debbie cupped her elbow in one hand, and rested her chin in the other. I don't have enough of a belly—okay, I have no belly, so definitely not enough—to create a makeshift table for my forearm, but it looked strangely natural and quite comfortable. She watched me intently, until I broke eye contact. "I know Lyle hurt you when he chose to take the job with Governor DeLonghi, but if you can't let it go, nothing good will come of it. She's doing good things for this city, like Prop. Twenty-Nine. If you try to sabotage that just to see her fail you—"

I flicked my cigarette butt to the sidewalk and pulverized it with my boot. "She's not doing anything for the city. She doesn't give a fuck about it. All she wants is to stir people up, get them divided, and laugh at the carnage. She's a goddamned wrecking ball, and I'm shocked nobody can see it."

Debbie smiled condescendingly. "A wrecking ball who used her authority to overturn the death penalty Governor Pete Shithead Ricketts reinstated? What kind of carnage is it that puts its reputation on the line to get wildlife protection bills passed? Maybe you've forgotten, but this is the home of Omaha Steaks. We're a proud community of red-blooded meat eaters. Trying to protect animals isn't much of a campaign strategy."

I knelt and scooped up the fiberglass filter. If I'd have put my arm in a blood pressure cuff the machine would've exploded. "You're ignoring all the other things she's doing that don't get news coverage. Land leases, mineral rights, building permits."

"And since when did you give two shits about politics, Lu?"

"Don't call me that!"

"Well?"

I'd hoped to back her down, but she was fit to see this out, and I'll be honest, I never thought Debbie would contradict me. "I thought you said you trusted me, and here you are trying to dismantle me and everything I'm doing."

Debbie made herself tall. "I do trust you, but I think your jealousy's clouded your judgement."

"Here we go again." I started down the sidewalk. Maybe Debbie would choose to let me go. I knew she wouldn't, but I wanted her to. "I'm not fucking crazy."

25

Turned out my orange jumper and Debbie's overalls were—if anything—too conservative. The crowd would've made peacocks feel underdressed. Just imagine, these people had been plucked out of *Boogie Nights*, dipped in glitz, dragged through a Roald Dahl novel, and poured into the vast conference hall like so many coins from a slot machine. What I wouldn't have given to be a fly on the walls of the employee service station at the Downtown Double Tree that night. Instead, I had to mingle, so I stashed a 750 of Magdalene in a potted Ficus, and found increasingly bizarre excuses to circle the edges of the room for a refill of my flask.

One man who stopped me when I'd slipped away from Debbie for a refill wore a suit jacket and pants made of genuine, one-hundred-dollar bills. He had to tell me a little-known fact that American currency was printed on a linen/cotton blend fabric, and not—in fact—paper, as was commonly believed. Before I managed to extract myself from his lecture, he let it be known even those who knew US currency was printed on fabric often had the blend incorrect. If you Googled the question, you'd be told bills were one-quarter linen to three-quarters cotton when the truth was closer to twenty-seven percent linen, one-percent pine pulp, and seventy-one percent cotton. That little bit of pine is what enables a clean tear when you rip a note in half, and now I will live the rest of my life with another useless fact keeping house in my brain.

The space had been rented at no small expense by the Nebraska Flyways and Waterways Coalition for the evening, and based on the necklaces, watches, rings, earrings, purses, and clutches in attendance— I'm talking five-pound diamonds, golf ball-sized pearls, fist-sized sapphires, platinum, gold, even a confirmed Alexandrite ring, which required its own entourage in the form of a security guard—the event would raise well into the millions.

I approached the bar, following one of my perimeter-checks after overhearing a woman say the cocktail tab would be astronomical and someone needed to send a thank you to Wildarmar—whoever that was —for providing the libations. The bartender wore an afro, and I wondered if he'd been hired for the night on that one style choice alone. I leaned in after a lady carried away two cloudy orange beverages in high balls. "What's your best bourbon?"

The bartender adjusted his black silk vest. "People seem to enjoy this Karl Kelley Five-Year."

I read the bottle he indicated. Anything under ten years better be named Magdalene, or it was a waste of money, but I almost swallowed my tongue when I got to the bottom of the label. "Nonalcoholic! What the hell? Who do I look like?"

The bartender raised his eyebrows. "Ma'am, this is an alcohol-free event."

I glanced back at Debbie, who was listening with amphetamine focus to a woman wearing a red lightning bolt and sporting a beehive hairdo straight out of Rocky Horror Picture Show. I went and rescued her, though she appeared perturbed at my intrusion. Perhaps I misheard her, but I think she said something about me going up in flames if she got too near me with a lit match. I did find straight lines to be somewhat more cumbersome than usual. When I'd brought her to the bar, I pointed at the row of bottles and described the issue as succinctly as I could. "Imposters."

She leaned past me, like I'd not said a word, rested an elbow on the bar top, and nodded to the bartender. "I'll take the Stars and Stripe, but can you do about half the grenadine?"

The bartender nodded and turned to mix her drink. I raised my hand in the universal WTF gesture. "You're kidding me?"

"Why would I be?"

I pointed at the menu. "You did see the part about nonalcoholic, right?"

Debbie beamed. "Thank goodness for a change. It's like I've died and gone to Debvana."

I couldn't gratify her nonsense with a reply, instead choosing to hit my flask for all to see, because my inhibitions were flirting with an all-time low. I told Debbie, apropos of nothing that we blended in, thanks to the worm shop, and criticized the rest of the population for caring more about their own glamour than anyone else's. I had half a mind to hide out and wait for my moment, which I think was code for wanting to drink more bourbon, but Debbie said she'd found my bottle and fed it to the trashcan. I nearly cried, and almost punched her in the nose.

After the bartender gave Debbie her pointless drink I asked for a glass with ice and a lime wedge because I figured there were only so many trashcans Debbie could have used. The bartender refused me, and I said I'd report his ass, reaching into the tip jar and retrieving a handful of bills. Debbie slapped my hand. The bartender watched as I released the cash, and kept his eye on me until I was well away from his tips.

Debbie took my arm in her hand the way a mother will her young child when a scolding is in order, and she grew very motherly. She said she'd already set aside her own values to help me, and if I embarrassed her on top of it all, I'd regret it. I asked if she was threatening me, and she said she had no need of threats, because the universe would defend her if I mistreated her. I wanted to ask which religious text she was pulling that nonsense from, but she was right that her role in the evening's festivities was already pushing a reasonable person's boundaries, so I let it go, and even apologized. I'm not always a monster!

I found the table with our names on it, and sat, sneaking a peak at the Magic 8 Ball. "You sure this is going to work?"

Yes. Now grow a pair and quit being such a coward, you drunken fool.

Even the 8 Ball found me pathetic. It was sexist, which appalled me. I shut my purse and hit the flask when Debbie was distracted. Things went a bit swimmy, and my tongue felt heavy. Would you believe me if I said I was nervous?

Debbie brought a young woman for me to meet: Jenny? Jenthica? Jessie? I remember her husband was an environmental lawyer, but not why that changed anything. My tongue felt thick and numb in my mouth. Debbie had to help me stand, and she led me to the bathroom. She pushed me into a stall and told me to purge. I told her I could hold my liquor.

"Do it or I walk."

I squinted at both of her, and they were equally pissed-looking. For Debbie to leave me with an ultimatum, I had to have really messed up. "Okay. Fine, fine, but you owe me." I pointed a finger at the space between both of her.

When we left the bathroom, I was feeling slightly more alert, even a bit horny with my stomach emptied. Don't ask.

From somewhere, speakers projected a man calling guests to their tables. Debbie guided me by the elbow, and I let her, though my vision had repaired from split screen to mono. I giggled, said it smelled good. "These are such beautiful people. You know? I feel sorry for them. They really believe they're saving the world. God! That must feel so good."

Debbie sat me down, told me to keep quiet. I nodded, and it seemed appropriate to give her a little salute. She told me if I didn't cut the shit, she was going to escort me out. I promised complete, utter, and total compliance.

If you could look past the loud colors, the white teeth, and the tanning booth complexions, there were some handsome men in attendance. Debbie pointed at my glass of ice water and told me to drink. I complied—one-hundred-percent. Water can be extremely tasty when it's wet enough. You never know when that's going to be. It kind of awakened me a little.

"Testing—" my head jolted toward the voice—"testing, testing." A man knuckled a handheld microphone. The thump, thud, thunk jarred my head like I'd skipped happy drunk and plummeted into Hangoversville. He put his lips so close to the microphone mesh, I imagined it felt violated. "Don't worry, folks, I'm not the main attraction." He wore a wool sport coat and blue jeans like an IT guy who'd gotten lost.

When he produced a tablet from a leather shoulder bag, my brain flushed, and I could've walked a tightrope. He placed it on the podium and shared with the audience that Bryan Bernitt would be speaking shortly. Then he invited the hotel staff to begin table service. I pictured what Lyle's reaction would've been when men and women in white collars and black slacks shuttled in, carrying plates with whole lobsters and tenderloin steaks. There were wilted green and fingerling potatoes to finish the plate.

Once the table service had concluded, the man of the hour took the stage. He wore an over-the-ear microphone, a pastel pink fedora, a lime green sport coat, and Carolina blue slacks with classic Birkenstock sandals. His greeting boomed, as he welcomed us with both hands extended. I tapped Debbie's shin with the toe of my boot and whispered. "Go time."

On the drive in, Debbie had asked why I couldn't just take the tablet when no one was looking, to which I'd asked if she'd ever noticed neither of our faces looked like Bernitt's. She'd asked what that had to do with the price of rice in Tokyo. After addressing her racism, I'd asked how she unlocked her phone. Understanding had dawned on her face.

She mouthed a question at me. I understood but pretended not to. She wouldn't let it go. "Because—" I whispered—"when there's something important at stake, my brain is always sober."

It was clear she didn't buy my claim, but I didn't need her to. I just needed her to do her part so I kicked her shin again and made my most serious eyes. She mouthed, *Really?* and I mouthed, *Now!*, because the guy was already starting his closing comments because no one wanted to eat cold lobster, and she mouthed, *Seriously?*, and I mouthed, *GO!!!*

She rolled her eyes back in her head, which is a trick I'd learned she could do from our stretch in the state pen together, and she fell back on her chair, making loud, passionate gargling sounds. First just the people immediately around us noticed, but as Debbie's gargling grew in volume, and she worked up a good lather of foam around her mouth, and some goopy slobber, panic spread out in a shockwave.

At the first squeal—a woman in a royal blue space suit type dress—I was up, out of my chair and moving for the stage. The NF&WC's CEO set his tablet on the podium just as the sexist 8 Ball had said he would. I approached it, feeling perhaps a bit more gelatinous in the legs than I'd expected to, but still clear enough and in-command enough to perform. The tablet reader was unlocked. I dug a dongle from my pocket and plunged it into the charging port.

Debbie was growling like a wild animal, and there were screams from the crowd assuming an unreported shellfish allergy. I opened my cellphone, closing Twitter and opening an app called Hacker 2k. It loaded, scanned for nearby devices, and found the dongle, offering a prompt to download. I selected *YES* and accepted the terms of service, which was hilarious given the legal status of the app. My phone showed a download window and a two-minute timer.

One man had taken charge of the Debbie debacle, announcing himself a doctor. He assured the captivated crowd he could help her. They had nothing to worry about. He dipped his ear to her mouth. Perhaps his breath hit her neck or his ear grazed her lips because her seizure impression turned briefly into a something resembling laughter. The phone timer showed one minute, nine seconds remaining.

The doctor announced Debbie was likely suffering a heart arrhythmia and stated his intention to begin chest compressions in an effort to reestablish viable rhythms. No sooner than he'd laced his fingers together, downfacing palm over downfacing palm, Debbie's eyes popped open and she sat up forcefully "No, no, no!"

Startled, the doctor lost his balance and tumbled backward, striking the back of his head on a table. He crumpled to the floor. The timer on my phone seemed not to have moved, as I still showed more than a minute to complete the download.

Meanwhile, the CEO had begun to back toward the podium, reaching for something to hold onto. His forehead perspired, and I had the impression violence made him woozy. Debbie fell upon the doctor, feeling for his pulse. The bystanders murmured. You could feel the crowd trying to make sense of what it had seen while remaining riveted to the unconscious good Samaritan doctor.

Debbie looked toward me. I shrugged, nodding my head toward the tablet reader. The CEO bumped into me, and I swung around, prepared to fight my way free if forced. He hadn't seen me however and seemed to believe he'd backed into the podium, a misconception I had no need to correct, but when his hand began feeling for the tablet, I was forced to improvise.

It's a felony to yell, "Fire!" in public, even if there is a fire, though if there is a fire you'd not be charged or convicted. But there was no fire, and so the sudden scattering of bodies, so much like a spun kaleidoscope, was a last-ditch effort. The CEO, near enough to touch, ducked and winced when I yelled. I reached for the dongle. Ten seconds remained. Debbie stood. The doctor was stirring. I'd been the cause, direct or otherwise, of too many unconscious people lately.

The CEO looked at me. I asked him for his autograph. He rubbed his eyes as if I was an illusion. I shot a glance at the dongle, and pulled it free: *Download Complete,* and I ran. The hotel would have security footage. I made a drunken fool of myself enough that I'd be remembered. My only hope was to expose Marva before someone put the pieces together and tracked me down.

I yelled for Debbie to run. She did. If I failed to secure the downfall of Marva DeLonghi, I'd take the fall for Debbie. It was the least I could do.

26

Debbie had an Uber waiting at the office though I'd told her she could just drop herself at her apartment, and I'd drive myself the rest of the way. She said she couldn't support drunk driving. I asked her if I seemed drunk, and she said it hadn't been even an hour since I was puking my guts out in the stall at the hotel. She had a point, but just.

After she'd left, I went around the van and got behind the wheel. The biggest part of me figured if I was going to end up in prison for an ill-concocted plan to bend the governor over a barrel, I might as well take a stab at seeing Lyle one more time.

But business first, because my thirst for revenge overpowered all else. I opened Twitter and warned the world it was about to see what a bad ass PI with a bone to pick could do, and I opened my phonebook and scrolled to *X*. If I dialed, I was all the way in, all the way and then some. My thumb hovered over the button. I tapped the phone number.

On the last ring the call connected. "Luluchuk! Rak Devushka. Mnogo zhizney."

I should try looking up what he says to me, but I can never remember how to pronounce the words much less spell something close enough for Google to translate, and I don't trust him to tell me the truth if I asked. "Did you get the download?"

"Does bear eat little children in woods?"

He leaned into his immigrant status as hard as anyone I'd ever known. "What do I owe you?"

"For you, I give. No charge."

"Not a chance, Phil. I've known guys who owed the mighty Ruskov, and I don't want to be one of them."

"You wound me, Lucia Evelyn. Mine is a rare generosity you refuse."

"I'm not buying your shit. Chances are I'll be behind bars by week's end, and for a long time so the last thing I need is an unpayable debt to a man who has half the prison system in his pocket for one reason or another."

"You flatter me." He coughed. "You were having that hard time?"

"You wanna know the truth? It was a total shit show."

He cleared his throat. "Too bad, that is. Here is what you should be doing. You get good strong vodka. Drink. Make everything better, big, big."

"The last thing I need is more liquor."

"Lies! Lies! We have a saying in Russia. "Peyte cherez eto.""

"Is that so? Well, I'll keep that in mind." I flicked my lighter and watched the flame. Fire, in any size, is calming. "So what do I owe you?"

"Why you are resisting so much? I am no dumb-dumb head. Lushenka is not made of money."

"I've been doing fine for myself. Not that it's any of your business. Name your price."

"You cut me deep, my Luluchens. If I am good only for whoring, I see what it is to you."

The thing is, I'd learned never to pity Philipe Ruskov, even if he pouted and acted the victim, because he would just as soon give you a Russian manicure, and I'm not talking about the kind they offer in beauty salons. "Cut the shit. I've got Venmo at the ready."

"These Venmos, these Pay Buddies, Cash App, they are so crude of tools. What ever happen to good old fashion counter check?"

He was wearing me out. "Look, I can mail you a check, for christsakes, just name your fucking price already."

"I was not knowing you had no loving for good friend Ruskovanya."

"You're a friend the way a leech is a friend. When you're needed, you're a lifesaver."

"That is what I am being like about you. Always the words in your mouth are truthful."

I lit a cigarette. "Even to a fault. Now what do I owe you?"

"How about we call it one hundred dollar?"

I remember hearing Warren Buffet would lose money if he stopped to pick up a hundred-dollar bill because every step he took earned him some ten-thousand. Of course, I'm sure there's more to it than that, but the point was clear. "Hey, stay dry, okay?" I hung up.

The sign off was meant to be nonsense. I sent a grand to Ruskov and followed it with a text message: *Now you owe me. Thanks for taking the job. You're good at what you do.*

With most people you could say something basically kind like *Thanks for the help*, or *You're a lifesaver!* But with Ruskov, to acknowledge kindness was to admit debt, and I can't stress enough what a bad idea it is to be in debt to him.

I leaned back into the driver's seat and rolled my shoulders, trying to release unshakable tension. When I gave up trying to relax, I dug in my purse and palmed the oddly cold 8 Ball. Though I'd established a dozen times it didn't need shaken, I shook it, perhaps a small act of violence to acknowledge it often seemed to plot a course that put me in the dead center of chaotic situations. "What next?"

27

Two men, one broad-shouldered and clean-shaven, the other thin-framed, wearing a lopsided scowl, snuck into the office. Kudos to the one who thought he'd picked my lock, though I'd been expecting them and left it open. Thin-Scowl pointed a crowbar at the couch. Broad-Clean nodded once, raised a baseball bat and sited the humanlike blob under a blanket. He seemed familiar though I couldn't place him.

Thin-Scowl didn't know he looked into my camera as the shutter snapped a long-exposure from the dark corner of my office. I snapped a dozen pictures as Broad-Clean wailed on the couch-blob with his baseball bat. After the fourth swing he shouldered his bat and reached for the blanket with his free hand. He pulled it back to expose a mess of rolled towels and Lyle's bowling ball resting on a pillow.

"God damn." Broad-Clean turned, scanning in the dark. His gaze swept past me, the dark hiding my form well. "She was expecting us."

Thin-Scowl opened his mouth like a silent scream, squeezed his chin. "That ain't possible. We wasn't even expecting us."

"Shut up, Bob." Broad-Clean readied his bat to swing. "She's in here, and if she knew we were coming, somebody snitched."

"Oh." Bob scratched his temple. "Wull damn."

Broad-Clean moved toward the window nearest the desk. "That should worry you, Bob."

Bob gave an airy chuckle. "If you say so."

"Shut up and look for her, dumb fuck." Broad-Clean slid along the perimeter of the wall like he'd been trained to deal with ambushes, which worried me. I could hold my own in a scuffle, but against a man as big as Broad-Clean I needed the element of surprise or Bob's crowbar, and the problem was, Broad-Clean was moving toward me. While the dark might hide me in stillness, if I stirred, he'd detect my movement.

I slipped my hand in my pocket and pinched the lighter between thumb and index finger. Picturing the stillness of a glassy lake, I drew the lighter up out of my jeans. With as swift and small a movement as I could, I flung the lighter toward the doorway. Its impact was dulled by the carpet but loud enough both men looked. I threw myself on Bob with the instant of distracted advantage, managing to wrest the crowbar from his hand.

Cold lightning charged through my back and I pissed myself, crumpling to the floor. I rolled to my back and instinct told me to raise the crowbar in both hands before my face. The bat splintered on the length of metal. Broad-Clean drew it back for another strike. I rotated the crowbar with all my strength and caught him in the knee as he was bringing the bat down for a strike that would've broke my elbows. All the power drained out of his swing when his leg gave and he dropped to the other knee.

I crab-walked backward, and tripped Bob, who was just flicking the light switch so he could better see their two against one advantage. Broad-Clean swore, standing but with a pained grunt. His hulking form filled my periphery. I scuffled with Bob, landing a punch on his nose, which erupted blood.

Falling left, I dodged the brunt of the baseball bat, as it glanced off my hip. Still, the pain was excruciating. Bob got around me and wrapped his arm around my neck. Broad-Clean spread his legs for one big swing. Bob laughed. "Make it hurt."

A smile bloomed, slow and full of anger on Broad-Clean's lips. He seemed the sort to pleasure in someone's pain. "Yeah, make it hu—"

A police siren shattered the witching hour. Bob's lips rounded into a caricature of surprise. "Them's—"

"For you." I sat up as he bolted, leaving Broad-Clean behind.

Broad-Clean lowered his bat. "I'll be seeing you, but don't worry keeping an eye out, cause you won't see me coming next time." He ran out the door and down the hall in long, lumbering strides.

28

Standing proved more painful than expected. My lower back had started to swell and tighten. The adrenaline rush had been everything, and I'd forgotten pissing myself, but when someone pounded on my door, my consciousness came slamming back.

"Police! We received an emergency alert for this address and are preparing to enter by force."

My pants were soaking, sticky, and cold. "I'm coming." It hurt to speak. I opened the door.

Two officers stood to either side of the doorway. I greeted them, wincing. One asked if I was alone inside. I told him the attackers had fled. He told the other to enter and clear the room. It seemed a cowardly approach, but for all I knew, he was simply following procedure. The other entered, sweeping his flashlight beam side to side, keeping it on even after he flipped the switch for the overhead lights.

The one stayed with me. "Something spill?"

I debated with myself if he was cruel or clueless. "My bladder."

"They scared the piss out of you, eh?"

I was leaning cruel. "A big guy tried to play baseball with me, except I was the baseball—" I gasped as something in the word baseball caused a fiery arrow to shoot op my spine—"and he was the bat."

The other officer came up alongside me. "All clear." He nodded at the one officer, scratched his mustache, then craned his head around. "Ma'am."

"Luke. You can call me Luke."

"Well, Luke. Um..." He scratched his head behind the ear. "Well, see, I only ask because you might be injured, um..." he looked away. "Maybe you're on your, uh—"

"Spit it out, would you?" The one officer stepped into the office.

Definitely cruel. Mustache asked if I was on my period, and even in my discomfort, I found his shyness endearing. I know women who think men that act awkward about women's reproductive cycles are blatantly sexist. Maybe that contributes in some cases, but I think, just as often, shy guys lack experience, and that's fine.

I told Mustache I'd been struck with a baseball bat. "Could've been the one with the crowbar, so I guess I'm lucky."

He shook his head. "Must've been scary."

Under normal circumstances, yes, but I'd known they were coming. "It was terrifying."

The one officer had circled the office, and returned. "Were these friends of yours who'd maybe had a little too much to drink, maybe got a little rowdy?"

"No." I had the sense this officer was the kind of person who sped up if he saw a squirrel crossing the street. "I have no idea who they were. Why?"

He looked toward the couch. "You just seem, I don't know, pretty calm for having been attacked by men with weapons."

His tone bothered me. "I'm a private detective. Seen my share of violence."

"Oh, sure, sure." He aimed his trigger finger at the couch. "Say. Mind explaining that little set up there? Kind of a curious thing."

I tried for casual with a breathy chuckle. "Yeah. New pillow. Trying to break it in."

"Right." He smiled, glanced over at Mustache. "And the blanket and the towels. I suppose you didn't want the pillow to be lonely?"

"How'd you know?" I shrugged. Why did it feel like I was being interrogated? "Lonely pillows make for strange dreams." I concluded my comments looking at Mustache. "I've always had a tough time sleeping, so I do whatever I can to make it easier."

Mustache nodded. It seemed he was about to say something, but the one officer wasn't done being an asswipe. "Why don't you walk me through the incident, cause I'm a little confused. You texted nine-one-one at one eleven a.m. about an armed B-and-E. We arrive at one twenty-six, exactly fifteen minutes after the text—"

"Slow I might add." I was starting to cook under the collar, which had its advantages since it dulled the pain in my side.

"We prioritize calls as a matter of policy, as text messages tend to suggest less urgency."

One thing you should never do is assault a police officer. "Less urgency? How about I didn't want to talk and give up my position?"

"So you were hiding?"

"When I heard them enter, you bet your ass I hid!"

"Where?"

"Where did I hide?" I scoffed. The 8 Ball had said nothing about this. "Ha! You know what? No. Fuck this. You come in here and from word one, treat me like I'm some kind of suspect, when the truth is, I was just ambushed, and as your partner pointed out, hit so hard, I pissed blood. So you know what? I'm going to excuse myself, clean my wounds, and see if I need medical attention, thank you very much."

I started for the bathroom. The one officer stepped in front of me. "Hold it. I just have a few more questions."

This had all the trappings of bad news. I thought back to my conversation with Shotz. Had he suggested OPD was positioning itself to oppose me? "Questions, you say? Aren't you supposed to take my statement? Get forensics out here? Set up an APB to find my attackers?"

Mustache raised his hand. I had the sense he'd just graduated academy. Endearing was fine, but I needed take-charge, and I needed it yesterday. "What?" I gave him just a hint of sass, something to try jump-starting his ego a little.

"I was just going to say, I'm a licensed paramedic too, and I'd be happy to examine your injuries to see if there's anything to worry about."

Hot dogshit on a stick! This guy gave a whole new angle to the good cop bad cop routine. "As much as I appreciate the offer, I think, until I've looked myself over to see what I'm dealing with, that feels unnecessary. I'd prefer not to show off my lady parts if I can avoid it. I'm sure you understand."

He nodded. "We'll wait."

The one officer rose both hands, palms splayed. "Hold it, hold it."

I shouldered past him. Whatever his agenda, I was going to face it in clean cloths, smelling fresh, and with a good stream of bourbon flowing through me. I'd thought sobriety was a reasonable precaution for this evening's festivities, and I'd been wrong.

A hand gripped my arm. I tried to pull away. It held tight. I turned. The one officer held tight. If I hadn't had a sudden and strong intuition he wanted me to hit him, I'd have hit him, and hard. "Let me go. Right now. Before I report you to the chief of police. Maybe you don't know this, but I have a direct line to the chief. I can call any time I want."

I held his gaze while he considered what to do. Something told me he knew my claim about the chief was a bluff, but I also suspected he knew I had a few ears in the department. Truth was, the longer this jackass was in my office, the more I had the sense he knew quite a lot about me, which I didn't like to contemplate. I gave my arm one more firm tug. My arm pulled free.

29

Stripped out of my pants, I tossed them on the shower floor along with the underwear. My mind raced. The Magic 8 Ball was out on the desk. I wished I'd grabbed it. The damn police officer had derailed my whole thought process. I focused on breathing, imagined being a compass, focused my energy on north.

I fished the backup bottle of Magdalene out of the closet. It was three-quarters empty, and don't call me a pessimist. I opened my throat and drank it off. The last swallow plunged directly to my bruised hip where its fumy fingers tickled my pelvic bone. I looked myself over in the mirror. Where the bat had struck, my skin shown hues of yellow, green, purple and blue.

I wetted a hand towel with cold water and scrubbed my legs. Something told me violence-induced incontinence was the least of my worries. I'd somehow found myself in classic frying-pan-into-fire-territory, and worse, I hadn't had to deal with something like this without Lyle before. Now, I know some of you will remind me I'm a powerful woman and didn't need a man to solve my problems, but I'd say to you we all have our strengths and weaknesses, and Lyle has always been stronger than me in the social context.

After taming my hair and dressing in fresh pants, I lit a cigarette and opened the door to find the one officer holding the 8 Ball. My stomach flipped. "Put that down."

"Where'd you get it anyway."

I blew smoke at the ceiling. "None of your business."

"I want to buy one." He laughed. "It's way better than the original." He nodded at Mustache. "Tell her what it said to you."

Mustache folded his hands at the pelvis, looking every bit as tender as I'd come to believe he was. Cops like him had short tenures. He'd be better suited to teach a classroom of rambunctious ten-year-olds. When he neglected to answer in what the one officer deemed a reasonable time, the one officer piped in. "Fine. I'll tell her. He asked it if you were single, and you know what it said?"

I figured I'd play into his dog and pony show. "Sorry, I don't answer questions about love."

"Ah! So it's got preprogrammed responses. Makes sense."

I felt my anger rising, because he'd not only not set the Magic 8 Ball down as I'd requested, but he'd asked it a question. Now, I don't know if the 8 Ball will work for everyone who holds it, but my guess is it won't discriminate. "It also won't share sports scores or lotto numbers."

The one officer put on a hungry grin, something that made me hope he didn't have a romantic partner or children. He was bad all the way to his shit hole. "Guess what it said when I asked it if you'd cooperate with us?"

I wanted him to put the 8 Ball down, and I was prepared to make him, which I couldn't afford, for so many reasons, to do. "I don't know. Maybe that you're doing a shitty job processing an emergency call."

Mustache laughed. "Worse." It relieved some of my stress. I had to imagine if they'd worked together more than a few days, Mustache had learned how to neutralize his partner, and I had a pretty good idea laughing at his expense wasn't part of the program.

The first officer set the 8 Ball on the desk, and I sighed relief. He looked at his partner. "Piss off," then turned to me. "It said it doesn't answer questions for petty ass wipes."

Now I understood why Mustache had erupted into laughter, and I fell into it with a childish kind of disregard for who it was at the expense of or how it might harm my already precarious situation. To my relief, the one officer said he knew how to be a good sport, but he had a question: Where could you buy this version of the toy, because it was way cooler than the traditional one, everything from the digital display to the cutting insults. I said I'd gotten it from someone else and didn't know. Then he said he was lying because he had another question. He wanted to know how the answers worked, and what ratios of the answers were specifically insulting, because the more the better. I said to the best of my knowledge the 8 Ball answered based on the person and the question, and I said I didn't know how often it insulted the person asking the question. I didn't mention that it had recently told me to "grow a pair," which was both insulting and sexist. I did confess it seemed to have infinite unique responses. He asked how much I wanted for it, saying his girlfriend would love him in every way if he could gift it to her. I told him it wasn't for sale, but I didn't say I felt sorry for his girlfriend just to be attached to him. When he pushed the subject, I told him I was borrowing the 8 Ball and couldn't choose who could have it anyway. He asked who I'd borrowed it from. I wanted to break a bottle over his head. Some people are hopeless. I said I'd borrowed it from a past client, which was confidential.

I put my cigarette out on the heel of my boot and flicked the butt into the waste basket. If there were Olympics for cigarette-butt-flicking, I'd win gold. "Hey, this is fun and all, but I think we should get back to why you're here, which is that two men broke into my office, assaulted me, and made off into the night." I lit a new cigarette, and snagged my phone from the back pocket of my clean jeans. "I got pictures of the burglars."

Mustache's head snapped toward me. "You what?"

"Look—my words were punctuated by puffs of smoke from my face holes—"not that you asked, but I happened to be awake when I heard noises at the door. I was in the kitchen pouring a drink to knock me out, so I hid there."

The one officer was machinelike in his transition from trying to be friendly to get the 8 Ball to being an asswipe, trying to interrogate me. "About that. I noticed no sign of forced entry."

He needed a taste of my right hand, which I'd named Attitude Adjustment. "I rarely lock up since the building's bolted at night, and I know everyone who lives here." Neither of these details were factual, but they were believable.

"You telling me you can't come or go after...what...business hours?"

I followed his logic. "There's an emergency exit out back." This was true, though I hadn't used it months. "You can retract the ladder if you're in for the night."

The one officer scratched his temple. "I see."

I finished my cigarette, and banked it in the trash. Mustache told me I was good at that. His attention to me confirmed his attraction. Perhaps that contributed to his quiet awkwardness. I'd always been the quiet type around men I found appealing—before Lyle.

Mustache could be an asset for me, but he wouldn't be a support, and so I needed to arrest the one officer's control and beat it down. I needed to demolish his authority. "By the way, gents, I hate to do this, but I need to see your badges."

The one officer rolled his eyes. "We don't have to do that."

Seeing as you've determined I'm not in danger, and there's no crime to report, I'm thinking it's time you leave."

The one officer puffed out his chest. "I'll decide when it's safe."

I punched the numbers 9-1-1 into my phone for both officers to see. "I hope you like days and days of paperwork, shit-for-brains."

Nodding, he spread his arms. "Fine. You want my badge?" He showed it to me. "Here's my badge."

"Officer Howard, rhymes with coward." I gave it back. Mustache handed me his. I examined it. "Officer Lance. You wanna dance?" I blew him a kiss.

His cheeks flushed. "What about those pictures you were mentioning, Miss Mia."

"Remember. Call me Luke." He was so smitten, it was adorable. I unlocked my phone screen and opened photos.

Officer Howard leaned in. He smelled like a Slim Jim, which probably meant he lived in his mother's basement and when he said girlfriend he meant mommy. "Kind of grainy, you think?"

Perhaps I have more violent thoughts than the average person, but if Officer Howard was subjected to my mind, he'd be left for dead in some dumpster in a dark alley. "What I think is that you're the worst cop I've ever had the horror of meeting, and you disgrace the badge."

He raised his eyes from the phone. Locked them on mine. "Here's what I think, detective. I think your text was fucking suspicious. You send a message to emergency dispatch with just enough detail to tell us nothing but get two squad cars lights and sirens to the scene. Shows some inside baseball. Then there's no sign of forced entry, there's a setup on your couch that's suspiciously like something made to look like a sleeping person, which suggests foreknowledge of a threat. Victim seems calm as a summer breeze, and she's hostile to any questions I ask, just to get a sense of what I'm dealing with. Any cop worth his paycheck is going to see it how I do. That's what I think."

"Maybe you ask the wrong questions."

"Hey, Jer." Officer Lance had taken my phone and was examining my photos. He aimed it toward Officer Howard. I leaned in. Officer Lance seemed unsettled in a way I couldn't describe. He pointed at one of my pictures of Broad-Clean. "Isn't that—"

"Gentlemen!"

I jumped. It felt like someone had netted my stomach and threw it fifty feet in the air.

A tall woman with long brown curls stood, framed by the doorway. "Out here. With me." She wore a slate gray blazer over a white blouse, black slacks and matt black flats—the standard uniform of feminine authority, stereotypes be damned. The two officers responded immediately.

I didn't know much, but I knew my predicament had gone from bad to worse. "Officer Lance."

He looked back. "What were you going to say about the man in the photo?" I knew he'd recognized Broad-Clean, which maybe for the first time in this case left me scared.

"Be right back."

The officers were so quiet, so compliant I knew the woman in the blazer was bad news. Whatever Officer Howard had been, Blazer lady was magnitudes worse. I nodded, felt for my flask, found it empty, and as the police stepped out of my office, I retreated to the kitchen to get my head on straight.

30

I filled a tumbler with Magdalene and drank from the bottle. If the 8 Ball had a neck, I'd have strangled it. There'd been no warning the police would come, agenda blazing, which would've been a helpful note, and I knew Suzie had warned me about the 8 Ball's appetite for mischief, but I felt things had been different between us. Maybe I'd thought I was special, or the 8 Ball could sense the unique justice of my objectives.

Officer Howard and the woman in the power suit opened my door and entered. I believe, because they'd exited, they needed to request permission to reenter, but something told me I was dealing with the invisible side of the law so I didn't bother with technicalities. "Where's officer Lance?"

The woman in the power suit showed her badge. It was shinier than the officers' and heavier-duty than mine. "I'm Lieutenant Bilson, and here forward you'll be working with me."

She'd mastered the politician's style of replying to questions without answering them. I uncapped my flask. "Great, so then you can inform Howard the Duck over here the difference between a victim and a perpetrator."

"Officer Howard briefed me on your attitude, and I want to let you know, it ends here." She pointed at the couch. "We've determined you aren't in need of medical attention, I believe."

My head hurt, so I guess it depended if bourbon counted as medical attention. "Do I have a choice?"

"Are you injured?"

"I got the home run treatment, if that's what you mean."

"We can get a paramedic out, if you'd like." Lieutenant Bilson had a hard-charging, keep-the-pressure-on, style. "Just say the word."

"I'm fine." I hit the flask again. "But off the record, I'd like to see how you'd feel after dancing with a Louisville Slugger."

Lieutenant Bilson coughed into her closed fist. "Is that a threat?"

I mock-slapped the side of my head. "Yeah. I'm a moron, and I'm threatening a police lieutenant now." I crossed my arms over my chest. If she wanted to play bold, I'd play bold. "Hey, tell me. What's Governor DeLonghi paying you?"

Lieutenant Bilson smiled—classic diversion. She wagged her head. "My salary's none of your business."

I winked at her. In detective lingo I was committing to the penny and pound technique. "Don't act stupid, honey. You know what I mean." I opened my lighter and flicked the flint wheel. "What'd she tell you? That I'm a threat because I see her for who she is?"

Officer Howard adjusted his collar. "See what I was saying?"

"Late-stage alcoholics do tend to suffer paranoid delusions." Lieutenant Bilson tugged her earlobe. "We see it all the time."

They *were* in her pocket. I'd only been half serious, but they were full-on-the-take. She'd sent them to deal with me. I didn't know who to be more upset at: the department for turning their back on justice, or myself for underestimating Marva. "Know what? I've decided I don't want to pursue this matter any further. Probably, whoever broke into my office is long gone, and after the fight I put up, they're not likely to try me again."

Officer Howard laughed. Lieutenant Bilson joined in slick as a snake. She clicked her tongue. "Well it's too bad for you we can't do that."

I had to start thinking about self-defense if they pushed much further. "And why's that?"

"Well—" Lieutenant Bilson shifted her weight from hip to hip— "even if I could ignore you accusing police personnel of active bribery, there's the fact that we've taken two suspects into custody and need your help to give a positive ID."

That wasn't possible. "Why didn't you say something sooner?"

Officer Howard picked at a hangnail. "It's not exactly like you've been a model of cooperation." He flicked his eyes up at me. "Have you?"

"How'd you act if someone barged into your office and start treating you like a criminal after you'd just been assaulted? Truth is, I'd rather my assailants walk free than spend more time with you, so just go ahead and take whatever notes you need and hit the road, all right?"

Lieutenant Bilson nodded. "Okay, okay, maybe we put you on the defensive, but it's not exactly like you're an unknown quantity around the department."

She'd come prepared, and I could practically read the assignment she'd been given in the reflection of her pupils. "Sure, I can respect that. OPD's had to talk me down a time or two—"

"A time or two?" Lieutenant Bilson laughed.

I rolled my eyes. "The point is, y'all had a chance to help a victim of a serious crime—"

"Come down to the office, and we *can* help you."

She'd started interrupting me to imbalance my thinking: same goal, new technique. "No thank you." I fumbled for my cigarettes. "You've done more than enough."

Officer Howard and the lieutenant exchanged a look. The lieutenant put her hands on her hips. "I didn't want it to come to this, but if you refuse to cooperate, I'm going to place you under arrest."

"For what?"

"Interfering with an investigation."

I lit a cigarette. "Interfering my ass!"

"Come on, Luke." Officer Howard hooked a thumb through his cuffs. "Give us thirty minutes and we can get this issue wrapped up and behind us."

"Fine." I figured at least if I got to the station there'd be witnesses and the bullying would stop. Marva couldn't possibly have the whole department on speed-dial. "Fine, I'll drive down and have a look at your lineup if you promise that's the end of it."

Lieutenant Bilson frowned. "I'm afraid we can't let you drive. You've had enough of that flask that I'd be afraid to light a match in here."

It might've been a clever joke if I hadn't literally just sparked a smoke. "I'll grab a Lyft."

"Hello?" Lieutenant Bilson did a kind of pseudo-jovial cross-eyed thing. "We're right here, and from what I understand you aren't exactly a Forbes Self-Made Millionaire."

Bilson's jovial act needed a lot of work. She practically had PREDATOR tattooed on her forehead, and the buddy-buddy routine only made it all the more obvious I couldn't get in a car with her. "I can afford a Lyft and it would be nice to have a few minutes to myself, no offense."

"We can't keep the suspects detained that much longer." Lieutenant Bilson crossed her arms. "Just think. If you'd worked with us from the start you'd already be back in bed and we'd have the bad guys in a jail cell awaiting booking."

"So let me get a Lyft and we'll go."

"Come on." She made like the big bad wolf and lied to my face through her big shape teeth. "I'll even let you ride up front."

The question wasn't *if* she'd hurt me if I got into her car, but how badly. I've known a lot of things in my life, but I knew at the most primal and alert of levels, Bilson and Howard wanted me quiet by any means necessary and they weren't going to suffer my stalling much longer, so I reached into my pocket, snagged my phone, unlocked the screen, and fired the only flare I had.

31

"Night Flight Pizza."

"Debbie."

"Luke?"

"How quick can you get to the office?"

"Ten minutes if I speed."

"Make it five." She disconnected. I lowered my phone and looked at Lieutenant Bilson. "That was my partner. She'll drive me to the station."

The stillness had me feeling for my pocketknife. How I missed it!

I reached behind me, running my fingertips over the desk lamp with its heavy-duty smoked green glass shade. It would split a skull. Officer Howard's fingers twitched, hand hovering between the cuffs and his firearm.

Lieutenant Bilson's lips thinned to pale whips. "You have fifteen minutes. If you're not at the station, I'm putting out a warrant for your arrest, and don't ask me on what grounds, because I've already let you slide on a dozen arrest-worthy offenses tonight."

I truly had no idea what she'd qualify as a crime. Nothing I'd done seemed even risky, but I figured she hadn't planned on me resisting quite so hard, and I could empathize with her situation. She probably got into law enforcement to make a difference for good, but when she realized the ladder was clogged with men who hated ladies in uniform, and promotions doubled your work but hardly put a dent in your salary, well, maybe she got an offer allowing her to take her kiddos to Disneyworld and all it required was for her to say yes ma'am when called upon. I can't say I'd not take an offer like that.

Bilson and Howard had hardly left when my phone rang. I answered.

"Where are you."

I snagged my purse and ran out the door. "That was fast."

The echo of her Supra's engine revving doubled in my phone and outside the building. "Sounded important."

I bounded down the stairs two at a time. "Thanks, Deb. I'm paying time and a half tonight."

"Hurry." She revved the engine again. "We can talk about that later."

I burst out the door and ran for her car. "You're a lifesaver." I hung up and hopped in. It smelled like burnt mozzarella and tomato sauce. Debbie's hair was gilt with flour dust. "Thank you for coming. You wouldn't believe the night I had."

She burned rubber out of the parking spot, but I told her to go the speed limit and follow every law of the road because the cops, at least a few crooked ones, were out to get me. The lights all up Maple ticked red in unison, which is a feature of downtown Benson. She asked me what had happened, and I told her the whole story from 8 Ball to Lieutenant Bilson. I even said the 8 Ball had gotten me in over my head, knowing full-well Debbie would preach on how she'd told me the 8 Ball was no good.

But she didn't. She apologized that my evening had gone so poorly and said I'd done the right thing in calling her. We discussed what might go down at the police station and agreed not to be split up under any circumstances. No one had broken any laws, and we were going under our own power, voluntarily, so any pressure they applied was empty threats. Debbie knew me well in saying she was surprised I'd managed not to take swings at anyone and reminded me to keep my cool inside the station. The only thing that rubbed me wrong was her saying "if" the police were actually on the take instead of "because". But she said if they were on the take they'd try to create division, put pressure on us, and even lie to get us acting stupidly.

She parked the Supra in a visitor's space and pulled the keys from the ignition. "This could get ugly if we aren't careful. You ready?" I said I was ready, checked my phone's clock and said we had enough time for a quick cigarette.

32

The officer working the front desk might've been sleeping when we knocked. He jolted upright when I hit the bell. His collar was half popped. He pressed a button and spoke to us through a small microphone on the side of his desk. His voice came out tinny through the panel in the wall. Debbie informed him Lieutenant Bilson was expecting us. He asked us to hold and raised a telephone to his ear. A moment later he began speaking at a fevered pitch. You never realize how much speech looks like two lips dancing until you see it through bulletproof glass.

He hung up and buzzed the door, telling us to come in. Before I could greet him, Lieutenant Bilson emerged from a hallway behind the front desk. She stopped and waved us back. I asked Debbie in a whisper if it was just me or if Bilson's eyes were fit to kill. Debbie granted Bilson had an angry look about her.

Bilson scanned a card at a doorway, and we passed through into a familiar chamber. I can neither confirm nor deny spending two separate occasions in one of the cells attached to the chamber. Bilson showed us into a darkened quarters I'd never visited with a mess of recording equipment. It reminded me of the studios you see in films about rock legends. A one-way mirror looked out into a small room with white cinderblock walls and a drain in the middle of the concrete floor. At least twice, but maybe three times, I'd been in that room. It gave me the heebs remembering those nights. If you've ever heard of a paddy wagon, you understand.

Bilson pulled a cellphone from her belt clip. She tapped a button on the screen and held the phone in front of her face. "Send them in."

I forgot to be cautious with her for a moment. "Is that some kind of high-tech police radio or something?"

She rolled her eyes. "It's just Zello."

I shrugged. She said anyone could download it from the app store. It had never occurred to me you could download a walkie talkie for your phone. I was going to say more, but a line of men, and somewhat confusingly two women, strode into the cinderblock room.

Bilson fanned her arm out, indicating the lineup. "Now it's important you take your time. Really examine the faces, the bodies, the postures. You were in a greatly heightened state of—"

"The one in the middle. Thin. Weasel-eyed. Permanent scowl on his face."

"Take your time, Detective Mia." Bilson pointed toward the window. "Make absolutely certain you get both men. We don't want to see a guilty man walk."

I noted she didn't mention a concern for seeing an innocent man locked up. I looked around the room. It was just Bilson, Debbie, and me. "The thin guy. That's one. The guy that actually assaulted me, he's not in there."

"Impossible."

"What do you mean, 'impossible'?" I think I'd recognize the guy who tried to kill me with a baseball bat. He's not in that room. Crowbar guy's that one." I pointed again to Thin-Scowl. A little part of me was saying my compliance was playing into their hand, but I couldn't think why that'd be an issue.

Bilson's shoulders slouched. It was more like what Hollywood tells you dejected looks like than what it actually looks like when someone feels frustrated and defeated. "Can we please not do this again?"

I looked at her without turning my head. "Do what?"

She tapped the side of her head with her index finger. "Make everything as hard as possible." She jabbed her finger in the direction of the lineup. "Just take a breath, look at every face. Who's the second assailant?"

Debbie stepped between us. "If this is what it was like at the office, it's no wonder Luke wanted you to pull anchor and sail. Here she positively IDs one of her attackers and tells you the second isn't in the lineup, and you accuse her of making things as hard as possible?"

Bilson put on a smug smile. "It must be a real cracking business if you need to work a night job to pay the bills."

Debbie's cheeks flushed. I could almost see her internal dialogue, *Don't hit the bitch, don't you do it, Deb*. She closed her eyes and inhaled, slow and deep. "Luke and I had a few professional differences. It happens. So I was on a brief hiatus from the agency, as if that's any of your business."

Lieutenant Bilson leaned on one of the shelves housing recording equipment. It was meant to look casual, laissez-faire. Instead, it came across awkward and uncomfortable. "Try this on for size. Say you pick up two men near the scene of the crime who act guilty as hell, and say you bring both of these men in for questioning, and both have previous records of breaking and entering. Then suppose you walk both of them into a room with a half dozen others for the victim to identify. Now, finally, consider the victim acts unflaggingly confident she knows one of the people in the lineup was one of her attackers but she somehow can't identify the second attacker even though he's standing in the room with his partner in crime. Suppose all of that and what conclusion do you reach about the motives of the victim?"

The way Debbie considered me with such intensity of focus, I could've believed she'd evolved x-ray vision. I felt naked before her. "I'd say—" she lingered on the hollow of my throat—"the victim is telling the truth and you've somehow mistakenly picked up one guilty man and one innocent man."

"Oh sure!" Bilson mock-laughed. "That makes perfect sense. A man who's just committed a felony just runs up to a perfect stranger and what? he says, 'Hey, buddy, wanna join me and run around looking guilty so the cops can pick us up and take us in for questioning?' Is that what happened?"

Debbie removed her Night Flight Pizza cap and held it by her side. She had a bad case of helmet hair that made it hard not to giggle. I am prone to occasional giggles when tired. She shook her head. "I'm saying, Lieutenant, that I'd believe your officers picked up one man running from the crime scene and another man who was drunken and disorderly, doesn't even have to be at the same time or in the same area, but maybe your officers knew what they were supposed to be doing and so they—"

"Let me just stop you right there, honey. It's late." She looked at her watch. "Fuck, it's early, and so I can imagine you're not thinking clearly, but accusing police officers of outright lying for no reason is a serious and dangerous path to go down."

"Oh, baby!" Debbie clapped her hands together and rubbed her palms in little let's-get-after-it circles. I felt warmed by the friction. "Maybe you don't know who you're talking to, but I spent the better part of a decade in prison for a murder I didn't commit because of a corrupt cop in your own department who lied and said he found ricin pills in my vanity. So don't tell me about corrupt cops."

Lieutenant Bilson cracked her neck. She wore a smirk I wanted to slap off her face. "I know all about your case, Ms. Lenvil. I know about your case and how Detective Mia brought evidence forward that exonerated you. I know that she disgraced the good name of an officer of the law who served his city and state with loyalty and honesty for twenty years and who died too young in the line of duty. I also know you were freed on a technicality and your case being overturned has nothing to do with your guilt or innocence. To be honest, I believe you murdered your husband and it's a miscarriage of justice that you're free. I believe you are a cold-blooded killer and it's no surprise the people you choose to associate with."

Debbie turned her face away. She was half in the shadows of the darkened room. "Your practiced cruelty is exceptional." Her hands were joined in front of her, fingers laced. She raised them, joined, and held them, just below eye-level, between her and Bilson. "Hear me now. We complied with your every whim. Now we're going to leave, and if you give us even *one* more speck of trouble, you'll be hearing from our lawyer. And trust me when I say, our lawyer is a pit bull who won't release his jaws once he's latched on."

As Debbie motioned for me to follow, my admiration for her swelled. I vowed in my mind and heart to never fire her again. I vowed to smoke a cigarette, to raise a flask, and to drink to Debbie's superb grit and courage.

33

I asked Debbie to just drive for a while. My body was amped, and though exhausted, I knew I wouldn't sleep. Debbie said it was risky driving around too much if I was bent on hitting the flask, as the whole of OPD now probably viewed us less than fondly. I told her to head west on Dodge toward Fremont, as no one knew me from Eve up there.

The day was already warming, with the first bits of sunlight, and the threat of summer had pumped humidity into the air. We sped past the Chik-Fil-A that always had a drive thru line at least ten deep and past the glazed glass buildings housing realty outfits, banks, insurance, and all the suburban-type employers that devour their employees in neat 8-hour chunks five days a week. Sometimes I wanted a job like that.

Around 168th Street, where all the car dealerships are, I socked Debbie on the shoulder and told her she was a kickass partner for whom I was elaborately, and extremely grateful. I told her she was like the female version of Mike Tyson except with her words instead of her fists and she'd handled Lieutenant Bilson like a cat with a mouse.

She said she was just happy she'd kept her head because in the thick of the interaction she'd had a few violent thoughts. I didn't mention Lieutenant Bilson's comment about Debbie having murdered her late husband was, in my opinion, a possibility, but I did say I could relate to Debbie's violent thoughts.

She signaled and passed a station wagon puttering along in the right lane. "Not to change the subject or anything, but how's it feel being a local celebrity, even if people don't know you're you?"

I paused, with my flask halfway to my lips. "Celebrity?"

"You know, hashtag Operative Cancer?"

I didn't know and said so. "What kind of name is Operative Cancer?"

Debbie switched back into the right lane. "Your alt Twitter."

I heard the words, but the brain failed to make sense of them so I opened Twitter on my phone, but all was as I'd left it. "Look, I've gone on my share of benders, but I think I'd know if I came up with some ridiculous pseudonym like Operative Cancer."

Debbie snatched my phone. She fiddled with the app, harrumphed, fiddled some more, and handed it back to me. The handle was @TruthyMia and the bio read simply #OperativeCancer. I scrolled to the tweets. The most recent read, *NF&WC wants your vote so they gave $1mil. to Scott Pendleton Mineral Exploration. Vote for #OperativeTruth.* This was followed by a shortened link. I scrolled further. "What is this?"

Debbie signaled to exit at the Love's travel center in Valley. "It's not yours?"

I reached out the window and scrubbed out the coal in my cigarette butt. "This is the first I've seen of it." And that was all I needed to know. Ruskov had decided to backdoor me. I didn't know if it mattered. If the purpose of pirating the documents from the Nebraska Flyways and Waterways Coalition had been to smear Marva, how the information broke couldn't matter, but it was a betrayal all the same, and I felt it. I'd never have been dumb enough to call Ruskov a friend, but this played more like the act of a competitor.

Debbie pulled up to a gas pump. I told her I'd pay, that it was the least I could do, but asked if she'd grab me a 750 of Magdalene and a pack of smokes. There'd been a time in my life where five bucks would get you five gallons. The way things had been going since COVID, we'd soon be filling our cars with bourbon to save money. Then I'd be jealous of the cars.

A strong north wind ripped across the pavement. While the tank filled, I returned to the car and dug in my purse for the 8 Ball. I asked it if it knew Ruskov was going to leak the information when it told me to port the CEO's tablet reader. The viewer swirled with that smoky blue swirl I'd come to interpret as it thinking. *Y/N questions are SOOOO boring, tee-hee.*

"How big of a problem is he going to be?"

I cannot answer questions on the subject of love.

"Go fuck a rusty razor blade. What do I need to do about Ruskov?"

I cannot answer book-length questions.

"Cut the shit woul—"

"Who you talking to?"

I turned to find Debbie approaching, arms laden with candy, nicotine and booze. "No one." I dropped the 8 Ball in my purse and hopped out of the car to put the gas pump away. In the space of twenty-four hours, I'd gone from feeling like the 8 Ball and I were in league together against the world to fearing it had an agenda not quite like mine. It had never hedged with me before, but if it was willing to hold back, what else could it do?

Debbie figured since it was early and I needed a diversion we should make a day of it and hit Sioux City. We could get potato soup, she said, at a delicious hole in the wall and then drop in on her mom, who lived there April through September. I put the kibosh on that quick as a flame on grease, said I was starting to feel sleepy now and maybe we should head back.

I could see I'd disappointed her and tried to soften the blow by saying we'd go visit once the whole Marva debacle was over. Debbie merged onto Highway 275 east. She was working something over in her mind. I refilled my flask. The bourbon fumes filled the car with a musky sweetness. It felt like I was supposed to say something, but I was tired, and wanted a good bath and twenty minutes with the Magic 8 Ball.

Debbie took the exit for Maple Street, which gives a straight shot two hundred blocks east to the office, but all the traffic lights make it a longer drive than staying on Dodge. I peeled the cellophane from the new pack of cigarettes. "You still think I'm wrong about Marva, don't you?"

Debbie glanced in her sideview mirror. "I guess I'm surprised you're so jealous over Lyle that you can't let her be."

"It's not about jealousy." I lit a cigarette. Jealousy made it easier, but I'd have done it if it meant walking on a bed of redhot nails. "Marva DeLonghi has only herself in mind, and she'll roll over anybody who gets in her way, including Lyle, but especially me."

Debbie tapped out a nervous rhythm on the steering wheel. "Look, Lu. About that. This is just one person's opinion, but I've given it some thought, and it seems strange to me—and maybe strange isn't the word —but maybe notable that you and Lyle saved her life, and she rewarded Lyle for being...you know...the one who was...um...who was there. I mean, what I'm trying to say and doing a terrible job of is that even all of her public comments at the time were very—well...warm toward you. And there for a little while she even—if I'm reading your case log correctly—she, uh, was trying to send you some contract work that you, that uh...that you declined."

I don't know how to measure smoke in units, but I have to imagine I pulled something in the neighborhood of a metric ton into my lungs as Debbie fumbled her way through what could only have been a speech she'd been prepared to deliver when the time was right. The only thing stopping me from going ballistic was knowing Debbie had, with all seven-billion other humans on earth, not maintained a memory of the Marva DeLonghi who'd have gladly thrown Lyle's and my body in front of a firing squad to further her selfish and hateful agenda. No, alas, only I had had the good fortune of experiencing Marva unfiltered. "You know what's unbelievable about the whole thing? Just absolutely, bat shit too crazy to believe?"

Debbie tensed. She knew me well enough to understand I was listing toward bad behavior. "What's crazy, Luke?"

I laughed. It did feel a little uncontrolled. I was tired and lonely. "It's crazy that you've seen the Magic 8 Ball unquestionably know things no toystore object should know. I mean, you've seen how this thing can do honest to goodness magic, and it's given us a pathway to expose Marva's corruption, and you still think she's maybe not so bad."

Debbie turned off maple onto 61st and made a sharp turn into the parking lot of the office. "Yeah. I've seen that. I don't doubt something supernatural's going on there. I've seen plenty of magic in my life. Real stuff. I don't even doubt what you said about dying all those times or the things you learned along the way. You knew stuff about me that there's just no other way you could've but that we got to know each other really, really well, because those things are things I'd never tell anyone, but I must've told you in a previous life. And—"

"You still think maybe I'm just jealous and being petty about Marva?"

"I think it's easy to look at a situation where someone takes something you really want in this life and that losing that thing can cloud your judgement and lead you down a not so good path."

"You have to understand this is so much more than that."

Debbie turned the keys and pulled them out of the ignition. The inside of the Supra began warming instantly. She looked away from me, out the window and down the alley. "What I think is that Marva hurt you, she took someone you love, and you want to believe she's some extremely dark and ultimate evil because you need that kind of motivation to justify what you intend to do. And I know how you're going to respond, but I have to say, I've seen you transform the longer you have that Eight-Ball. It's drawn out all your anger and all your hate, and it's tearing you down."

I uncapped my flask and drank. "Who's jealous here?"

Debbie chuckled sadly. "There's not a jealous bone in my body, and the Luke I know knows that about me." She wiped the back of her wrist across her mouth. "Won't you give the Eight-Ball back to Suzie before something irreparable happens? Think of it this way. Chances are good, now that the Russian has his hands on all that stuff about the environmental coalition, Marva's going to lose her foothold on the state anyway."

34

Her store smelled of incense and wishful thinking. Across the middle of the floor, Suzie had assembled three clothing racks with every variation of tie-dye imaginable. These garments were of the impossibly flowy sort so it was impossible to tell at a distance what were skirts, shirts, dresses or robes, but as I browsed the collection, I found examples of each. Along the walls Suzie offered hemp purses, hemp bracelets, necklaces, headbands. She had crystals for luck, wealth, health and sexuality. There were beads and baskets of foggy polished stones. She'd assembled miniatures and metal discs with various inspirations carved into their faces. Around the windows, she displayed wind chimes, dream catchers, prayer flags and a handful of Bob Marley decals.

It was easy to get the sense of the kind of person who gravitated toward Suzie's shop, but I wondered how far outside her typical clientele she'd reached using the Magic 8 Ball. After she'd helped the first couple of people with her fortunetelling, word of mouth would've spread. You might think the average fortunetelling is impressive if you don't understand how a person solicits information without appearing to do anything, but there's simply no substitute for genuine foreknowledge, and when you see the future foretold, you can't deny its implications.

A young girl stood behind the cash register, smiling at her phone. I approached. She finished whatever video she was watching before setting the phone face-down on the counter. "Help you?"

"Suzie Q. in?"

"Whose asking?"

I matched the girl's skeptical expression. "I'm the PI from the office down the hall. She hired me to find Boaze."

"Oh, god! You're *her*?"

"The very one."

"Yeah, wow! You saved her life. I swear, I've never seen someone so depressed as when she lost Boaze."

"She in?"

The girl lifted a corded phone nested beneath the counter and dialed a number. I hadn't seen a live corded phone in years. It made me feel old in an unselfconscious way. Her eyes shifted from glassy to alert. She nodded. "That detective wants to see you." Her lips parted slightly. "Yep." She hung up. "I'll show you back."

I've never been gifted in geography, geometry or really anything starting with geo- but the hallway through the door behind the checkout seemed to defy all the geos. My brain told me I was walking out over Maple Street, and the stretch of hallway was some twenty-feet long, brick walls, and distressed, thick wood plank flooring. There was one door at the end of the hall. The girl told me to head on up.

Up also confused me, because I'd been under the impression my building was a two-story affair. But when you're standing on solid ground and in spitting distance of sober, you don't doubt your five senses, so I opened the door and headed up the stairs. There were nine of them: steel with rusted rivets on the risers and treads. A door at the top of the stairs stood slightly ajar. I knocked. Suzie coughed. She asked me to enter.

Pot smoke hung in the air. I stepped into the cloud. "I thought you hated smoke."

She gestured with a glass bowl. "Just ciggys."

Like everything else she surrounded herself with, it seemed, the glass bowl was many colored. I cracked my knuckles. "Didn't peg you for a stoner."

"I can't remember the last time I was awake and not at least a little bit high."

This was supremely relatable. "Are you the kind of person who thinks pot is somehow different than all the other drugs and so you judge people who drink and smoke and pop pills?"

"If by pills, you mean opiates, I'd say it's not the best idea to get hooked, but generally speaking I view drugs as a gift. Just so happens the smell of tobacco doesn't agree with me."

I didn't say I felt the same about pot. For a moment we both stood in the stillness being still and considering the other. Something passed between us. If I had to put it in words, I'd call it camaraderie. She aimed the stem of the bowl at me. "You want to know if the Eight-Ball means you harm, don't you?"

For being without the 8 Ball to tell her why I'd come, her insight chilled me, but then again not, because she'd experienced it, been under its sway. I imagine she'd asked herself the same question before. "I guess, more or less, that's my question, yeah."

"Sit." She aimed the bowl at a hanging hammock chair. "It's not an easy one."

I remained standing. "I might get stuck. If it's all the same."

"I never wanted anything from you." She tapped her nose with the bowl's stem. It functioned as a nervous tick for her, I think. "I mean, other than finding Boaze." I followed her eyes as they scanned the room. The cat slept on a floating shelf mounted to the wall. His front legs hung halfway off, but he slept with the confidence of nine lives, daring the precarious ledge.

"Okay." I sat. The chair swayed, settling into a gyroscopic motion that soothed me. Perhaps the pot smoke was seeping into my blood. I decided I could tell a kind of bare truth I'd most of the time filter for the audience. "I wanted plenty from you. It's not every day you land a client who pays the kind of rate you did."

"Money's nothing." She sparked a Jumbo Bic and tilted the flame to her pipe. If nothing else, the crackling of burning leaf is invigorating. After holding the smoke for a moment, she coughed and exhaled. "But you know that now, don't you?"

The 8 Ball seemed to love reuniting pet owners with their animals, and people who loved their animals that much paid for it. "Why does it still feel so good when it's so easy?"

"Everyone loves looking like a genius. You feed on that."

I found I didn't want to ask what I'd come to ask, the real question nagging at me, so I treated it like a swim in a cold lake, and plunged. "Why did it get mean all of a sudden when we were getting along so well?"

Suzie nodded. "You know better."

"Know what?"

"Have you thought about following up with the people the Eight-Ball helped?"

This was the answer I'd not wanted her to give. "Who gave it to you?"

Suzie chuckled. "I was on Craigslist, looking for a used crystal ball."

"It must cost a fortune."

She tapped out the bowl into an ashtray and reached for a baggie of buds. "Enough that I figured the owner understood the power of placebo."

I fished my flask from my jacket. "Why'd you pay?"

"My life was at a crossroads, and I figured it would be a fun story."

"And why didn't you give it back when you realized its appetite for mischief, if that's the right word?"

She asked if I'd ever had Chala Wine. I said I hadn't. She asked if I wanted to try. I asked what it was. She said it was slightly psychedelic wine brewed from Skullberries. A Skullberry seemed dangerous, and I enjoyed living wild. She meandered to a standing cabinet. From it she produced a clear bottle about half full of deep purple liquid and two stemless wine glasses. She poured us each two fingers and toasted to Just Boaze's health. I drank. Sour notes and a subtle sweetness emerged. It finished burnt and bitter and I winced. She laughed at my expression. "That's the gods."

"Oh?"

"One of my clients gifted it to me. She said the mood of your heart when you drank would determine the aftertaste of the wine."

I felt duped. "Is that right?" I finished what she'd poured me, the bitterness near intolerable. "How's it taste to you?"

She hummed out a longish note. "Smooth."

I decided not to linger on the Chala wine or what it might say about my psychological health. "When did you know the Eight-Ball was—or —when did you know it had its own agenda?"

Suzie loaded her bowl, tamping it with her thumb. "I guess I think I suspected it almost from the start, but I couldn't ignore the consequences after the shoe store manager."

I scratched my chin. She kept her eyes on me even as she put flame to the bowl and inhaled. I shrugged. "What happened?"

The manager had been one of Suzie's long-time customers. She'd bought the crystals and the wellness beads and the teas and she really felt Suzie had been instrumental in improving her life. Then, on one of her visits for a reading, she'd told Suzie about this district manager who had been pushing for a sexual relationship, and the manager had run out of ways to put him off because he'd recommended her for a promotion she'd received, but she felt that wasn't reason enough to ignore her sense of personal agency, and so Suzie had decided to use the 8 Ball and the 8 Ball gave the manager a simple two-step plan to make the DM issue disappear. For two months following that visit, Suzie hadn't seen her customer or heard from her. Then one day the lady barged into the office wailing and sobbing. She said it was all Suzie's fault, and she threw awkward but angry punches that landed on Suzie's arms, chest and shoulders. Suzie half meant to keep her face from taking a fist, and half meant to comfort this hysterical woman who'd always been the picture of calm and poise. It came out that the plan to deal with the DM worked, worked too well. He'd been so ruined by what the manager had done that just days later his wife found him hanged and lifeless with a bathrobe belt around his neck, body hanging from a doorknob. And the thing was, the guy was a favorite among the shoe store managers in the district. He'd brought a lot of young women up the ladder and empowered them. His sexual pressure had either been confined to his dealings with the store manager or the other women had welcomed his advances. So when news of his death circulated, all the managers filled in the blanks. Sure, the DM had been reported anonymously, but it didn't take Sherlock Holmes to see who'd been behind the accusations. The weight of judgement wore the manager to bones and dust, and she decided to quit her job to get away from the judgment and coldness. The best she'd been able to do after the incident, as far as Suzie knew, was shift lead at a department store in North Dakota. "After that, I put the Eight-Ball away, pretty much until Boaze went missing."

I rubbed my jaw. Suzie's story wasn't what I'd been hoping to hear. I'd wanted her to say the 8 Ball was a harmless trickster or it had a mischievous streak. "Suppose it wouldn't be the worst thing if Marva offed herself, though." I gave a half-hearted laugh.

Suzie fixed me with a stern expression. "That's not funny." She scowled and held it.

I felt like a scolded puppy and broke eye contact. "I told you I wanted the governor dead when you offered the thing." All the good feeling had leaked out of the visit, and I wanted to flee. "Maybe you want it back?"

She told me I could hang onto it as long as I needed it. "You just need to understand the Eight-Ball is no joking matter, that's all."

We made a bit more small-talk, weather and the like, but at the first opportunity, I gave an excuse and said I had to run. I closed her door behind me and sat on the steps to catch my breath. No matter how I tried, I couldn't shake the feeling Marva committing suicide would be the most fitting end for her. I've had two family members kill themselves, so I don't view suicide lightly, and in it there is a form of self-judgement I wanted to see inflicted on Marva. How well would I sleep knowing not even she could stand herself, in the end?

35

NOBODY CRIED MORE FREELY THAN MY THERAPIST. HE gently wept, blowing his nose into a premium tissue from the box he always kept at his side. He went through tissues like a chimp in captivity, which I really am going to have to tell that story someday.

At any rate, he dabbed his eyes with a fresh tissue and recovered his pad of paper and pen. Once he mastered his emotions, I asked if he'd seen the whole thing about #OperativeCancer. He asked if it was that flash mob debacle. I said the flash mob was the farthest thing from a debacle, that it was the sort of action this state needed.

He said we weren't on the clock to talk politics but he'd close this query by saying respectful discourse began with two parties in dialogue. I didn't care how we spent our hour. In fact, I preferred if we made like vampires and did away with all the self-reflection bullshit. I said a dialogue required two willing parties and since the Governor's office refused to consider the flash mob's requests, their protests were the only rational response.

He dabbed the corners of his eyes tossing another lightly stained tissue in the wastebasket by his chair. "You smell drunk. You sound drunk. You look drunk. Are you drunk...again, Detective Mia?"

"Kiss me. Then you can find out if I taste drunk too." I smiled. "What do you think drunk feels like? I mean, can you touch it?"

He shrugged. "You know I have...to mark in my file...that you are arriving at these sessions...intoxicated and unrepentant?"

"Cheap entertainment, as far as I'm concerned."

"Is that...what this is...to you?" He marked something in his note-book. "Just a time...to play around...and act silly?"

A small part of me felt guilty for the way I treated him, but it was small enough to toss under foot and stomp out. I reached into my purse and palmed the 8 Ball. There'd been two days of heavy drinking since my run in with Suzie, and I still hadn't managed to get the numbness out of my fingers and toes from how things had ended. Sometimes you'd rather navel-gaze than face how someone you cared about considered you, which was the case with Suzie. In her, I'd confronted the part of me better left hidden. The funny thing was, I had this sense Marva might actually break the curse and set me free if she offed herself, but my wanting that somehow revealed the part of me that scared people away.

I showed Sir Bucket 'O Tears the 8 Ball. "This is the million-dollar secret behind Hashtag Operative Cancer." I lightly joggled it before him. "Ask it any question. It'll tell you the unvarnished truth."

He scratched something on his notepad. "For you...this is marked regression."

"Oh?"

"You're using toys...as a defense mechanism...to avoid discussing...yourself."

I asked the 8 Ball what the therapist had eaten for dinner last night. An answer swirled onto its viewer. *Pork springrolls and cheese pizza.*

His eyes popped. "If this is your way...of telling me you know... where I live...I'll have to report you...to the police...Detective Mia. And I must say...I'm more than a little disappointed...that you've escalated your disfavor...of our therapy."

I told him his interpretation was looney. "I don't care where you live. When I walk out of this office, I forget you until the following week. That's a fact." I stood and brought him the Eight-Ball. "Here. Ask it a question I couldn't know the answer to. That way you'll see." He said we were wasting time. I reminded him it was court-mandated and insurance funded. "So the only wasted time is my own, and I'm here, aren't I?"

Tentatively, he received the 8 Ball. "If I do this...we can get on with therapy?"

I nodded. He sat up straight and his face took on a thoughtful complexion. "All right. Does my wife...think these pants...are cheap-looking?" He shook the 8 Ball.

I put my hand up. "You don't need to do that—shake it. And it's not going to answer your question, because—"

Please don't ask me questions pertaining to ai.

"Artificial Intelligence?"

"Ai. It's Japanese...for love." His composure seemed intact but faltering. A tear rolled from his eye and down his cheek. He took a tissue and dabbed his face. "I did not know...if I still loved her." He cried some more. "What kind of magic...is this?" He held the ball out for me to take.

I received it. It was not lost on me that the 8 Ball had placed me, for the moment, in the role of therapist. I wasn't going to lean into that, though. For example, I didn't mention how the 8 Ball hadn't said he loved his wife. It'd only said the question pertained to love, and given his surprise at its answer, I thought chances were better than good his wife loved him, but the feelings were not mutual. "So you want to do therapy?"

He seemed to find himself becoming aware of the room, his context, and he screwed his face into a mask of professional neutrality. "Yes... More than anything."

I replace the 8 Ball in my purse. "Good. Then I have a question about morality."

He hesitated. "Okay?"

"So, I have this Eight-Ball, and it's shown me how to right some terrible wrongs, but I'm starting to realize when I do what it tells me to, people get hurt, people I care about."

The therapist's lips rounded and his eyebrows raised slightly. "This is...very good. You're speaking...of caring for others."

"For fuck's sake! Of course I care about people."

He scribbled a note on his pad. "But other than...your expressed obsession...with Mr. Kupfernact...you avoid all mentions...of caring... until now." He lowered his voice as if someone might be eavesdropping. "And just think...it was a clever toy...that brought about...this break-through."

I weighed the pros and cons of punching him in the face. "Cut the shit. Can I ask my question?"

He leaned forward. "You may—" I opened my mouth to continue, but he raised his hand, pointer finger extended. "Aht-aht-aht...but first... I want you...to take ownership...of your feelings."

"Cut the crap."

He smiled a tight-lipped smile. "Say, 'I care...about others.'"

I could take the stubborn path and dig my heels in, or the expedient path and give what was requested so we could move past it. "I fucking care about people. That's why I'm a private investigator." I crossed my arms. Expressing my care felt good, but I wouldn't let on. "Why is that so hard for people to understand?"

"Ask...your question."

I considered how to phrase it. "I'm one choice from exposing the worst criminal I've ever known, and if I do, I'll save countless thousand of people pain and suffering, and I might even prevent murders and violence, but the same choice will hurt people I love, hurt them in ways they may never forgive me for."

He seemed to be reading his notes. I felt exposed and wanted him to break the silence. He left us suspended in all that quiet for so long my hair began to hurt. At last he looked up. "Have you ever...heard of...the Hippocratic Oath?"

I nodded. "Do no harm."

"Yes that...but also...a less often considered element...of the oath... each physician swears to uphold...is to give only those treatments... which will benefit...their patient."

"I'm not a doctor."

"No." He leaned back and filled his lungs. "But you are...interested in matters...of right and wrong...and the Hippocratic oath...is the height...of morality."

I looked off to the side. Warmth swirled in my chest, stormlike and tense. "But if someone has a tumor, they need cut open. That's a kind of harm, right?"

"Perhaps." He put his pen to his lips. "But whenever surgical procedures...are the preferred course...of treatment...the patient must consent...knowing the outcome...may cause harm...sometimes... even...death."

I perked up. "So you're saying it's okay if the point is to help?"

"Not at all." He aimed the pen at me and swung it like an orchestra director. "I'm saying...if your choice...will cause harm...in any way...you would want...to inform...those involved...and ensure...their consent."

"But what if telling them would invalidate my choice?"

He shook his head. "I'm not sure...I follow."

I reached for my flask, recalled where I was, and stopped. "At least one person's too close to the crime to understand what's happening, and even though h...even though they're not guilty of any wrongdoing, they're also not able to see how the other person is, and so they'd rat on me if I asked permission?"

The therapist pinched the bridge of his nose. "Have we been...this whole time...dancing around...a question involving...Mr. Kupteshanik?"

"*Kuputchnik*. I never said that."

"But that is...who we're talking about."

"It's just a hypothetical."

Captain Sobsalot tented his hands. "Then I would say...hypothetically...that whatever...you are considering...the chances are too great... your own feelings...have compromised your ability...to act in anyone's... best interests...and the only moral...and ethical...response...is to give the police...any and all information...you have...about an impending crime... and allow them...to handle the situation...as they see...fit."

I hung my head. Whatever I'd hoped for, I'd lost any chance of. I glanced at the clock on the wall. "Well look at the time." I stood. "Thanks, as usual, for nothing, pal."

He stood, considered a reply, seemed to decide better of it, and told me he'd see me next week. It was the same every time our session ended. I told him not to hold his breath, because this might be the last time he ever saw me.

36

After leaving the therapist, I needed a drink or five so I hit the nearest Kum & Go and grabbed a bottle of Magdalene. I had extra cash, and Lyle hadn't sent any smokes lately so I bought a carton myself, like a big girl. I rediscovered how liberating it was to fund my own addictions.

While I got good and drunk, I worked the 8 Ball on some open cases. A golf club owner thought his accountant was skimming. The 8 Ball agreed. A man living off of 120th and Maple had been accused of stealing his neighbor's mail. Right again. As I delivered the damning evidence to my clients and collected my fees, I wondered what ill would come of them gaining justice. Though I'd hoped it'd be different, I had to accept the 8 Ball left no life unpunished.

It was closing in on dusk, and I was getting to that close-an-eye-to-keep-the-road-from-doubling drunk, so I decided to call it a day and headed for the office. From where I'd been, it was fastest to take Blondo up to 66th, so when I turned off 66th onto Maple and the street was clogged with police cars, ambulances and fire trucks—multiples of each—something like a sandstorm swept through my gut. Adrenaline mimics sobriety.

I parked by the 402 Collective because it was as close as I could get to my office. Bystanders milled around the caution tape border. My building seemed the subject of interest, as the tape encircled any entry to it. I asked a man who was smoking a cigarette what had happened. He said from what he was hearing a woman had been murdered.

The options were limited, and a cold terror gripped me. I ran forward, pressing into the caution tape. My fear sprouted legs and fangs when Lieutenant Bilson came striding around the back of a forensics van. I had to know, and so I ignored the urge to hide from her. Sometimes I wish I had taken a different path in life. I called out, waving my hands over my head. When Bilson seemed not to notice, I yelled louder.

She spotted me. For a moment, she seemed caught in indecision. She turned, speaking to someone who was obscured by the van. I couldn't make out what she was saying. A moment later Officer Howard emerged. It was as if the things of nightmares had been distilled and poured over me. I struggled for breath.

Officer Howard advanced on me. He told me to step inside the perimeter. I did. He seemed so calm. I tried to mirror his attitude, but I trembled. "What happened?"

He drew a deep breath, sighed. "Miss Q. was found dead in her apartment around two PM this afternoon. We're still waiting for final details, but the team is marking the time of death at around noon."

"Just dead?"

"*Just*? What'd be worse?"

It hadn't sounded like I'd meant it to sound. "Dead or murdered?"

"Ah." He demeanor almost read jaunty, and it put me on razor's edge. "Murdered. Someone had a bone to pick. Very personal from the looks of it."

"Fuck."

He'd led me toward the van, and there, leaned against it, crossing one foot over the other as if the name of the game was Get Awkwardly Comfortable. "Say, where did you happen to be at noon today?"

The most important question was whether Officer Howard was involved in Suzie's murder or simply taking orders to gain leverage over me, but surely they'd have checked my schedule if they pegged me as a suspect. "I was with my therapist, across town."

"She'd verify that?"

"He."

"And where've you been since? Seven hours is a long therapy session."

Where airtight alibis are concerned, you couldn't have had one better. I was with clients just about every hour on the hour all day, too far from the office to present any opportunity for the police to frame me. "I'll provide you a complete list of my whereabouts with contacts so you can verify, but right now I'd sure like to see the scene since she was one of my clients, and I may be able to help in the investigation."

Officer Howard shook his head. "Sorry, babe. Not—"

"Don't call me babe. It's sexist, unprofessional, and condescending."

"Oh, great. Another lesson from an uptight feminazi."

I managed a hateful smile. "Right. Can't teach an old pig new tricks."

"Pig. Creative." He stood tall, perhaps unconsciously trying to reinforce his masculinity. "The killer bashed in her skull, but not before slapping her around and breaking a few bones. Best guess is, someone thought she knew something and tried to beat it out of her. When we got here, a cat was lapping up her blood, and having its best day ever."

I looked out over the street. "Sounds like the cat isn't the only one having a grand time." I fixed him with the most intense gaze I could muster.

"Hey—" he held his palm up—"ninety percent of the time it's paperwork and speed traps. Am I happy a chick got exed? No. Does it add a little color to my day? Sure."

"You disgust me." I decided the world was a lost cause so I might as well leave a mark however I could. My fists balled, and I visualized the haymaker, but just as I was loading my hips for the swing, someone called my name loud enough it rose above the thrashing blood pulsing in my head.

31

Debbie stood at the caution tape. She wore the scent of fried chicken like nuclear fallout. I raised a hand, loosening the fist into an awkward finger sprawl. She motioned for me. My last visit with Suzie ended poorly, and that was how she left the world, tortured, and murdered, believing I was without love or heart. I thought about waving Debbie off, but something gave me pause.

Officer Howard chuckled. "If it aint the chubby Wonder Woman."

I figured the Wonder Woman part was because she'd come to my rescue at the police station. For the chubby part, I hoped he'd soon get a slice of street justice, like meeting me in a dark alley. "Hey, how about you step in front of a speeding car, fuckface." I turned and aimed for Debbie without waiting for a reply. He'd disappoint me with some generic comeback anyway.

As I drew near to Debbie, I put on a hard face, because that's what shame requires. "Didn't I fire you already?"

She looked at her shoes. Whatever she said it failed to rise above the thrum of busy bodies all around. Maybe all the years of nights tossing in bed because my thoughts wouldn't stop screaming in my head had dulled my hearing. "What'd you say?"

She pursed her lips. "I'm working for Lyle, actually."

My hearing must've gone bad, because I could swear I heard her say she was working for Lyle, and I told her so. She said I'd heard right, and she said he'd sent her to collect me on important business. Maybe Marva was a disease. You hung around her too much, and then you started behaving like her. What else could explain Lyle hiring away the only person I could trust? "I must be fucking cursed."

Debbie glanced over my shoulder. I followed her eyes. Lieutenant Bilson was approaching. I can't remember who said it, and I'm probably going to butcher the quote, but it was something like, when you're trapped on the fiftieth floor of a burning skyscraper and the only way down is out the window, once the flames get hot enough, you'll always choose to jump. I winced. Bilson had fire in her eyes. "I can't go." This was the last thing I'd have pictured myself doing. "One of my clients was murdered and I'm probably to blame."

Debbie gripped my elbow as I tried to turn. She squeezed. I reached across my body and grabbed her wrist. "Let go."

She squeezed harder. "If you stay, you're going to jail as the primary murder suspect. If you want justice for Suzie, you come with me ASAP."

Between Bilson and Howard, it wasn't prison I worried about. "She never did a thing to deserve this."

"Who does?" Debbie nodded. "Come on. Now."

Leave it to the universe to take the one time I meant to face the waltz and force me to flee. I glanced behind me. Bilson was closing fast, reaching for her pair of cuffs. My relationship to all things spiritual is slippery at best, and I don't know what comes after we kick the bucket and stay kicked, but I apologized to Suzie and promised her she'd have justice as my top priority.

38

"When's the last time you ate?"

I lit a cigarette. "Liquid breakfast count?"

She tossed her hat on the dashboard. "Dos De Oros?"

If you've spent more than a few hours with me, you know I survive on bourbon and smoke, but if you tempted me with the one true taco, I couldn't resist. "They went out of business."

"Pay attention to the news much?"

I shrugged. What else was there to say?

"They got bought. Look it up. It's a cool story."

I hit my flask. It was too early to call it, but I think Debbie had changed since she'd worked for me. "What's this about Lyle hiring you?"

Debbie passed a Toyota in the right lane. "It's complicated."

I pressed her for details, saying complicated was my forte, but she mimed zipping her lips and tossing the key. When it was clear I couldn't coax her to spill it, I gave up and Googled Dos De Oros.

The Omaha Reader had run a two-page spread from December of '22 titled "Los AfortunadDos De Oros". COVID had been, to them, like so much of the restaurant industry, a catastrophe. The owner, Jesús Diaz, had almost guided his two taco trucks through the pandemic where so many other restaurants had failed, but when one of his grills

"""

broke, he'd couldn't afford a new one so he put the business up for sale, and that'd been the last I heard of it.

What I hadn't known was, unlike most restaurant owners, Jesús caught a streak of good luck. "Señora Evalda Turñal from who knows where"—*The Reader* had referred to her exactly that way—offered to buy the business, but only if "Chewy continued operating the business because the soul of a taco is in the man." All Señora Turñal wanted was to recoup her investment in one-hundred-dollar monthly payments. *The Reader* noted that at the agreed-upon repayment schedule, Señora Turñal would need to live for just under a thousand years.

Señor Diaz's good luck was only slightly blunted when the O'Reilly Auto Parts store where they'd parked the second truck for over a decade chose not to renew its lease, and finding a second location was taking time, but Señora Turñal encouraged Señor Diaz not to rush. *Lugares, lugares, lugares. That is what I tell him todos los dias.*

I butted a second smoke and tucked it back in the pack. "You have to wonder what her long game is."

Debbie parked at the curb about a block from the truck that was still serving. "Whose?"

"That Evalda lady."

"Maybe she just loves good tacos." Debbie shut the engine off and palmed her keys. "You ready?"

"Listos."

There was only one thing I'd ever found that bothered Debbie, and it was mixing Spanish words and phrases into conversation. She rolled her eyes. "Come on."

Margarita was taking orders. When she saw me, she cupped her hands around her mouth. "¡Señorita Fumadora!"

It was unclear if I'd earned the nickname because she'd always seen me smoking or if she found me incendiary. Either way, I liked it. I waved. "¿Que onda, Margarita?"

We caught up while they prepared our orders. Even after so many months, they remembered my usual. Margarita said when she hadn't seen me in so long, she figured I'd finally walked down the wrong alley and tangled with the wrong gangster. I asked how the new owner was treating her. She said there was no difference, said I'd probably love the lady, whom she'd never seen without a lit cheroot.

Marcos came out of the truck with our food. His hug was a wrecking ball. How he managed it without spilling my food is one of life's great mysteries. I asked about his family. He asked about Lyle. I deferred to Debbie, letting slip just the slightest bit of coldness. Debbie said it was complicated, which as mood killers go, fell somewhere between admitting on Twitter you still look at Facebook daily and telling your uncle who reads the New York Times you voted for Donald Trump.

We managed to recover some warmth in our goodbyes and Marcos made us promise not to be strangers. I told him to give my best to his wife and children. As we retreated to the car, I asked Debbie why she'd gone all weirdo about Lyle, and she said she'd been hoping to avoid the subject until after we ate. I gave her hell about her secrecy, but she wouldn't bend.

She sat behind the wheel and pulled the foil off her quesadilla. It was the most generic offering on the menu, but I didn't care to critique her. Native Nebraskans seem to find ethnic food too flavorful, as if such a thing was possible.

I opened my paper clamshell, tore the lid off, and nested the base inside the upturned lid. The sweet tang of carne asada filled the car. I squeezed a lime wedge over the diced onion salsa. Through a mouthful of warm corn tortilla and juicy steak, I managed to enunciate enough to ask what the big secret with Lyle was.

Debbie swallowed a gloopy bite of quesadilla. "Governor DeLonghi fired him this morning."

I'd dreamed of the moment Lyle would be free of Marva's clutches, but her firing him wasn't how I'd imagined it. He was supposed to see the light and quit, giving her the finger as he went. "Is he blaming me?"

Debbie finished the first half of her quesadilla. "Governor DeLonghi said she was tired of the Flash Mobs embarrassing her on the news every day."

I drenched my tacos in salsa rojo. "That's it?"

Debbie finished her quesadilla and wiped her palms on her jeans. "She may've felt you were a problem."

"*May* have?" I decided to take a quick break from eating to address my nicotine deficiency. "In what way?"

"I think it's not a leap from @TruthyMia and #OperativeCancer to Luke E. Mia, PI."

"Why didn't you tell Lyle that wasn't me?"

"It was you."

I pounded my fist on my knee. "You were in on it too, and Ruskov spilled the beans."

"Lyle understands that, and I apologized already."

"Apologized?" I examined the coal glowing at the tip of my cigarette. "I'm not going to say sorry for something I didn't do, and Marva firing him because she did something illegal is bullshit."

Debbie drew a line with her finger on the steering wheel. "You made choices, Luke."

Some moments in life catch you so totally off guard you wonder if the universe has consciousness, and it finds you repugnant. I'd given my life for Lyle, and as payment I'd lost his partnership, his friendship, and the only other person I'd cared about chose him over me. "Can you remind me why you came to get me, because I was in the middle of something important?"

Debbie's shoulders slumped. "I'm sorry about Suzie."

I flicked my cigarette butt out the window because the world was burning around me anyway. "Sure."

Debbie shifted her weight in the driver seat. "It's just..." She sighed. "Things got out of hand."

I bit into a taco, but it might as well have been sawdust. "You think?"

Debbie gave a soft exclamation. I looked up from my food and startled. There was a man standing outside Debbie's window. I leaned down for a better look. Heat filled my body. It was no use. I burst into flame. Tossing the clamshell on the dashboard, I flung my door open.

39

Lyle held a plate heaping with tacos, a torta, an overstuffed burrito. He had a bag in his other hand—roasted jalapeños, I knew from our many previous visits—and a bottle of Jarito's Mandarin pressed between his forearm and ribs. As I ran around the car, he arranged his food on the roof of Debbie's Supra. I hugged him. "You have no idea how sorry I am. I fucked up royally."

He held me, and I felt I belonged. "Little late for that, huh?"

I pulled away, searching his face for anger. There was none. "She's crooked, Putch, crooked as my mother's teeth."

He bit into the torta. Pork grease dribbled down his chin. "Don't talk that way about your mama."

"Will you forgive me?" It's easier apologizing when you feel you've gotten what you wanted. And it's even easier borrowing someone else's words. "Things got out of hand."

He turned his body and leaned against the Supra. Folding a taco in half, he ate it in two gaping bites. "You got in the middle of some bad shit, Lu. Marva doesn't like being messed with, and you kept giving it to her and giving it to her. Relentless as ever, huh." He finished a second taco and belched. "Did you ever have times when you doubted yourself, wondered if maybe you were just reading into things?"

I wiped my face on my jacket sleeve. "You forget I've been watching her for years. I mean, I'm a proverbial Marva expert." A cloud passed over his face, and I resented myself for bringing up the lives. He'd never taken to it. I tried to pivot. "Maybe it was hard for you to see what she was doing with a six-figure salary clouding your vision."

He said the money had been okay, but he'd have accepted the job for half. It was about the challenge and how he'd discovered he wanted higher stakes than the pets and infidelity M&K had to offer.

Saving Marva from attempted murder unlocked something in him. I wanted to say he hadn't saved Marva, that he'd only gone where I told him to, but I wasn't about to spoil a happy reunion on technicalities. At the same time, I didn't know what to say because I felt he'd taken the job from Marva without having told me he felt bored or dissatisfied.

I hit my flask. "So look, we can catch up on shoulda-coulda-wouldas as long as you want, but I'm thinking you didn't send your newest employee all the way out to get me so we could shoot the breeze over tacos.

He finished his fourth. "God, I missed these, huh?"

I nodded. He crumpled his paper plate and tossed it back in a bag and produced the cup of roasted jalapenos and several raw radishes. He ate a jalapeno whole and chased it with a hunk of radish. I missed his appetite. I'd missed his smell and his long body. Ten minutes in and I had zero regret about all I'd done to peel him away from Marva, and now—now we'd have the best of it all, because I knew I could show him how deep Marva's darkness went, how she needed the full weight of justice. "Hey?"

He'd peeled the foil off his chili verde burrito. "Yeah."

I parked a cigarette between my lips, but refrained from lighting it, because I knew he preferred I not smoke while he was eating a meal. "Now that you're back, maybe I can show you what I'm working on with her? She'll regret canning you, that's for sure."

He devoured half the burrito, replied with a full mouth. "What'd you have in mind?"

I looked over my shoulder like someone might be listening. "I happen to have—"

Debbie interrupted. "Can I get out?" She'd rolled her window down, because Lyle'd trapped her by leaning against the door.

He stood and apologized, spilling carnitas on the cement and cursing.

She opened her door. "Just a little awkward being in there while you two chewed the fat out here."

Lyle apologized. He offered her his bag of pork rinds, which she accepted. I asked if she was okay being involved in the political assassination of Marva DeLonghi. She looked at Lyle, Lyle at me. I said maybe assassination was a poor word choice, and started in on how if he thought #OperativeCancer was bad, the other stuff the 8 Ball had given me was twice as fucked. I said I wouldn't even be surprised if Marva was involved in Suzie Q.'s murder.

Debbie raised her palms and gentled us like horses. We needed to talk about Suzie, but Suzie was a separate issue. To Lyle, she said she could vouch, the 8 Ball was the real deal, but she also worried because it had its own agenda. Lyle asked about the 8 Ball. He seemed more interested in it than I'd have expected for a guy who shrugged off all my other mentions of the supernatural. I ignored my discomfort at his easy go-along and gave him the two-minute rundown while he sipped on the Jarito's and started in on the last of his jalepeños. "So let me see if I'm following you, huh. You actually think this toy of yours is giving trustworthy takes on Marva's so-called corruption?"

I stiffened. Lyle wasn't the type to question me. We hadn't always seen eye-to-eye, but when it came to investigating, we were simpatico. "Come on. Ask it a question." I started to reach in my purse.

He held up a hand. "It's okay. I'm just curious. Hey, where'd you get it from anyway? It's one hell of a bar trick if it does what you all seem to think it does." He finished a taco, wiping his mouth with the back of his wrist.

Lyle seemed too interested and too casual at once. I wanted to understand my feelings about it. "Who's *you all*?"

He shrugged. "Oh whatever. You. Deb. Miss Cleo. Deb, you believe it's magic, right?"

She nodded. I wanted to hit her. What was with the half-assed support? Okay, so maybe I'd jerked her around one too many times with the hiring and firing, but she'd still seen what the 8 Ball could do. "Come on, ask it a question."

He surveyed the area and changed the subject. "You been slowing down on the drinking?"

I looked to Debbie as if this was proof of her betrayal. She shrugged. I clenched my teeth. "I'm not drinking any more."

"Haha." He rubbed a spot of dirt off a radish with his thumb. "You're not drinking any less, either, though."

I blew a jet of air out of my nostrils. There needed to be a way out of this dilemma of Lyle treating me like a curiosity, because I was so flustered by it my brain was telling me he had hidden motives. "Since when do you care how much I drink?"

Lyle spat on the pavement. "Can't a guy worry about you?"

I lit my cigarette because a radish didn't count as part of dinner. "You just don't seem worried."

Debbie squeezed my shoulder. "We're all on edge."

Lyle nodded. I said the only reason I was on edge was because we were standing around doing nothing, like we had no urgency. Debbie asked where we had to be? I said if we didn't have anywhere to be, they shouldn't have pulled me away from Suzie. Lyle asked about Suzie, and I gave him the rundown, her connection to the 8 Ball, and how she'd probably died because someone thought she was me. I hadn't thought that last bit until I said it. You can get to feeling awfully sad when you accept you're the problem. It's one thing to have a problem, another to *be* the problem. Hey, it's me. I'm the problem. It's me.

Lyle said the situation with Suzie was horrible, and I said it sounded too fucking casual when you referred to it as simply horrible. Debbie asked if I was dead-set on nitpicking everything Lyle said. I took issue with her ganging up on me and said the only thing I was dead set on was understanding why Lyle had decided to meet us for tacos, and I wanted to know sooner than yesterday.

Debbie rolled her eyes. She was in a hellish mood, like none I'd ever seen her in before. Lyle swiped his finger through the salsa on the bottom of his plate. He licked his finger. He cut the tension by saying he'd hear me out about Marva, that it was the least he could do. I told him I hoped he wouldn't be offended but I really didn't think I was in a place where I wanted to share my scoop with a person who still seemed to be Marva's biggest supporter.

He asked why I thought he supported her. I said maybe it was how he'd justified every behavior of hers, and questioned me like an interrogation. Debbie said Lyle had come to me first thing after Marva had fired him, and she asked me what more I needed to see to know Lyle was trying to get on his feet and figure out his next move. She said he might be inclined to hear me out about Marva's corruption if I stopped treating him like the enemy. I looked to him to judge his response.

Lyle said we'd come to this place and that was what we had to deal with. He asked what I wanted to do about Marva. I told him exactly what I had in mind, saying she was lucky I couldn't snuff her out after all she'd done. He considered my comment without his typical flippancy. She'd changed him.

I asked what he knew about Marva's relationship to climate activists in Nebraska. He told me a lot of details I already knew like how she'd invited the board members for the Heartland Game and Wildlife to the Governor's mansion and how shortly after that meeting they'd received much needed funds for a restoration project that had looked to be headed to the bone heap, and though the funds were given anonymously, he thought they might've come from a company with interest in mineral exploration because just weeks later, at a public rally for a drilling operation no one from Heartland Game and Wildlife appeared to voice opposition, which was unheard of so Lyle was just putting two and two together.

Part of me admired him for seeing those things without the 8 Ball but the other part of me wondered why he'd not felt it was a problem enough to question his boss earlier. I mean, we'd been less than virtuous back in the agency's glory days, but Lyle never pulled punches when telling me he thought we'd crossed a line. I lit another smoke and held my breath until the nicotine assaulted my brain like a roundhouse kick. "What about Kewit's Initiative for Sustainability, Strength, and Maximum Yield Association? And was that on purpose?"

Lyle crumbled his empty wrappers into the foam clamshell and stuffed it in the bag. "Was what on purpose?"

"You're honestly telling me, in a world of acronyms, nobody stopped to check that one?"

I loved his face when it fell to deep thinking. "Oh, jeez!" He cracked a smile. "I might keep that to myself."

Debbie said she didn't get it. I told her she was too friendly. While the gears in her skull cranked, I asked Lyle if he'd happened on any proof Kewit's initiative had bought votes in last fall's election. He said Marva didn't buy votes, and I caught a whiff of defensiveness but ignored it.

I ashed my cigarette. "That's not what the Eight-Ball says."

"Well, listen, I'm—I mean I was—in her office on a daily basis, and she talked about plenty of handshake deals, but even the Hashtag Operative Cancer reports aren't conclusive proof. Other than a few angry words, she never stressed about those allegations." He pushed up his fedora and wiped sweat from his brow. "I mean, I still know as much about politics as I do about baking cakes, but I'm pretty sure buying votes is a felony."

I didn't say news flash, moron! Buying votes is the tamest felony she's committed. He might've been fired, but he still thought highly of her, which was cause for concern so I squeezed at his feelings to see what would ooze out. "If she'd hire you back, would you go?"

He shrugged. "I think right now, I'm too angry to even think about that."

Lyle sucked at lying. "Even if you think she's got her good points, you have to have seen her playing both sides. On the one hand she's running a campaign on clean water, clean air, and clean living, and on the other side she ran smear ads with contributions from the Geological Society of Mineral Wealth, and we're talking seven figures. You can't tell me that didn't influence her advocacy for our state."

"It's politics, babe. People have to work with all kinds to get things done."

I turned away. I felt cuffed, or bound. "Yeah, but not the way she was doing it. Her way would be like a research lab working on cures for lung cancer, taking donations from Phillip Morris."

Lyle shrugged with his lips and eyebrows. "Cancer research is cancer research."

Debbie interjected to say she was getting cold. Lyle said he'd booked a hotel downtown. They had a good restaurant in the lobby. Debbie asked how he could be hungry after all those tacos. He rubbed his belly, said maybe he was eating for two. I wanted the time to think anyway. Something was askew. "We'll meet you over there."

40

It struck me, on the way to The Magnolia, I hadn't wanted to ride in Lyle's car, which was when I accepted my bitterness toward Marva had wrongly estranged me from him. I could picture her, cozy in her dark office, late at night, relaxing in a high-backed armchair, hands tented, quietly cackling as she savored how she'd poisoned me against Lyle. She'd taken everything from me. I wouldn't give her that. Whatever Lyle wanted I'd give him, even if it meant abandoning my fight with Marva.

Debbie parked in the garage beneath the hotel and placed the parking stub on the dashboard. She asked how I was feeling. I guess it was a reasonable question after a silent drive over. I stubbed out my cigarette and flicked it in a nearby trashcan. "Everything's upside down."

"I thought you'd be happier to see Lyle."

I didn't say he seemed like a stranger to me. "I was happy to see him, but he's changed, or I have, or we both have."

"He did just get fired."

I gave Debbie a cold glare. "Don't worry. I'm over it. I just needed a minute."

Lyle was waiting for us in the lobby. He'd tamed his pompadour and shed the suit jacket he'd been wearing. Though he'd most always worn a fedora, before his time as a big wig, he'd opted for jeans and v-necks or casual button-downs untucked.

I approached. "Fancy seeing you here." It was easy to smile and to mean it.

He held a tin of mints and offered me one. "They're curiously refreshing, huh."

"You saying I have bad breath?" I took one and gestured to Debbie.

Once upon a time he'd have playfully elbowed me in the ribs and fired off a comeback, but perhaps his sense of humor had gone into hiding, working for Marva. He jerked a thumb toward the restaurant. "I called ahead."

The host led us to a booth on the patio. There were heat lamps overhead. Still, we were the only party outside on a beautiful night. The host took our drink orders. Lyle asked for sparkling water, which I refrained from teasing him about. We made small talk about the Cubs great first month, how unexpected Swanson's bat had been, and the emergence of Velázquez.

In a quiet moment, Lyle asked Debbie if she'd mind getting a folder from his car. He said it had some of the environmental outlines I'd been referring to. He gave her his car keys and directed her to where he'd parked. "Sorry. It's a bit of a jaunt, huh."

As Debbie rose, I asked her if she'd grab my purse. I'd forgotten it in the car and wanted to have my money so Lyle couldn't trap me with charity. She asked if anyone needed valet service or perhaps a gentle foot washing. I laughed. Lyle didn't. Marva had murdered his sense of humor, if I haven't already noted. Debbie sauntered off. I liked it when she was sassy.

A cool breeze stirred. I folded my arms and shivered aloud. I couldn't not look at Lyle, but his face reminded me of my failures. He wanted me one-on-one—a good sign? My heart fluttered. I imagined apologizing to him for the hell I'd put him through and him saying he knew it was for the best. The host brought Lyle's drink. I asked where my bourbon was. She said it was coming. Her expression said she was worried about my thirst. I waved it off. "Hey, no rush."

Lyle grabbed his glass. I'd never seen him show such restraint. Usually he'd have a bag of peanuts in hand and a block of cheddar within arm's reach. I pointed with my eyes at his empty hands. Must be a hell of a restaurant if you're waiting to eat."

He looked me up and down. I thought there was sadness there. He sipped his water. "If you had a chance, and you knew you could get away with it, would you take Marva out?"

I gave a breathy laugh. "You mean like assassinate her?"

He looked at his hand, holding the glass. "Sure. Whatever it takes, huh?"

"She wouldn't stay dead in the first place..." I looked up as I was thinking, and he was focused elsewhere. It took a special kind of stupid to ignore what was happening. I pushed a lock of hair out of my face. Whatever part of me is always picking up clues, it had been firing cannonballs at my unconscious, but I'd ignored them. "Jesus fuck!" I pounded the table. "And I was planning to tell you who the Flash Mob Organizer was."

He folded his hands on the table. "You always drank too much, Lu."

I gripped the empty salad plate in front of me, slowly raising it. A storm passed through me. A lot of things stopped mattering. I brought it down on the table, and it shattered, slicing my palm. I hardly felt the cut. "Just tell me, is Debbie in on it? Does she know?"

Lyle shook his head, slowly. He stood. "I never thought anything would get the best of you, Lu. But you're paranoid, and jealous, and you let it completely overtake your better judgment."

I looked over my shoulder. A woman was coming followed by a man. I couldn't make them out, backlit in dim lighting, but I knew. I fixed Lyle with a hardened look. "Tell me. Was Debbie in on it?"

"No. I didn't tell her. Despite everything you've done, she'd still defend you."

I closed my eyes to slow time. "You used to be like that, but Marva broke you."

"I'll have her visit you in jail."

"Ha! Jail? You're something."

Hands seized me. I didn't look to see who'd grabbed me. If I'd been at the office when they came, Suzie might've lived. I saw the whole play in my mind. Some random goons went looking to silence a pain in the ass private eye, but they'd found instead a seer in a mystic shop. "Your boss had Suzie Q. murdered, and now she's got her sights on me. Don't let this happen. Pay att—"

"Shut up." A hand knocked the back of my head. Cold cuffs closed around one wrist and I was pulled up and back with force as the second cuff clamped around my other wrist.

I kept my eyes fixed on Lyle. "This fun for you, Howard?"

"*Officer* Howard, you bitch."

Lyle winced. He didn't know. I couldn't be mad at him. He didn't know. To him, I was the betrayer. He'd gone and gotten a dream job, and I'd given him nothing but shit from go. Drunk, wild, how many times arrested, firing and rehiring Debbie like it was a game. Then I come to him with some story about a magical toy. "Hey, listen—"

Howard jerked the cuffs down and away. "Shut up."

Lyle jolted forward. "Let her say what she's gotta say, huh." He pulled a travel-sized box of raisins from his pocket.

I smirked. "Hey, if you can pull your head out of your ass in time, figure out what happened to Suzie Q." Howard pulled me back hard. I yipped because it hurt. "And tell Deb she owes me big time. Can you do that?"

41

The night was fragrant with lilac and abandonment. My wrists stung, but I knew asking for help would only show weakness. Officer Howard pushed me into an unmarked car. Lieutenant Bilson sat in the passenger seat. I wondered what Debbie had thought when she returned to the table, or what Lyle had told her.

Howard drove for a while before I decided what needed saying. "You're going the wrong way for booking."

Howard threw an arm over Bilson's headrest and craned his head around so the car was piloted blind. "No shit, Sherlock."

"I just didn't want to die with you thinking I was a moron."

He laughed. It was high-pitched and nervous-sounding. "Wow. And you thought I'd be impressed that you had me pegged as a crooked cop?"

"I'm not looking for you to be impressed. I just want you to know I had you pegged from the first."

Lieutenant Bilson adjusted the rearview mirror and locked eyes with me. "You've proven yourself an adequate investigator, and at this point I don't mind telling you so."

I think I'd already resigned to where our evening was headed, and I wondered what happened if Marva outlived me—a whole lot of quiet and maybe stillness. Snuffed out, never to return. It was just that I'd be beaten that bothered me, but if I was obliterated from the future, nothing would bother me so even being beaten didn't bug me too much. Maybe Debbie and Lyle had been right, not that I was crazy to trust a toy, but that I'd let my feelings for Lyle cloud my judgment. If I'd been harder, more alert, not so sentimental about my feelings, I'd have let Lyle have his fancy title and moved on.

A six-year-old named Theodore who pitched legendary fits if you tried to call him Ted, Teddy, Theo, or Dory had brought us together. I'd been fresh off the case that'd won me my pocketknife and resentful it hadn't made me a household name—the case, not the knife—as the lawyer who contracted with me had promised. It's since been suggested I might've ridden that case to fame if my taste for bourbon hadn't been so pronounced. If that's the deal, I'd ask why it matters how much a person drinks if she's the best mind for the investigation.

But, add that to the list of concerns I'd soon be leaving behind. I asked if Bilson or Howard would spot me a cigarette. Neither replied. I asked if they'd consider turning down the air conditioning as my toes were cold. They said nothing. "So, look, if you're going to kill me anyway, why make it such a boring experience?" Their silence unnerved me.

Silence is what they gave, though. We carried on another twenty minutes, west on I-80 through Lincoln, before Howard took an exit that advertised no services. I hoped they weren't going to march me into a cornfield and shoot me. It's probably not the kind of thing you've thought a lot about, because getting murdered isn't a subject to dwell on, but take it from me, if someone's going to end your good times, you kind of want it to be a dignified affair.

Howard headed north long enough my mind began wandering and a stab of boredom pushed through the ache in my wrists. I decided if they were going to give me the silent treatment, I'd give them my version of AM talk radio. "We're coming to you live from Butt Fuck Egypt, folks, and boy do we have a show for you today, but first, let's send you over to Nancy for a weather update." I raised the pitch of my voice and gave it some nasalality, if that's a word. "Thanks, Luke, and, whoo-eee! I've got just three words for you: Hot, hot, and hot! It's hot out today." I clicked my tongue because I couldn't snap. "Back to you."

When my routine failed to provoke a response, I pushed it further. "Thanks, Nancy. Hot indeed. You might even call it hellish. In other news we've been reporting on a rogue contingent of corruption in the OPD headed by one, Lieutenant Jennifer Bilson. Sources tell me she's a soulless whore who h—"

Bilson came all the way around and clocked me in the side of the head with a slap jack. My vision blipped out for a moment and it returned with a high pitched smell and something that sounded like burnt eggs. I hard-blinked until something resembling monovision returned, though the edges of everything remained blurred. I'd had at least one concussion in my life and knew the signs.

Howard turned right onto a dirt road. He was smirking, and I felt angry at myself for giving him the pleasure of watching Bilson strike me. "Let me out of these handcuffs—" my words tasted like hot copper and electric current—"and let's see if you're so eager to take a swing on me again."

It was back to the silent treatment though, which was fine by me because nothing is quite so exhausting as dealing with someone who's got nothing to lose. "Hey again, folks, seems we had a brief power outage up here, but we're back on the air with all the hottest takes from the coolest voices in radio. Now where were we? That's right, the soulless whore, Wynona Bilson, and let me tell you—"

She swung the blackjack again. It must've been something about calling her a whore, are maybe she really dislike people getting her first name wrong. Either way, I was ready for her, and when her arm flew I ducked, so the strap of leather glanced off the side of my left ear. It stung something fierce, but the pleasure of eliciting a reaction outweighed my pain.

We crested a hill, and in the distance there was an old farmhouse. Howard turned when he came to the rock driveway. I tried a quick narration of the events, but Bilson had wised up and she came down with the slap jack so it rang my crown.

Howard parked. Bilson said to get me into the room. Howard said it was his pleasure. I can't say why it was a relief for them to speak. Howard opened the rear door and hauled me out of the car. I tried to catch my footing, but he tugged too hard, and I fell. With my hands cuffed, I had no way to catch myself and my face broke my fall. A tooth popped out, and I spat it into the dirt. Under different circumstances I'd have been angry about that tooth because I've always had curiously perfect teeth. We're talking cavity-free, straight pearly whites. It's my winning, genetic lottery ticket.

I had little time to consider if my face was going to swell before Howard reeled me to my feet. He pushed me toward the house. I asked if he was well-liked on the police force, but he was winning in the stubborn category and refused to answer. He shoved me toward the porch steps, and I almost ate it on the treads, but someone caught me by the arm. Broad-Clean lifted me bodily the last two steps. I felt nauseated and relieved at once. "You bastard!" If I'd been smarter, I'd have asked the 8 Ball when I could, who this guy was instead of feeling smugly satisfied I'd known he was coming to rough me up that night. Part of the 8 Ball's gig is making you lazy toward the small things. Where you usually rely on minute details, when you have an all-knowing Magic 8 Ball, you neglect to get all the answers, instead focusing only on the big rocks so to speak.

He raised a phone to his ear. "She's here." As Howard pushed me inside. Broad-Clean took the car we'd arrived in and backed it out of the gravel drive. He was important, and I hated that I'd never know why.

Howard flung me across the dark and swampy entry to the farmhouse. Apparently, no one cared about air conditioning. This was a place no one lived in, but one that saw plenty of use. The floors and windows were generally dust-free, the windows clean. The lightbulbs modern.

It didn't take long to guess at what its use was. Howard pushed me into a room with a solitary wood chair. Bilson stood behind it. Jackson Pollock might've decorated the floor in blood. I figured sterile procedure wasn't a top priority in this place. He spun me so my back was to the chair. I stepped to the side to catch my balance. "Silly me. Here I was thinking you took occasional look-the-other-way money, but you're a—"

Bilson drove a fist into my kidney, and I collapsed to my knees. She hooked her hands under my armpits and hoisted me up, pulling me toward the chair. I clenched my arms so she had a tough time getting them behind the chair's uprights. She open-hand slapped me across the face "For being a pain in the ass."

I licked blood off my lips. "Is this why you got into policing so you could slap people around?"

She looked at Howard and told him to leave us. When he did, closing the door behind him, she answered my question. "I joined the force because my father was a cop. They fired him for shooting a robber in self-defense."

I was sure she'd left out important details and said so. She backhanded me. Her knuckles came away blood-soaked and left my cheek hot and throbbing. When I collected myself, I spat. "What is it you hope to get out of this?"

She straightened, circling me once. "I'm glad you asked." She leaned forward at the hips until we came eye-to-eye. Her breath had the ghost of decay in it. "Governor DeLonghi says you took something that belongs to her, and she wants you to know it makes her very, very, very, extremely angry."

I thought about the copy of Brian Bernitt's tablet. It was ironic that something I'd never seen had brought me to this place. The Magic 8 Ball was merciless. "You're wrong."

Bilson laughed. "Whoa, now!" She pulled the slapjack from her back pocket. I'll decide who's wrong." She raised the leather strap over her head and brought it down in a chopping motion across my knees. The pain thundered up and down, simultaneously. My ears popped like a case of the bends. "You might not know this, but if you take enough nerve damage below the waist but above the knee, you'll eventually lose the ability to walk. It's actually a fascinating process. The muscles, the tendons, the bones, they all remain perfectly healthy, but because your nerves burn out, you lose coordination and remain an invalid."

It sounded like a torture myth, though I hoped not to be the one to disprove it if so. "Probably doesn't really matter though, since when I leave here it'll be in a pine box."

"Oh, honey." She relaxed her lips into a pout. "That's up to you."

Adrenaline was an overlooked superpower. You could be in agony, but it enabled your mind to hold on. So maybe more of a curse. "You won't let me live. You'd be too worried I'd rat on you."

"That's where you're wrong." She crossed her arms, letting the slap jack hang from her fingers, a pendulum at rest. "We let people walk every day. From our prisons, from our interrogations, from this house. Murder's overrated." She shrugged. "Now, sure. As a last resort we can bury you out back. You'll be in good company. If we determine a person's beyond rehabilitation, it's an option. But if you cooperate, everybody wins." She smiled. It was authentic. This gave her happiness. "How's that sound?"

It felt like someone had set a hot cast iron pan on my legs. "I can't give you something I don't have."

Bilson coiled and she was a cobra with her strike. Blood dripped from the cut in my brow and my tongue throbbed in the soles of my feet. She stepped back. "You let that sink in, Detective Mia." She retreated, looking back with her hand on the doorknob. "We know you have the Eight-Ball. Suzie told us."

42

In what world can you accept a coincidence of this kind? Suzie Q. manages to be the person who rents the Magic 8 Ball from the owner who happens to be none other than Marva DeLonghi. There are bad odds, and there are odds like those, but I wasn't given much time to consider it. Officer Howard replaced Bilson, and the expression he wore suggested he found personal enlightenment through hitting people, but especially women. "Candy tells me you're playing dumb." He stretched a length of rope between his hands and made it twang.

They'd taken Lyle from me. That was an accomplishment I never could've believed possible. I had nothing left to lose—if you didn't count my teeth or my life—so I mirrored his smugness. "Candy? Oh, that's so adorable. Are you two going steady? You seem perfect for—"

He stomped my foot. The bones in my toes shattered like so much glass. Heat engulfed my head. He lowered his arms and let the rope hang from one hand. Its ends coiled on the floor. "You might want to excogitate the value of smart assing. Because that—" he pointed at my toe— "was just a warning. Next time you piss me off, I won't hold back." He came closer and gathered the rope in both hands. "I think we're wasting our time with you." He knelt to bind my feet to the chair. "But she thinks you can be reasoned with so—"

I kicked with both feet and met a special kind of agony. If there'd been any unbroken bones in the smashed toes, I'd remedied that. My consciousness blinked out for a moment, and when I came to, Howard lay sprawled on the floor cursing. I struggled to stand, fighting a wave of nausea that climbed my legs. "Excogitate?" Somehow, I managed to untangle my arms from the chair. "Who the fuck're you pretending to be?"

Howard rolled, trying to regain his feet. I lifted my maimed leg and hopped on the good one, leaning forward, gaining momentum. When he lifted his front knee to stand, I threw myself at him. The center of my forehead met the soft hollow of his temple, and as we clunked heads, golden bell tones spilled from my ears. I thought I'd made a foolish decision, but when I rolled away, Howard's snoring suggested I'd had at least a lick of luck. But any positive feelings faded when I considered the challenge of sitting up with my hands cuffed behind my back.

If there were justice in the world, though, Howard would have the handcuff key on his person. I didn't allow for thoughts of how I'd manage to unlock the cuffs even if I could find the key. One step at a time, I told myself, because if I could manage to free myself before Bilson returned, I just might live to tell the story. Maybe.

I inched my body around, alternating a thrust of the knees and a tuck of the hips until my hands were more or less buried in Howard's crotch—and by "more or less" I mean my knuckles were pressed against his erection, which told me everything I needed to know in regards to his relationship with violence. I contorted my elbows, a challenge given I had to lay my weight on one of my arms to get in the correct position. My fingers explored until they found what seemed to be a crease in the fabric of his pants—a pocket. I managed to dip my index and middle fingers into the pocket, but reaching in far enough set me to panicking. The cuffs prevented me from gaining the necessary leverage.

After accepting I'd run into a dead end, I considered a plan B. You might struggle to believe this, but picturing Lyle, kept me going. Likely a delusion, but I thought if I could just get to him, I could show him how he'd been played. That kept me going, but there was this inconvenience of my wrists in cuffs.

I'd have to roll Howard on his back and mount him on mine so I could use my hands with less restriction. Depending on how traumatic his concussion, my weight might rouse him, but no plan C existed. Inch, by painful inch, I positioned his body, then my own. His breathing grew labored, but it remained even. I worked my fingers into his pocket and at last hooked my index finger through a keyring. I rolled off his body after I'd worked the ring up to my second knuckle and made a hook of it.

Then there was the question of finding the right key by feel, somehow manipulating my hands to plunge the key into the lock, and twisting it to free the tumblers. As I put myself to the task, Officer Howard's breathing grew ragged. My time was waning.

I closed my eyes to tell my brain vision would be no help, and it is a strange thing, because humans are, if nothing else, visual animals. We rely on our sense of sight as much as all our other senses combined, but as any good detective will attest, no one has eyes in the back of her head.

In the darkness, my hands found themselves. The cold, slick groove of the key's polished steel. I singled out the smallest of the bunch, worked it to the top of my hand, pinching the base between my thumb and forefinger. I fished the key in compact jabs, at last finding the opening in the left cuff, and I wriggled the key back and forth until it met the lock cylinder. My breath created a problem, so I held it, and I flexed my fingers to the fullest, every cell electrified, and the key drove all the way in. Even still, twisting it required a painful precision I scarcely believed my hands could execute.

Howard moaned. He was rousing. I gave everything to my fingers and the left cuff popped with a squeak and sigh. I brought my hands around and stood. The throbbing in my legs from where Bilson had struck me made standing a true test, and the first bit of weight on my broken toes scraped a groan from my lungs, but adrenaline countered any reluctance my pain put up. A gun would've increased the odds of my escape, but Howard's eyes were coming open, so I hobbled for the door and took the knob.

The brass was cold in my palm. How in the hell was it possible, of all the people in all the world, the Magic 8 Ball just happened to belong to Marva? It was the kind of detail one could only accept if she'd already been the subject of magic before, and when the magic is connected to one specific woman, you start to get ideas.

I squeezed the doorknob, twisted it, and pulled the door open. Warm light spilled from the vast room. I stepped into the void, and I bounced off a sturdy, uniformed officer.

43

MIKE SHOTZ TOOK ME BY THE SHOULDERS. "LU?"

First Lyle. Then Debbie. But this? It's hard to describe what utter defeat feels like, though one-by-one losing the people you thought you could lean on is about as close a description as I can imagine. "Michael."

He spun me. A mix of surprise and resignation made me more pliable than I should've been, but Mike was muscle and force in the flesh. He'd been trained how to engage with hostiles so enforcing compliance was a matter of leverage. He pressed my free wrist back into the cuff and returned me to the room. I was pudding held together by cheese cloth. He arranged my arms over the chair's back and sat me down.

In the corner of the room, Howard was rousing. He rubbed his head. "The bitch took a cheap shot."

Shotz winced. He knew how I felt about that word, but I wasn't going to be enlightening anyone about sexism—not here, and never again. Ever, after all, was pretty short for me. He turned just his head toward Howard. "You ignored my warning. She's the toughest buck-and-a-quarter I've ever seen, and I've taken on chicks bigger than her doped up on PCP. Luke'd trash any of 'em."

There was performance in his comments. If I hadn't already resigned myself, if I had something to fight for, I'd have missed the truth behind the scene. Mike felt fondness for me so he was trying to be nice, but I also knew he wouldn't let me free. Whatever had led to this moment, he had greater debts to Marva than what he owed me for covering up his murder debacle with Dickey Hollars. He knelt and gathered the rope Howard had brought. It took a kind of bravery I admired to look me in the eyes as he bound my legs. I spat in his face. "How long?"

He swiped his chin clean on his shoulder. Howard stomped over and he raised his fist to strike me, but Mike threw his elbow back and up. Howard crumpled. Mike glanced back. "You had a chance. And she still has hers to do it easy." I'm not sure Howard heard any of what Mike said, given his balls were somewhere in his throat at that moment.

Shotz stood after checking his knots. He'd been a Boy Scout, no question. Both ankles were bound separately, and tied to the leg of the chair, but the rope between my legs made a slipknot, so if I struggled, the binding cinched tighter. Mike brushed his hands on his uniform pants. "To be clear, I'm the easy way. This is how it goes. Tell me where the Eight-Ball is. Candice tells her guy, and when he says they've got it, you walk."

I tried a punch of caustic laughter, but it wasn't in me. "You don't actually believe I'm making it out of here alive, do you?"

He posted his hands on his hips. "You can walk out of here, absolutely. How do you think we're in the same room? Sometimes you end up on the wrong side of a bad situation. And I'll be honest, I'm no fan of Big D, but she's fair enough. Tell me where it is, and I can take you to the hospital. Lu, we can be at Bryan Medical in twenty flat."

I scoffed. "You're telling me you sat in this chair, and lived to tell?"

He pointed to a splash of blood on the floor. "I didn't even get a warm up act. They started me with The Professional, and let me warn you, don't let it come to him, because he'll give you two choices, and you won't want either. Just tell me where the Eight-Ball is."

I tried to adjust because my back was throbbing, but the ropes were merciless. "You're lying. Suzie wouldn't be dead if there was any other option."

Mike fixed me with such an intense gaze blood boiled behind my eyes. He hunched forward and raised his hand, pointing at my face.

"Suzie lent something that didn't belong to her so she got a different offer, and for the record, she chose the hard way."

I shook my head. "Was it you? Did you cave in her skull? Is that the price you pay to stay alive? You become one of her hired killers, because no thank you."

His face contorted in curiosity. "Seriously?"

I looked to Howard. He was a fish out of water, jaw chuffing noiseless O's. It left me wondering if blunt-force trauma to the testicles caused brain damage. Time would tell, but Howard for sure was somewhere else for the time. "Which ones are his bloodstains?"

"Fuck. I don't know. Maybe he chose the easy way." Mike looked at his shoes. "What I do know is I wish someone had given me the chance I'm giving you."

I know the truth when I see it, and Mike believed his line. He somehow thought Marva's way was stern but reasonable. I wet my lips with my tongue. "You ever met her in person, spoken face-to-face?"

"Sure. Couple times. Why?"

"It's her yellow hair, you know? The first time I met her she was in high heel shoes. A guy named Larry'd made her black and blue. I remember feeling sorry for her. Boy, she knows how to play it." I fluttered my eye. "I bet you had a crush on her, right?"

"Hey, now. I'm not doughy-eyed like Lyle, thinking the governor's a saint, but she's doing a job, and if you don't get in her way, she leaves you alone."

I did laugh. "You don't seriously think of that as a selling point?" My split lip bled freshly. It stung. "Must be easier to live with yourself when you make shit ass excuses."

"There's people like Lyle, and there's people like you and me. Lyle sees the world as a consequence of his character. You and I are going to go out and get what we want, character be damned, but if you want to keep up the self-righteous nonsense, be my guest. In a weird way, I think I'm a better person after The Professional went to work on me. Maybe you need that."

I rolled my head, cracking my neck. "You always struck me as a bit naïve but I thought you could at least see the difference between milk chocolate and shit on a stick. Tell me, Mikey, does it hurt?"

He crossed his arms. "What?"

I imagined pulling on a menthol filter and inhaling gallons of smoke. "Having your head so far up your ass you can see tomorrow's breakfast."

"Hey, whatever. We don't have all day. You've got the Eight-Ball, and as soon as I know where it is, we'll get you out of here. All that blood, your head's gotta be throbbing."

I ignored his delusion. "You never answered my other question."

"Oh, boy, I can't wait. You'll have to jog my memory."

"How long have you been a lowlife Judas?"

He palmed his forehead and drew a long breath. "Is that what you think?"

I turned my head away. "This isn't betraying me?"

He mock-gasped. "This is you fucking yourself like you always do, Luke Mia." He tapped his temple. "First you go off and save the future governor from an assassination attempt, and in the same day, you take down her biggest political rival, by proving he paid for the attempt on Marva's life, and you've got pretty much everyone from Ryan and Kelly down to the Corner Drug calling you a hero, so you go and start fucking it up by talking trash about Marva and stalking your old partner after he takes a job working for her."

I closed my eyes and focused on finding calm within myself. "Answer my question. How long have you been planning to throw me under the bus?"

He gestured to the room. "This?"

I nodded. "This."

He crossed his arms. "I got the call this morning. Before that, I didn't even know you were on her list. But listen, I promise, in a couple days this'll all blow over, and you'll wonder why you spent even one extra minute in those cuffs. I swear to god. Fess up, and let's get you to a doctor."

"Yeah, a doctor. You me and the duck over there. We can all ride together in a apple-red Vanagon and sing Kumbaya."

Mike's expression didn't change. He really believed I'd cave and be a little lackey in Marva's growing army. Maybe they all did. Me and Bilson, Howard and Mike, we'd all start having drinks at the end of a long hard day of torturing anyone who thought differently. Boy, wouldn't that be fun! "Listen, the Eight-Ball was in my purse. If your stupid coworkers hauled me off and didn't even check to see if they got everything I brought with me, I can't take the blame. You can't fix stupid. But I'm sure you're in luck, cause I bet Lyle's grabbed it. Go ahead and relay that to little miss Candy Corn, and when she still has me killed me in cold blood, I'm going to stay here as a ghost and haunt you until you piss blood and pull out all your hair with tweezers and sulfuric acid, but just so we're clear, I get the last laugh, because even after I'm dead, the releases from At Truthy Mia aren't going to end. I might've helped start the story, but I'm not the one pushing it out there so just make sure to pass on my regards to Marva DeLongfuck, won't you?"

Mike looked as confused as an unlit match in a gas can. "You think Lyle has the Eight-Ball?"

I'd been hit in the head a few times over the past hours. Maybe I was slurring or something. "Am I not enunciating my words? The Eight-Ball was in my purse. My purse was with me at the hotel. Your fellow officers of the peace—har, har—seem to have neglected to take my purse. Therefore, unless Lyle just abandoned my bag, it's in his possession."

"Okay. Okay. I find that strange, given we've been in contact with him, and I'm pretty sure he'd've mentioned the Eight-Ball his boss is tirelessly searching for, but why don't I just go out and tell Candice you think Lyle has it? See what she wants to do." He half turned toward the door. "But, uh, if it turns out Lyle doesn't have it—and I guarantee he doesn't—then it won't be me who comes back into this room."

I had a good idea Shotz's replacement was going to be a hell of a lot worse, and I really didn't care about giving up the 8 Ball. If Marva wanted her stupid toy back, what did I care? As far as I was concerned if I actually did walk out of camp-tortures-a-lot, I'd buy the first ticket to outer space and disappear in the middle of the Cartwheel Galaxy. "Yeah. Sorry. I'm calling bullshit. There's no way Lyle would knowingly give me up to a bunch of brass-knuckled douche canoes."

"Oo! Good one." Mike rolled his eyes. "Thing is, I agree about Lyle, but as far as he knows, you're in processing at the State Pen. Threatening to kill the governor is yet another serious offense in a long line of them."

I might as well've been talking to a wall. "Is this the big-lights comedy show, or what? Because telling me I'm making serious offenses when you're a twisted cop, that's just funny. Am I right, or am I right?"

Mike waved a hand in the air. "We can split hairs all you want, Lu, but the truth is, time's ticking, and I can only help you if you work with me." He slipped his phone from his pants pocket and glanced at the screen. "Five minutes, in fact."

I had no interest in being stubborn, but maybe Shotz needed his hearing checked. "Why don't you text Lyle right now and ask if he grabbed my purse?"

Mike plunged a hand in his pocket. "I can't do that."

I stared him down. "Can't or won't?"

He looked over his shoulder at the door. "Three minutes."

"He doesn't know you're involved in this, does he?"

Mike winced. "Lyle doesn't have the Eight-Ball so what's it going to be?"

"I hope you get yours, Michael. You stand here pretending there's an easy way, but when I tell you the one-thousand-percent, unvarnished truth, you act like I'm trying to give you the run around. Well I'll tell you what, you better hope you're right, and the next guy lets me walk out of here, because if he doesn't and I'm tossed in a dirt bath, my ghost is going to haunt you for the rest of your days, and I'll make it my personal mission to fuck you over...or wait, you're screwed either way, you turncoat traitor mother fucker. And if I don't get to do it myself, make sure to tell Lyle I officially hate his guts."

Mike looked at his hands. "I hate to say it, Lu, but Lyle was your last defender. Nobody, and I mean nobody held out longer. Your drunk driving excursions, your stalking the capital at all hours, your week-long benders, your crazy-ass conspiracy theories, the way you'd look right into a camera on live news and tell the whole world Marva DeLonghi had killed you ten times but you refused to stay dead, Lyle defended you through all of that, and then you go shitting all over her about a few measly fucking goddamn votes."

A thrill raced through me. "Whatever it takes. You said it yourself.

Marva's twisted. Don't get me wrong. I've got no problems with a little wink and nod, but Marva picked a fight with the wrong bitch."

He tugged at his earlobe. "Wow. You threw away your life for a stupid grudge."

Part of me wondered if I had thrown everything away for a petty grudge. What did it matter if Marva got Lyle? If he wanted to be her lap dog, what did I care? Because it suddenly seemed like the dumbest thing in the world to suffer for. Months of love-sick-puppy all so I could end up tied to a kitchen chair. Halle-fucking-luiah! "At least you admit I'm a goner."

"That's not what I said, retar—"

"Don't you say that word!"

His eyes went wide. "Sorry. I forgot I was with the PC Police."

My guts were running laps in my belly. "Hey, Shotz. Do you even know what the old Magic Eight-Ball does that Marva's so keen on getting it back?"

Mike stood tall. "Doesn't matter."

"It tells the truth"

"Damnit, Luke." He shook his head. "Cut the fucking games, unless you wan—"

The door opened. Bilson stood framed by the opening. Mike turned toward the noise. She asked why Howard was laying on the floor. It neither seemed to surprise nor upset her. Mike said Howard lost his temper and tried to assault me so he'd stepped in. She nodded, reaching into her pocket. I held my breath, but she was just grabbing her phone. She dialed a number and raised it to her ear. When in connected, her eyes narrowed. She told the person on the other end Steve needed attention.

After she disconnected, she asked Mike if he'd gotten what they needed. He said I'd been playing dumb, but he was positive I was finished playing games. I said if they wanted the 8 Ball they should've made like actual cops and not dragged me away without checking to see if I had my shit. I locked eyes with Bilson. I told her I wasn't a fool and I knew she was going to have me murdered, and I asked her to tell Mike the truth, that no matter what I did or didn't do, I was a dead woman this very day. When she showed no signs of even hearing me, I clacked my cuffs on the crossbars of the chair back. "Candice Bilson is a terrible name, by the way." I affected a laugh. "Did your mother hate you?"

"That's it." Bilson stepped inside the room. She sipped off a can of Diet Coke. "I'm sending him in."

Shotz's face tightened. "No." His head might've been on ball bearings the way he shook side to side. "She doesn't understand what she's saying." He turned to me. "Luke. Tell her where it is."

Bilson clapped her palms together and held them clenched. "I'm sorry, Mike. We tried your way. And I'm not going to go to the governor and tell her we failed her because we didn't feel like doing everything necessary. Detective Mia is an obstinate fool." Bilson pointed at me. "But she'll listen. It's just a matter of pain, isn't it, honey?"

She didn't know the first thing about pain, how betrayal hurt worse than any slap jack, how physical pain can't touch your mind if you don't want it to, but losing love is hell. They'd lost all bargaining power the moment they took Lyle. "You can't hurt me."

Bilson came alongside of Mike and examined me. "I'm tempted to prove you wrong, but I'll leave your body to The Professional." She turned, reached across Shotz body and started to walk him back.

He used my full name. "The Eight-Ball. Spit it out."

I clenched my teeth. "What kind of game is this? I told you. Lyle has it, and if he doesn't someone stole my purse." As he and Bilson closed the door, I hung my head. Injury ends at death. I focused on the finite nature of my nerves in that context. Feelings ends at death. What was this game they were playing? Pretending they want an answer, ignoring what I told them.

44

The man stood eye-to-eye with me, though he was standing and I sitting. He had knees where most people had shins and a face like day-old rye bread tossed in a mud puddle. With a polyester handkerchief, he dabbed at his glistening brow.

He examined Howard, who, I began to wonder, might've been the first ever death by testicular trauma. This man did not introduce himself, the one Bilson had referred to as The Professional. He replaced his hanky in the pocket of his tweed jacket. I wondered where they made suits for miniature humans. He raised a hand with two fingers extended. "There are only two things. My job and your job. Your job is to provide information."

"And what's your job?" I knew what his job was.

He adjusted his glasses, gold wireframes with round lenses that seemed to float on his weathered face. His cheeks were a map of grooves and rivulets. His forehead had five expressed lines, even at rest. "My job is to teach." He removed his jacket revealing a red silk vest over a white oxford. He draped the tweed over one arm. "Shall we start with the pliers or the hammer?"

So much for pleasantries. "You pick."

"I am sorry." He sniffled. "You must choose. Remember? Your job is to provide information. I teach. You inform. Do you understand how it works?"

"What if I choose neither?"

The muscles in his lips appeared to operate individually. First one side of his face smirked, then the other. "Mahahw—" lifting the coat from his arm, he held it out before him. "Mahahw, mahahw, mahahw. You are a funny young lady. Hear my laughter? Mahawh." He spread the jacket over my head. A sharp, musty aroma punched at my nostrils. "That is not an option."

I told myself I could breathe just fine, but it was as if my nostrils and mouth had been taped over and punctured only by a pinprick. I opened my mouth all the way and forced a yawn—the body's hard restart—but still I was left disoriented, and hot. *Take control of yourself.* "Not choosing is a choice."

He pressed a firm object against my forehead. "I am not like your friend, the police officer. There is no clock by which I am working."

If you've ever had your head dipped in liquid concrete, you know exactly how I felt. "Come on. Teach me already. I'm an eager student."

"Ah." There followed a metallic clacking. I imagined scissors opening, closing, opening. "A teacher cannot teach if the student will not share. You may think of this as enrollment and I'll be introducing you to tools of the trade. I think you will find my style is very collaborative."

Tingling, sharp, angry sensations raced along the branches of my nerves. The forced blindness created a sense of trapped urgency. I needed fresh air. Who had first called this man The Professional? "But how can I give you information without knowledge?"

His voice had a depth that gnawed on you. "That is a common misconception about learning. Every time you do something for the first time, you are giving information without knowledge so tell me, what will I teach you?"

My initial inclination was to choose pliers, because I couldn't think of any use of a hammer I could recover from, yet I couldn't bring myself to choose either. Even when I reminded myself pain ended at death and so the hammer's haste would probably be the more expedient choice. Even when I tried to tell myself physical pain was a choice, I remained horrified silent. My own recycled breath grew hot and suffocating. My pores vented stale smoke and sour alcohol.

Time became a living beast crawling my head and nibbling at the walls of my veins—each heartbeat a second on the clock. The Professional occasionally sniffled or shifted. He breathed. At some point the door opened and closed. People grunted. Shoes shuffled and scuffed along the wood floor. The door opened and closed.

I believed myself strong enough to hold silence, but almost against my will I called the man psychotic. He disagreed, saying rather he was professionally trained. I contemplated kicking back in my chair and leaning my head back. The impact might crack my skull and escort me to the grave on my own term, but it might just as well give me a headache and two broken arms. Time perched on my throat, stitching its thread around my neck, tightening moment by moment. I gasped. "I'm suffocating!" I knew I wasn't but couldn't stop myself from believing so.

This failed even to gain a reply.

Less time gathered between outbursts. I told him I hoped someday someone would repay him for his cruelty. His reply was a buoy in the ocean of my torment, a moment of relief. He said men of his sort always paid their debts, and he would die by violence, but he had made peace with his end many-many-many years ago: three manys as if he were countless centuries old.

I tried counting to a thousand to fight the sense of eternity. I made eight hundred and asked what would hurt worse, the pliers or hammer. It seemed he might let this question, like he'd let the one about suffocation go, but after a short delay, he replied. "Yes."

"That's not an answer."

"It is also not not an answer."

I tried pleading with him, then. I realized with horror I wanted the 8 Ball to tell me what to choose, and this was its cruelest turn of all, paralysis of the unknown. He asked if I had made my decision. I became adamantly animated I was, in fact, incapable of choosing, and I said if he would simply tell me what to pick, I'd pick that. I'd pick either and be glad, if only he'd tell me.

This, he left to sour in my stomach. I tried to gather myself, but having broken into so many pieces, I found it impossible to be whole again. I tried to shift the power, though if I thought in terms like power, that is lost to me now. "It's been proven physical torture produced false confessions."

Again, he gave no reply. I then surprised myself utterly by breaking into song. I sang Creep by Radiohead. What the hell was I doing there? The Professional said I sang with conviction. I believed him, had even been told this by others so I asked for a cigarette. He said I might never smoke again unless I could choose between the hammer and pliers.

"Why won't you just choose for me?"

"Because choice is what you came to learn, and you must remember, I am a teacher." He neared me, neared enough that his body heat mingled with mine and his breath seeped into my nose. "If I were to choose for you, you could blame me for your pain, and this is the down-fall not just of you, but of all humankind. We resign agency so we have someone else to blame. Coca-Cola is the reason I'm fat. Netflix is the reason I have no friends. Alcohol is the reason I'm sad. Those who can't teach. Those who teach inflict maximum pain with pleasure. On and on and on."

It was agony and truth. "Hammer." I chose the hammer because it said I couldn't be beaten. "Now get this fucking jacket off my head."

His feet scraped against the floorboards. He pulled the jacket from my head. The air I'd formerly considered sticky and close felt so cool and fresh I may've been reborn. "Time's wasting, boss."

He reached into his pocket, seeming to fondle himself a moment. "Almost everyone chooses pliers. Did you know that?"

Of course I knew that. There's only so many ways you can dance with a hammer and have a face left to tell about it, and most people prefer to keep their faces. "I buck trends. What can I say?"

"I admire you, Detective. Though before we are finished, you will doubt that, I am sure."

"Can we get started? I'm kind of antsy now that we've settled on a tool."

He retrieved from his pocket a pair of pliers with red, rubber-coated handles. The clacking of metal buzzed the inside of my skull like static electric shocks. "Um. Did you hear me wrong? I said hammer."

"And so we move on to your second lesson." He clamped the pliers onto my eyebrows and tugged, a smooth, slow pressure, puling the skin into a tent, before a clump of hair ripped free. "What do we do when our choices produce unpredictable consequences? I like to think of it as the woman who is given fifty-fifty odds of survival from a cancer if chemo is used, but as a result of chemo, she is so crippled by debt all her belongings are taken and she is left physically weak and destitute."

A seepage of blood mingled with my eyelashes, and I blinked furiously. I suppose, if you've waxed before, you have some idea how I was feeling just then, and if you haven't waxed you're likely a man. I closed my eyes and focused on breathing. "Does everyone who chooses pliers start with hammer?"

Either a mercy or a further cruelty, but he clamped the pliers on my thumbnail and pulled. I've burnt myself in a wind, trying to light a smoke before. It was kind of like that, magnified, like leaving your hand in the flame after the nerves had reported the heat, but it was also a stinging sensation, the way you feel when a hangnail brings a strip of living flesh with it. My whole body seized, and my lips drew back in an involuntary grimace. "Okay, okay, okay." I focused on my lungs. They still worked, though if my senses were true, lungs and nailbeds have a direct connection.

"What you're really asking is if your choice caused my action, is it not?" The pliers clamped onto my index fingernail and tugged. I screamed. He let the nail fall to the floor. It landed like a hollow coin. "All good things come in threes." He clamped my middle fingernail.

"Nuh-nuh-no!"

He pulled. My eyes fluttered and began to roll back in my head, but a firm slap to my neck roused me. "No sleeping in class, my darling."

He circled my chair. "Are you ready for the hammer?"

If I could've found my voice, I'd have declined, but my voice was hiding. I shook my head. He slapped me across the face so hard my ear bled. Hot, wet, sticky and yet somehow slightly ticklish, the flow of blood down the side of my face. I groaned. It was no relief to consider an end of pain. There was only that moment, nothing before, nothing to come. Spiders had replaced my blood, and the screaming I thought was ringing in my ears from the slap was the air from my lungs in full flight.

The Professional replaced the pliers in his toolbelt. He took my face between his palms. "I want you to know that most people are not ready to talk after their first class, and so I do not expect you to cooperate yet, but I am a sensitive teacher, and I want you to have every opportunity to prove you have learned."

The joke about a henway clanged around inside my throbbing noggin. It felt absurd. I couldn't remember the punchline, but the point was simple. If you can't understand the terms, how can you answer a question? I had a hard time finding my words. "What do you want to know?"

"Perhaps the hammer will jog your memory."

This was a kind of psychic terrorism. "A man named Lyle Kuputchnik turned me over to your associates." Talking hurt. I thought about the hammer. "They failed to collect my purse inside which's where you'll find the Eight-Ball. I've told this to Lieutenant Bilson and no one will listen."

The Professional reached behind his back and produced a hammer. It struck me the way cheap magic would. He examined its handle. Stained ash, and a well-oiled claw. The head caught light from the window and reflected it in my eye. "Do you know the last person I introduced to this hammer?"

My eyeballs hurt. "I doubt you're married, otherwise I'd say your wife's assho—"

He slapped a shoelace of drool out of my mouth. Tears filled my eyes and rolled down my cheeks, stinging as they fell. "I can't say I'm surprised. No one is ready to cooperate so quickly." He tucked the hammer back behind his back. "The answer I was looking for was Tsopan Shauerov." He plucked the pliers from their holder. "You need another class session with these. They can be very persuasive when applied to your nostrils." His comment was punctuated by a gunshot sounding nearby. I wondered if the whole farmhouse was full of captives like me being tortured for sport. A burst of bullets from a semiautomatic rifle made The Professional startle. He narrowed his eyes and pursed his lips, and resheathed the pliers.

That the gunfire took The Professional by surprise scared me. He turned as a volley of explosions sounded. The only window in our room turned to dust and my tormentor's head burst, splattering my face with bone, brain, and blood.

I was tied to a chair, covered in human remains, in the middle of a firefight. Sitting around waiting for answers or a bullet in the brain seemed foolish so I shoved down with my legs. Considering all the pain in my face and hands, I hardly noticed the agony in my toes. The rope tightened, but I gained enough leverage to tip backwards. All my weight in the chair landed on my arms, and bones broke: the chair did too. I'm not a doctor, so I can't say what physical processes occurred, but I know my body surged with numb power, and springing to my feet felt as natural as an Olympic half tuck. Simone Biles had nothing on me. I waddled toward the door.

The ruckus had awakened Howard, and he called after me to wait. I chose not to look back. It was my tortured hand that gripped the door handle and twisted. I walked the door open. As I passed into what would have been the living room, I tripped over Mike Shotz. A bullet had passed through his neck and two through his chest. The walls were peppered with holes through which daylight poured. It's hard to explain my gratitude, but I'd learned some physical pain couldn't be ignored, which left me with a profound thankfulness for guns.

"Hey."

I turned. Lieutenant Bilson lay half on the floor and half on the stairs leading to the second story. One of her arms was separated from her body, laying by the wall, pale and bloodless. Her stomach was a mess of guts. "What?" I felt woozy.

She pulled in a breath wetly. "Faults grabber."

"Okay." I'd think on that later if I had anything to think with. I considered myself both dead and alive, and I waited for the bullets to aerate my body as I started again for the front door. The urge to just step out of the house and die in the open air was greater than I can manage to convey.

Mere feet from the door, I stumbled back as it burst open. I believe I had attained supernatural abilities through my hunger to leave that place that I had used my mind to open the door, but in its frame, haloed by a burst of light so bright it blinded, was the girth of a woman. She turned her head and gestured to someone. "If that's being careful, I'd hate to see your people casual." And that was when I collapsed.

45

The woman is clouded in rich smoke thick as velvet and sweet as caramel. It fills my whole body with warmth and life, and I try to make out her face or any feature at all, but she is obscured by golden light and that heavy smoke, and she tells me I have died too much for this life, and I ask if I am dead but she says I am not, not this time, not really even close but rather just exhausted, although she isn't a doctor and says so, and I ask who she is, and she says I will know if I must, but for now she wants me to go back home, and I say I would rather not, but she says I can't stay, and though I try to resist, I am pushed by a powerful force out of the light and smoke and into deep, cold darkness, and I awake with a gasp.

Debbie looked down on me. "There you are."

I tried to piece together some idea of how this could be happening that I was with Debbie in a van—not the Savana—alive after being abducted and tortured by Howard and Bilson. "Mike Shotz."

Debbie apologized. "How did he find you?"

I told her he'd been with Lieutenant Bilson and Officer Howard. "But he treated me kindly." I'd gone to his wedding and attended his children's baptisms. Now he was dead. "How did you find me?"

"The Eight-Ball." I was surprised and showed it. Debbie told of how she'd returned after failing to find the folder and how Lyle had told her about my arrest. She said she'd felt gut punched and betrayed, and he said that is why he'd sent her away for the arrest, but that it was the all-around best choice out of a bunch of bad ones. He reminded Debbie I'd said I could see myself assassinating the governor. I tried to push back on that claim, to clarify, but Debbie said it was water under the proverbial bridge. She told me to put pressure on my arm. Until then I hadn't realized I'd been shot. My whole body was pain.

Debbie must've seen the mounting panic in my eyes because she assured me I was going to be fine: pretty banged up, but fine, probably a scar or two, but a pretty face like mine could use the character. I squeezed the bandage wrapped around my arm and gagged at the squelching sound my broken elbow made.

Debbie crooked a finger under my chin and turned my head. "Don't look at that. It looks worse than it is."

Why didn't it hurt? "How do you know?"

"I just do."

I considered the fall in my chair. That my left arm seemed unharmed was a marvel of its own. I blinked to moisten my eyes. "What happened then?"

She said she'd asked Lyle if the whole being fired thing had been an act, and he'd said it was and wasn't. Governor DeLonghi had given him a last chance to solve the Luke problem. He said he worried your hate for the governor had grown so deep it'd finally overcome your better nature, and that he'd decided to test you. If you showed violent intentions toward Marva, he would hand you over to the police, and if you didn't he was ready to let his job go. The way it turned out, he was just hoping a few years of prison would sober me enough to get my life back on track. Debbie said she felt sad for me, but if she was honest, she thought I'd become unhinged too. Though, after a few hours something still felt wrong about the whole thing so she decided to ask the 8 Ball what prison the police had taken me to because she thought maybe being able to picture me in a cell would calm her nerves.

I adjusted my weight and yipped. Pain zapped through my body. "You hate the Eight-Ball...Wait? How did you end up with it?"

Debbie glanced toward the driver. He was a squat man with hair everywhere but the top of his head. "Can you give it some gas, pal?" She looked back at me. "Hold your horses, Dirk Gently. One question at a time."

"Dirk whonow?" I gave a half-hearted shrug of the eyebrows, and that screamed with pain too. Fucking pliers!

"Maybe you should read a book someday."

I closed my eyes. "Hey, maybe you forget I'm injured. Spare me the B-S, would you?"

Debbie gently cupped my hand in hers. "I'm sorry."

It was too sincere, and I winced. She released my hand. "How did *you* get the Eight-Ball?"

She explored her knuckles like the answer was written on her skin. "This is going to sound too absurd, but do you remember how you asked for your purse last night?"

Until she'd mentioned it, I hadn't. "Okay."

"Well." Debbie looked out over the fields of corn rushing by. "I captured a certain keen interest in Lyle's eyes when you mentioned the purse and it bugged me. He's a lot of things, but observant isn't one of them, and so even without thinking much about it, I snagged the Eight-Ball and all your cash and left them in the glovebox."

Debbie was an incidental genius. I smiled, splitting my lip and didn't even care. "I could kiss you."

"Well, so, when I came back you were gone, and Lyle explained what'd happened. I called him all kinds of dirty names and swore to hate him forever. And—"

I coughed into my fist. "Ahh-bullshit!" Trying to be funny had a good deal of physical pain to it. "Like you said, it's over. You temporarily lost faith in me and thought I was crazy. Then something happened that changed your opinion so you saved my life. Let's just accept what happened and move on."

She smirked. "Fair enough. You're right. Though I really did dump the Eight-Ball for the reasons I said. I guess I just had this notion that a person like Marva DeLonghi would be a big problem with a thing like the Eight-Ball."

I thought she was going to have a coronary when I told her who the 8 Ball belonged to. "I can't imagine."

"Right?" The driver exited the interstate for downtown Lincoln.

"Well, so, Lyle said your purse was part of an open investigation and needed to be submitted to the department. I gave it over, and he looked through it and asked if that was it. I think I knew then I'd done the right thing, and it made me wonder about Lyle."

I asked if Debbie could help me sit up more. We abandoned the idea when my arm spontaneously burst into flames. I cursed. Debbie apologized. I focused on my breathing until I felt something other than pain. "So they've got my phone, a tampon, and my lip gloss?"

Debbie smiled. "You're curiously optimistic for having been subjected to the inquisition."

I scratched behind my left ear. "I'm still vertical." Debbie laughed. I was laying down. "Metaphorically."

"That still doesn't explain how you got from questioning Lyle to getting back to the van and making fast friends with the Eight-Ball."

Debbie's eyes went wide. "It's not my friend. Oh, no. Thing's effing crazy. But to answer your question, when I got back to the van, the window was busted in and everything had been cleared out."

"The Eight-Ball?"

"Everything."

"What? Who? How'd you get it back?"

Debbie looked at her wrist where a watch would've been, but like us all, she didn't wear one. "You and your questions. There's a guy I know in German Town who works at Gerda's Bakery over on the restaurant side, and he tends to know things."

"Things?"

"Important things."

"Okay?"

"I'll tell you the whole story another time." Debbie swatted at my curiosity like a bothersome fly. "It was a couple of guys. They were up to no good. Made trouble. We took care of it."

I couldn't believe my ears. "You *took* care of it?"

"We're here aren't we?"

How do you even respond to such a thing? "So you get the Eight-Ball back. And?"

"And as the night progressed, I kept thinking about Suzie and the more I did, the more I didn't like where the evidence around her murder pointed, so I made a pact with myself if I asked the Eight-Ball a question no matter what it said, I'd still make you get rid of it the first chance I could."

I felt like this was a story about someone else. "What did it say?"

The driver parked out front of a house in a neighborhood. Debbie had locked onto me like a missile. "I can't forget its reply."

She held a beat. I wanted a cigarette. "Don't keep me waiting."

"It said, I swear, it did. It said, *Official? LOL. No way!!! Hahahaha.*"

"Of course it did." The 8 Ball thought our lives were a joke. "So you asked it where I was, but how'd you find all the firepower?"

Debbie smiled. It was the first time I'd seen her self-satisfied, and I kind of liked it. She pushed her glasses up the bridge of her nose. "When I asked it where you were, it said you were surrounded by armed police officers who'd open fire at anyone who approached, and when I asked where those officers were, it provided an address." She narrowed her eyes in thought. "You know, the—" she lowered her voice to a whisper—"the Eight-Ball is mega creepy."

I was just coming to appreciate how creepy it was. "All right, cut to the chase. You're boring me with all the details."

Debbie looked hurt. I told her I was joshing with her. She doubted that, I could see. "Once I knew where you were, I figured I'd need help so I asked the Eight-Ball who'd have no issues going against corrupt cops in a mission to rescue you, and that's when Phillip came up so I called him and he said he'd be more than happy to help."

"Phillip? Is that your German friend?"

Debbie laughed. "Maybe you're more roughed up that I thought." She massaged the webbing between thumb and forefinger. "You know? Ruskov."

Oof, my life was going to cost a fortune. "How could you afford that?"

Debbie said Phillip called himself my friend. "He agreed to do it as a favor."

Until your blood has actually done it, you don't fully appreciate the phrase blood running cold, but at that moment it did, and I can promise it's best to avoid it. I pointed with my eyes to the driver. "Wait, wait. You let *him* do *us* a favor?"

Debbie nodded, smiling big. "These are his guys."

"Welp." I closed my eyes. "Turns out you should've let me die back there."

Debbie examined me. "That's not funny."

"Good, because I'm not joking." I opened my eyes. The driver sat quiet and attentive. He wore a slight smirk, and he held my gaze with pride. I spoke to Debbie, but held the driver's gaze. "He's not someone you want to owe."

Debbie scrunched up her face. "But you said he was a life saver when you went to court against Magnus."

"I was doing him a favor." I shivered with pained anticipation. "That's the only way it works with Ruskov. You do him favors and he gives rewards. Occasionally, I'll ask him for opinions if I'm dealing with really bad people, because Ruskov has a lot of personal experience in that area, but you never let him do anything for you without first agreeing on a fee."

Debbie remained breezy. "Fine. So then let's pay him. I'm sure—"

"It's too late. He's already performed the act. Now any money we give him will be a pointless donation."

"I'm sure he'd underst—"

"He won't."

Debbie gave an exasperated sigh. "Would you really have rather I let you die back there?"

I thought about it. The driver made a show of unlocking the doors. He cleared his throat. "Is doctor."

Ruskov had prepared for everything. A private physician so I could avoid answering questions about my injuries and keep my name out of the public, where Marva would be on to me. In for a penny in for a pound, they say. "Well, I guess let's get me sewn up then."

47

AN HOUR LATER THE DOCTOR HAD SET MY ELBOW, CAST IT, booted my foot, fished the bullet from my arm, sewed it, stitched two separate cuts in my brows, and dressed the fingers on my right hand. The pain when he disinfected the nailbeds rivaled the nailectomy itself. I left with a bottle of oxy and a script for refills, but what I really wanted was a jug of Magdalene and a pack of smokes. The doctor gave me the name of a dentist who could get me implants and an optometrist to check if my retina was detached. I guess when you have a lot of blood in your eyeball, it's cause for concern.

The Savana was parked in the driveway waiting for us. I hobbled toward the passenger side and told Debbie to find the closest c-store. While she buckled, I nicked her phone and dialed Ruskov. While the phone rang, I asked how she'd gotten Ruskov's number in the first place. She said the 8 Ball knew it. "Now that's creepy."

On the last ring, the call connected. "Lupnachenka!"

"How'd you know it was me?"

"I can always feel who is it that calls by the way the phone is ring in my hand."

There was no way that could be true, but there also wasn't a better explanation. "I don't suppose you'd take my money after the fact and call my little rescue mission a paid job?"

"Luluchevna, no, no! I have made want to giving favor for you many long year."

Did he purposely string nonsense words together? "But I didn't ask."

"In heart of yours you are knowing otherwise."

I felt my spirit melting. "Nope...I'm pretty sure my heart knows no such thing."

"I cannot make you to seeing truth, Luciachevka, but it is change nothing. You and the lady friend are to me indebted."

"There's got to be another way."

Ruskov sighed heavily into the phone. "Why does working with Philipe bring such upsetness to my Lulu?"

"Because I know what happens to people who owe you."

"I am nothing but kind, Luluchek."

"You don't seriously think I haven't heard about Carl Vinton, or Allen Paige, or Sally Mullak, or—"

"Okay. Yes. You are right. Some people are not grateful to Philipe, and that can cause frictions." He'd dropped some of the thicker Russian affectation in acknowledging the fates of those he'd done favors for.

"Maybe you ask too much."

"I have business to run." His voice grew edged with anger.

There was a risk pushing him, but I decided to take it. "Look, I already paid you for something you never delivered. And just who the fuck is At-Truthy-Mia and who said you could do that?"

"You wanted Marva DeLonghi smeared, and I blyat' isportil yeye."

His affectation had disappeared then morphed into Russian. If that wasn't a sign I'd pushed far enough, what would be? I pressed my shoulders into my seat's padding. "I wanted proof Marva had committed felonies so I could show Lyle who he was working for."

"And how did that work out for you?"

I needed a cigarette more than breath so I muted my phone as Debbie pulled into the Kum & Go parking lot and asked her for two packs and a handle of Magdalene. She nodded. I unmuted my phone. How did that work out for me? I can't tell you that because you went and fucked up my plans."

There was muted laughter. "Mr. Kurfutchik knows does he not?"

I felt deflated. "But not the way I'd planned on telling him, so it doesn't count. You made me look like a jealous, petty, coward who cares less about people's wellbeing and more about hurting a woman I'm angry at, like some kind of personal grudge when it could've been so much more!"

Ruskov must've sensed I was off balance because he let me cook a little. My mind spun. I was about to rant, just to fill the silence when he cleared his throat. "I had for you kept back the best part, but now I am not being sure you deserve."

The return of his thicker accent suggested my pressure had paid off. "I'm all ears."

"I am not sure you are deserve knowing."

"You can't keep it back. Save us both a phone call. Come on. Cough it up."

Debbie returned and I tore into the cigarettes, peeling the cellophane off and opening the clamshell. I plucked a filter between my lips and dug for the lighter in the glove box. Smoke was salvation. Debbie asked where to, and I told her the office.

Ruskov chuckled, which is something he rarely did. "Well, Luluchik. For you, I will forgive. Please you are to enjoy this." It turned out one of the documents on Brian Burnitt's tablet was a direct email from Marva DeLonghi promising to have her people plant false evidence of corruption in the offices of The Society of Grassland Protection of Illinois so that Burnitt's leading competitor would be removed, paving his way to a cabinet seat for the United States president if he delivered on his promised vote tally.

I told Ruskov to send the document. He said he just had. I told him we'd be in touch. He said he knew. I didn't like it, but I couldn't undo Debbie's doing. After I hung up, I opened my bottle and drank to catch up on lost time. Debbie asked if I knew about the office.

"You know." I capped the bottle and lit a cigarette. "With friends like the Eight-Ball who needs Marva DeLonghi?"

48

From floor to ceiling, the office had been ransacked: couch cushions sliced, stuffing discarded everywhere, desk overturned, chair gutted and tossed aside, walls sliced and dug into, file cabinet drawers emptied—files strewn about. The laptop was missing, as was the hardline phone. It smelled of garbage and rot as the refrigerator in the kitchenette had been left open and all its contents thrown out. Not a single dish had been spared.

I'd underestimated how badly Marva wanted the 8 Ball, which left me all manner of curious, because why had she rented it out in the first place? Her people had left nothing undisturbed, though a minor miracle gave me some hope. We found the accounting lamp with its green glass shade still intact and no worse for wear when we righted the desk. It was even still plugged in, and the lightbulbs worked.

Debbie offered to help clean, but I said I hadn't had a moment to myself in so long, I forgot what stillness felt like, and plus, I'd be more productive at cleaning by myself. She asked how I meant to get anything done with my bum leg, the shoulder, the hand, my bum head. I said I'd manage and told her to meet me at Leo's at six the next morning. I said whatever we were going to do, we had about another twelve hours before Marva knew all the buckets had been kicked by her collection of crooked cops, so we needed to work fast, but to work fast, I needed rest and relaxation.

Debbie told me to take it easy on the booze, and I asked her what good that would do. She couldn't think of a thing. I thanked her for saving my life and told her I needed the 8 Ball. She asked why we couldn't take it easy and work some straightforward cases for a change. I said detective work was all twists and turns, and she said I was taking her comment too literally. Regardless of what she was hoping for, I said, I needed the 8 Ball.

For a while, after she left, I managed to clean and organize. I got most of the couch cushions restuffed and back in place. I covered them with sheets and towels to hold everything together.

But not long after, I had to pop an oxy and three fingers of bourbon. It's not easy getting around in a boot, and my broken arm throbbed like the postcoital clit with none of the pleasure from the leadup. As the oxy hit my system it felt like the golden hour and my self-consciousness faded to a dull buzz. I grabbed the 8 Ball and lay on the couch. The stupid thing had led me into all kinds of trouble, and I wished I could bury it and be done, but it was my burden, and until I knew how to dispose of it safely I had no choice but to guard it from others. Meanwhile, I figured asking it questions couldn't hurt.

Did it think I'd manage to outsmart Ruskov? It said it wasn't in the habit of answering novel-length questions, but it could say he'd cause me sufficient problems. I didn't care for its reply but that was becoming the norm. I asked what would happen if I posted about Marva's email. It said she would take considerable public criticism. I asked if criticism was the worst of it. It said degrees of badness were relative. I told it I had no issues introducing it to a sledgehammer, if it kept giving evasive replies, especially after what it'd done to me with Lieutenant Bilson. I asked if the criticism would lead to Marva losing her governorship. It said she was just as dangerous outside the governor's mansion. I considered that a bonus answer but in a downer kind of way. I asked what it would take to get Lyle away from Marva. It said as long as she was able to vote Lyle was at risk of following her.

I lit the last cigarette from my pack. The ashtray was stuffed with butts. "What am I supposed to do, then?"

Did you know a perfectly aimed 8mm can cause a person to fall into a coma. You can't vote if you can't wake up!!! ROTFL!!!

"How could I ever know what perfect aim is?"

Go for the left ear, silly!

"Okay. But even then. How would I get close enough with a gun? She's surrounded by security."

Go tomorrow at 3pm.

I smoked my cigarette to the filter. "And what's so special about three o'clock tomorrow?"

In the words of John Hiatt, have a little faith in me, tee-hee!

The night grew late, and then early into the next morning, as I drilled the 8 Ball for answers. Somehow, the one thing I'd meant to do—get sleep—was the thing I neglected. I looked out my window at the dawn. Debbie's Supra was just parking on the street. I lit another cigarette and walked to the window looking out onto the street. When Debbie opened her door I called down to her to get us a table and order me coffee, bacon, eggs and toast.

She waved. I finished smoking and took the 8 Ball once more in my hands. "What are you not telling me about this afternoon with Marva?

If I told you, then I wouldn't not be telling you. Har, har!

I dropped it in my purse, filled my flask, hit the bottle and covered my head with a Cubs hat. There's a certain feeling that comes with resolving to commit violence, and I was glad after breakfast I'd have an hour with my therapist, though I figured he might not enjoy what I had to say about things.

49

Debbie had an easy job. She needed to be at her apartment, with her laptop and phone at the ready. She'd receive a text message from Doctor Shulgin with an email address and a four-digit code. She'd send the email and verify it with the code. And that was it. When we'd had our way with Governor "Jailbird" DeLonghi the hen's would be home to roost. She'd be a lame duck spitting feathers with an albatross around her neck. Her nest would be fouled, her wings would be clipped, her goose would be cooked, and her chances of recovering, well, that wouldn't be anything to crow over.

But there was plenty to do before then.

I parked out front of the clinic, stubbed out my smoke, finished my third flask of the day, and popped a handful of mints, because I knew how my therapist felt about me showing up drunk for our appointment.

It was a windy morning, but the sun felt oppressive already. I wanted to believe I could hold up my end of the day without losing nerve. I popped my shirt collar and made for the entrance. With the walking boot on, I got around like a pirate.

When I opened the door the receptionist looked up to greet me and covered her mouth with her hand. "Lucia, what happened to you?"

She'd always used my name as it was on the intake form, and mispronounced it to boot—Lew-shuh instead of Loose-ee-uh—but I never thought I was a long-term customer, so I didn't bother correcting her. I pushed a bit of hair from in front of my eyes. "Would you believe me if I told you I got my ass kicked by a dwarf?"

She squinted one eye and bit her lower lip. "I don't think I would believe that."

"Well then. I guess I got abducted by a crooked cop and dragged out to the boonies and tortured by a dwarf."

She shook her head. "You have a strange sense of humor, Lucia."

"So I've been told."

She hooked her thumb toward the back of the room. "He's expecting you."

You probably think it was indelicate to cop to how I'd gotten my injuries, but when media coverage did start on the deaths of Bilson, Howard and the rest, a significant portion of the specifics would be held back from the public.

I went down the short corridor and knocked on the office door. "Come in...Luke."

I pushed the door open. He was sitting where he always did, with that box of tissues on his lap, gently crying. I wondered what kind of evolved tear ducts he had that he could weep so freely, not to mention the acute emotional sensitivity. He motioned for me to sit. Most of the time, I'm fine seeing others cry, but on occasion, I get sympathy sadness and it's hard to hold back. I found myself swallowing extra hard to keep from joining the sobfest, but I must've betrayed a chink in my armor, because he offered me a tissue. I grabbed one on my way to the chair.

Dabbing at the corner of my eyes, I thought about the way we all hate to be seen as vulnerable. It takes confidence to shed tears with strangers. I'm not sure that confidence is well-found or useful, but it is to be acknowledged. I balled the tissue in my fist. "Do you think there's any significance to the fact that there's only one space between Therapist and The rapist?"

He adjusted his glasses. "Are you drunk already...this morning? Because that isn't funny...and you should know...better."

"I know it's a bad joke. And yes, I'm drunk. I had a long few days, as

I'm sure you can see, and things are about to get a whole lot better or a whole lot worse so."

He uncapped a pen and opened his notebook. "Will you be honest... with me if I ask... about your injuries?"

"Yes."

"Were you...driving drunk?"

"No."

"Operating...a motor vehicle?"

"No." I scratched my arm. "I was abducted and tortured."

Any doubts he felt, he scratched in his notebook. "For...what?"

I gave him my most significant look, as if to say without saying, don't effing question me. "You remember the Eight-Ball?"

"You mean to tell me...these abductors...caused you great physical harm...over...a clever toy?"

I rolled my eyes. "It's not just a toy. You saw that."

He jotted a note in his notebook. "Why did you not...just give them...what they asked for? Were you afraid?"

His questions were two very different questions and yet I saw in them something I'd neglected during the torture. "I wanted them to know I was stronger than they were."

"That seems to be...a common theme...for you."

I nodded. "And now you're going to tell me that strong-willed is a weakness." I scratched my nose, even though it didn't itch. "But you don't know what it's like to be the only person who gives a shit enough to actually put up a fight. Maybe if you'd ever once in your life put that stupid ass pad of paper down and stopped your teary-eyed bullshit long enough to see some people drink because if they didn't they'd have to face the fact that nobody else is even willing to step up to the starting line, and fuck you if you mention mixing metaphors."

"Hold...please...I need you...to understand...that you are...assuming the role...of persecuted victim. Do you believe...you can be...both victim...and survivor?"

I said it didn't matter what I believed, it mattered that I'd gone through some seriously messed up crap, and I still had holes in my jaw from where two corrupt cops and a sadistic fucking munchkin had worked on my face. If it was all the same to him, I had a few more details to wrap up and I'd be turning in my detective's license and exploring other career fields that had a lower rate of physical violence, like boxing or tackle football.

He told me it seemed like a good idea to explore other career fields, which of course I bristled over since it's one thing to say you want a new gig and another for someone to suggest you aren't cut out for the one you've got. We covered the basic outline of every visit from there. Had I reflected any more on my relationship with alcohol? Nope. Did I see a path forward that didn't include booze? Not at all. Were my feelings toward Lyle at all changed?

The therapist made notes like mad when I said that though my basic feelings for Lyle were unchanged, I no longer saw myself trying to prove I was the better woman or any such nonsense. He tried to keep me there, but I hurried past it instead thanking him for his always-calm, consistently kind, gentle listening. I guess I don't pay compliments too often because my words stopped him short and made him cry like I hadn't seen before, and his tears got me to cry so he had to give me more tissues, and the tissues made me feel better in ways I had never felt better, which caused me to think about my childhood, provoking more tears and more tissues. I said he must go through gobs of tissue boxes and should probably try to get a sponsorship for them or something, and he said he'd been using the same tissue box for fourteen years. I hadn't pegged him for a jokester, but gave a token laugh anyway.

We were a few minutes early to wrap up, but I asked if we could call it because I had a crazy day ahead. If he only knew. He conceded we'd had a good session and told me to book for the next week before I left since he had limited availability. I didn't say I might never see him again, because that's a quick way to extend the session to its full time, but I did want at least a proper farewell. "You're a good therapist, Doctor Matsui, and I appreciate you."

A fresh tear appeared in the corner of his eye, and I made a quick escape before I had any more unwelcome emotions. At the front desk, I slowed just long enough to tell the receptionist to put me down for anything Thursday or Friday and just email me the time. She said something but I didn't slow to hear. I felt absolved and ready for what lay ahead.

50

Sol's Pawn Shops have always rotated billboards advertising to Omaha's downtrodden and needy. They're stocked with stolen laptops, cameras, and jewelry from broken marriages, as well as reasonably priced name brand appliances repoed from evicted apartment tenants—all that and school supplies like AR-15s.

I debated over a pocketknife in the main display case that looked similar to the one I'd loved and lost, which, for the record, it may not be better to lose than to never have had at all because you can't miss what you never had.

Donald finished ringing up a woman who'd bought two full bags of hair products and accessories. He asked if I wanted to buy the knife or make love to it. I said I was in the market for a burner phone. He asked if I meant to make some prank calls. I said anything was possible. He showed me a couple phones. I picked one that came with a black case and three hundred minutes. Donald asked what else I needed. I said I happened to be looking for a reliable handgun.

"I thought you didn't use guns."

You get a reputation, and it's a good thing until you need to change what you're doing. "Times are changing, Don. Wha'd'ya got in the way of eight millimeters?"

"Other than my ex's new boyfriend's prick?"

"Haha. That's a tongue-twister, metaphorically speaking." I snagged my lighter from my pocket and flipped the lid open. "Come on, bud. I'm on a tight schedule today."

He crossed his arms and tilted his head to one side. "You're a buzz kill, you know that?"

"I do what I can."

He pulled a cellphone from his back pocket and punched its screen then held it to his ear. I waited with that awkward sense you get when you feel you're intruding on someone's privacy. A moment later he nodded. "Yeah. Got a chick up here who's looking for a piece." He nodded. "Eight mil." He nodded. "She checks out." Again, he nodded. "I'll send her back."

Donald led me to a small gated office behind the cash registers. A compact lady with crescent moon readers and hair like a drain clog sat behind a well-worn desk. "Donny tells me you're looking to rob a bank."

She kept a straight face and an even posture. I looked behind me like I expected to find a camera recording for some streaming reality show. "Nah. I'm more into political assassinations."

The woman stayed in character for several more moments, just long enough I thought I'd chosen the wrong approach. She broke into a smile that grew until all her front teeth shone bright. "Call me Zanfurdeh."

I offered my hand. "Luke."

"You're brave, Luke."

I could almost believe she'd seen into my heart and perceived my plans. "Probably just stupid."

"Man trouble?"

At first, I didn't follow what she was asking. "Oh, the gun. You could say that. I'm just looking to um, you know—"

"You've got the look of a lady who can handle herself, so it must be some kind of asshole to get those over on you."

Half because of the bourbon, half because of the oxy, and the other half because of my resolve to follow this day through, it took me a minute to understand that *those* referred to the cuts and bruises. "You know I've got a killer hook, but I guess there still ain't nothing wrong with a little self-defense."

"Couldn't've said it better myself." She showed me one handgun at a time until I stopped her and asked which was the best bet for a person who'd never fired a gun. Technically I'd fired guns, but I was, for all intents and purposes, a novice.

She put all of the guns she'd shown me away. Instead she produced one from a locked box in a secret cabinet at her feet. "This one never misses."

"Is it an eight-millimeter?"

She smiled like I'd annoyed her. "Why does the caliber matter?"

I didn't say, *Because a Magic Eight-Ball told me I needed an eight-millimeter to put the governor in a coma.* "My boss told me I have to have an eight-millimeter."

"Then you're in luck."

"I'll take it." I felt a thrill I wouldn't have expected. "Do I get bullets from you or..."

"Do you have a background check with you?"

"Uh." I scratched my head. "Do I need one?"

She nodded. "And you didn't hear this from me, but you can grab a box across the river. My sister works at Bear Arms in Council Bluffs."

I thanked her and told her I was ready to go. She called Donald who came back to collect the gun and walk me up front. He gave me twenty percent off the phone because I'd showed him something he never thought he'd see. I paid and thanked him for the help. He told me to be careful and always lock the gun and to keep it clean and to never point it at anyone unless I meant to shoot him, and if I meant to shoot someone, I better understand bullets didn't give do-overs. I assured him I understood, and I walked out into the world with every intention to point my gun at someone without the safety engaged.

51

I had two hours to get to the capitol, and a lot of shit work ahead. I jumped on 90th toward Papillion, lit a cigarette, and tore open the plastic packaging on my new phone. It felt like they should've had a sell-your-soul-for-easy-set-up option, and I think the only reason I managed not to crash the Savana was because I had to look up at the road to ash my cigarette every few moments so I guess, in a way, you could say smoking saved my life.

When the phone was finally operational, I dug a scrap of paper from the breast pocket in my jacket and dialed the number on it. It rang through to the voicemail, and I left a message. A few minutes later, as I was passing Abelardo's—also known as Lyle's favorite breakfast burrito in town—the phone rang.

"This is Luke."

"Who're you?"

His voice sounded like a caramel lollipop tastes. I moistened my lips and breathed in slowly. "Hello, Doctor Shulgin."

"What do you want?"

My heartrate slowed, but it jarred my ribs with every pump. "Same thing you do."

"I think you have me mistaken for someone else."

"Then you wouldn't mind if I tipped the police to your connection with the flash mobs."

"I have tenure at the university."

People will think of the most irrelevant details in a moment of genuine shock. "Maybe you should've considered that when you started poking the beehive."

"Beehives at least give us honey."

"You know how bad she is, don't you?"

He sighed. "Bad enough, I'm afraid."

I liked him. "But you've never had the kind of concrete proof you'd need to face her publicly."

"And there's my family's safety to think about."

"Of course." I fished the flask from my jacket pocket. "So, here's the deal. I need your help, and I want to give you a document you can share among your network that will ensure the bird falls from her nest. You won't have to come forward yourself, and the document will come from so many sources no one will be able to trace its origin."

"Why?"

"Because we want the same thing like I said."

"But why me?"

"I need a mob, and I need them in—" I pulled my phone away from my face to see the time because the clock on the dashboard had died years ago—"seventy-five minutes at the capitol, on the southeast corner."

He laughed. It was the kind of laugh you'd hear in a gritty fast food ad. "That's impossible."

I turned into a neighborhood. "You have lots of connections and once you let your phone chain know what's to gain, we both know you can do it."

"You don't understand the organization that goes int—"

"Forget the signs and the background music. Just get bodies on the streets and have them chant something simple. I'll take care of the rest."

"How do I know you're not doing something illegal."

"*I'm* doing something illegal so you don't have to."

"That makes me an accomplice."

"You don't know me. There's no evidence you spoke to me on the phone, and this number doesn't exist two hours from now."

"You'll blackmail me."

"I already am, remember. But no. I assure you, my deepest desire is to see Governor DeLonghi plucked and roasted. Nothing would bring me more joy." I lit a cigarette. "Okay, there's one thing, but it can't happen. Anyway." I told him I had a direct email from Marva DeLonghi promising to plant evidence of corruption in the offices of The Society of Grassland Protection of Illinois so Brian Burnitt's leading competitor would be ruined, paving his way to a cabinet seat for the United States president once he delivered on his promised vote block.

Dr. Shulgin asked why any more charges against her were necessary given the voter buying accusations. I asked if he trusted the DA to really do its job and show the voter fraud. He said he understood my point. For a time, his breathing was the only thing letting me know he hadn't disconnected. "Well, miss, seems I have no good choices. You've got me good and cornered. Can I ask, how'd you figure out who I was?"

I could've told him the truth, that his hand-written signs pointed to a person with myopia and Type 2 Diabetes, that his choice of protest music pointed to a man of a certain era, that the wording his protestors used was highly academic, and that the Flying Worm Vintage Clothing boutique had sold a gob of clothing to a man who matched his description and that if he'd wanted to remain anonymous, he should've spread out his purchases to avoid notice, but honestly, if it had been anyone other than me who cared, they'd never have found him. I'm good at what I do. So I lied. "With the help of a little Magic Eight-Ball."

"Yeah. Sure. And a Ouija Board, I bet."

"Nope. I don't believe in that nonsense." I went on with the specifics as I parked out front of a split-level house with cream brick and a bump-out bay window. Only after the doctor provided the requested diversion would he receive a text message with a phone number to call. When he called that number, my friend would take care of the rest.

"I'll have to run it by my wife. She's the rational one between us. Seems I might be better off not compounding my problems by breaking any laws."

My mind raced. Panic crouched nearby. "A good man is hard to find, Doctor, but the life you save may be your own." I disconnected the call, killed the engine, grabbed a box on the passenger seat, and stepped out onto the curb. Leaning against the van, I opened the text message app, typed out an apology for being the kind of person who never listened, who never supported, and who made betrayal the only reasonable option, all of that and a confession, which I ended by expressing that any rational person would be sure to find an excuse to avoid the capitol building that afternoon, and I sent it to the only phone number I'd memorized. Then I dropped the phone on the sidewalk, and crushed it beneath my boot heel.

52

She opened the door just a crack like she had people to fear. I held a box up for her to see. "Mrs. Shotz, this is from your husband." I let her examine it. "He was a colleague of mine, and so I know you didn't always get along, but I also know he thought the world of you. You may hear some things in the coming days that are false, even hurtful, but you have to trust what's inside this box is the real truth."

Mrs. Shotz opened the door so we stood squared off with only the storm-door between us. "What do you mean he *was* a colleague."

Setting the box on the stoop, I backed several steps. Inside the box was ten thousand dollars—all the surplus I'd earned from the cases I'd solved using the Magic 8 Ball, because I figured as much as anything, he'd died on account of the 8 Ball—ten large and a note explaining that Mike had given his life to save mine. I detailed how he'd learned of my abduction and found me, but in trying to save me was shot and killed. "I'm sorry for your loss, ma'am."

53

I parked at the G&G Smokeshop with ten minutes to spare, so I popped in, bought a Cuban Cigar and a pack of Export A's because I was feeling international. Outside, I lit a smoke and started toward the Capitol. I dug the 8 Ball from my purse as I walked, and I shook it for old time's sake. "You're telling me I can just strut across a hundred yards of open lawn and no one's going to notice?"

Chances look good, haha.

I dropped it back in my purse, slung my purse over my shoulder, and hobbled across the road as fast as a couple oxys and a grip of bourbon would allow. The handgun, tucked into my waistband, cut into my hip bone. Sweat beaded my brow though the day was unseasonably cool. I pulled my Cubs hat so low I had to tilt my head up to see ahead. I hopped onto the curb, crossed the sidewalk and began traversing the Capitol lawn. My body tensed with anticipation.

The 8 Ball had its agenda. I had mine. Marva DeLonghi had hers. Lyle Kuputchnik just better not cross my path, which I hoped I'd settled by defying the Magic 8 Ball's plan for him, that I would tell him to meet me across town. I'd seen enough of its games to know there was exactly zero chance the 8 Ball would give me a real plan on how to avoid him, and so I tried the truth because if he knew to stay away, and he was there anyway, I was going to shoot him for his own good, and I'd want him to know I tried to avoid that.

Crossing the lawn felt like the longest ninety seconds of my life. It was the furthest thing from inconspicuous I'd done since running naked through The Slowdown at a Bright Eyes concert on a dare my senior year of high school. And, believe me, I know: thinking of me as a high schooler fractures the brain.

At last, I came to the Capitol steps, which I mounted in a thousand painful motions. Even Oxy doesn't repair a broken leg. Magdalene does allow you to forget the future though, which is when pain comes to haunt.

I buried my hands in my pockets and wondered again what kind of idiot trusted a toy enough to carry a loaded gun into a government building. The main entrance was two doors fashioned from the hearts of gargantuan ash trees. Each door had to have been twenty feet tall and five feet wide. The handles were thick around as my wrists and as long as I stood tall, polished copper. I opened the one to the left and stepped in sure to keep my head down, though I'm unsure if I believed I'd somehow make it through security without showing my face.

But there were no security personnel. The scanner was powered down. Anyone could have walked in uncontested. I had no way to check the time, but figured it was three o'clock and an eerie kind of discomfort settled in my stomach. If I got out of this conundrum, the 8 Ball was going into an incinerator, because no one could be trusted with power like this. Especially not me.

Rather than produce the gun and risk it being seen in a security recording, I hopped the scanner belt and walked into the Capitol lobby without going through the metal detector. The 8 Ball had told me the Governor's office was on the third floor in the east wing. I followed a spiraling staircase up to the second floor. There were no people in sight as if I'd passed out of this world into a dead world—a clean and orderly dead world.

On the second floor, I followed the balcony to a richly carpeted corridor with paisley wallpaper and brass sconces every three paces. All the light fixtures gave the impression the building had a potential for great illumination. I followed the corridor to the very end and used the last doorway to take access stairs up to the third floor. My footsteps echoed barren on the concrete steps.

It occurred to me the absence of people might include the governor. Perhaps the laugh in the 8 Ball's plan was to see me step foot in the governor's office without resistance, but to what end? I opened the door onto the third floor. The quiet held. What was I going to do if I found Marva absent?

According to the 8 Ball, the set of doors to my left were the doors to Marva's office. To know this was itself a kind of violation I found unsavory. Why had it taken this for me to see how dangerous my games had been? I placed one hand on the grip of the gun in my waistband, and I took the door handle with my other hand. If I allowed myself to think too hard on what I was here to do, I would back out.

I opened the door, stepped forward, produced the gun and aimed it at the chair in which Marva DeLonghi sat, as if she had been waiting for me and had cleared the building so we could be alone.

54

"Luke." She pushed her chair back and stood. "There's no need for violence."

Her calm enraged me. "This has all been a game to you." I hated her soft, unblemished face, her piercing brown eyes, the health and volume of her hair. I wanted nothing so badly then as to shoot her between the eyes and destroy a work of art. Death though, is emphasis, which she didn't deserve. Not to mention my life followed hers. "Tell that to Candice Bilson."

"How'd you manage?"

"You aren't surprised to see me."

She took two steps to her right. "Very little surprises me."

My aim followed her. "Don't move."

"You won't shoot me."

I smiled. It felt good to know things she didn't. "If I aim for your left ear you'll finish your life as a vegetable in a hospital bed."

She drew a shape in the air with her index finger that I recognized. "Doesn't that sound romantic?" She winked at me. "Do you think vegetables dream?" She answered her own question. "Of course they do. I sometimes think my life is a dream inside a life I'm living somewhere else. That would explain so much, how I feel I've lived a thousand times a thousand times."

"You're stalling."

She blew me a kiss. "What do I have to stall? I'm just waiting for you to pull the trigger, darling—if you want to, that is."

You could call it jealousy, what I was feeling. Marva DeLonghi behaved so casually, so calm with a gun pointed at her as if she truly couldn't care less. "I'm not sure who I believe, and if you die, I'm a goner—"

"Oh! Is this—" she make smoochy lips—"is this that silly theory Lyle was telling me about? Let me see if I remember. He said you believe your life is—how did he put it? —tied to mine." Mockery dripped from her tongue so thick I could spoon it. "I think that's it. If I live you live and if I die you die. How did you come up with such a strange fantasy? Do you really believe—"

"Shut up!" I waggled the gun barrel. "Shut up, shut up, shut up!" She deserved to be shot, not because she was a corrupt politician, not even because she'd stolen Lyle from me, but because as long as she lived, she'd dispose of any person who came between her and the things she wanted. But for me, killing her wasn't an option, and I hated that Lyle had told her so. It was one thing for the rest of the world to call me crazy and an entirely other for him to believe I was nuts. "I don't know how, and I don't know why, but our lives are all tangled together so I can't kill you, but if you don't die..."

Marva smiled. She seemed happy, even thrilled. "Ransom would be your number one fan."

"Marriage on the rocks?"

"Since the dawn of time, sweetie-pie."

I longed to shoot her smug little face, and I knew I could. She'd fall into a coma, sure as the sun would set and rise, because the 8 Ball told me so, but following instructions hadn't worked so well for me where it was concerned, not in the long run, so I obeyed my instinct, because it had done right by me in the past. "You know what?"

Her pleasure challenged me. "Tell me?"

I fumbled with my bad hand in the pocket of my jacket and snatched the flask. "You lose, and I just wanted to look you in the eye and say I win. I win. You lose. Eat shit. You sent your goons after me, and I survived. You underestimated me, and I'm going to sleep like a queen knowing I'm the disease that rotted your world."

She swatted at the air. "Get over yourself. If you don't shoot me, I've already doused the voter buying accusations. Mwah. Kiss it goodbye. I saw you coming from a mile away."

Now it was my turn to play calm and collected. "I figured you would, but you'll have a harder time slithering out of the report in tomorrow's paper that shows you offered Keegan Smith a cabinet position with the president in exchange—"

"You!" Marva made claws of her hands and fangs of her teeth. If I believed in horror stories, I'd have said a monster lived within her skin suit.

"Thought you'd like that. I bet you'll be even happier to know it was your Eight-Ball that told me how to play it." I kept the gun aimed.

"You think I don't know that?" She tapped the side of her head with her index finger. "But the real question is, have you realized yet that for every act of help it gives you—"

"It takes a shit of equal or greater value on my head?" I nodded. "Yup." I felt a bit of a thrill. "I'm pretty sure I have it to thank for the work you your friend, The Professional. The fact that you work with those kind of people..."

She started around the desk, and I backed into a wall made of human flesh. I turned. Broad-Clean stood between me and the stairwell. "Fancy seeing you."

"Shall I kill her, Ma'am?"

"Get the Eight-Ball first."

I looked into her eyes. Curiosity overwhelmed everything else. "Why did you rent it out in the first place?"

"Why not? Because it's fun to see people thinking they've won some cosmic jackpot only to have their world crumble." She smiled as a hand clamped around my wrist holding the gun. "There's more to it, but we're short on time and it's a long, long story."

Large men are the easiest to overcome because they have the least concern of resistance. I used my cast as a bat and clubbed his cheek. He released my arm and stumbled back.

With determination, I turned and ran for the stairway, discharging a shot from the gun to awaken anyone nearby. It was a case where I preferred either escape or a public capture. I scampered into the stairwell and started down.

As I'd hoped, when I came out onto the second-floor, the shot had brought a handful of Capitol employees out from behind closed doors, which if you know anything about active shooters is the worst possible response, but in a way, it makes you feel good knowing there's still a lot of us who aren't so shaped by gun violence we know how to respond in crisis.

Haste proved much more challenging than I'd expected, and I know Broad-Clean would catch me, barring a miracle. And it was there, crossing the regal carpeting of the second floor common inside the state capitol that my brain chose to ask the obvious but untimely questions like *why?* and *what's the point?* or *what did I gain?* Then the biggies like *was the fucking gun really necessary?* and *how many cameras got a good enough shot of me to pull a positive ID?* those and a dozen others. I think I'd really believed right up until the moment I faced off with Marva that I was going to shoot her. The only question I'd actually been wrestling with up to then was whether I'd aim for the left ear or the center of her heart.

As I approached the banister overlooking the main floor, two separate voices called for me to stop. I'd tucked my handgun back into my waistband before they'd seen me, but to be careful I raised my hands as if to surrender, the universal sign language for *Don't Shoot*. I kept on moving though, because I had no plans of surrendering.

Marva called for someone to stop me. As I closed on the stairs to the main floor, two security guards at the main entrance looked to see what the commotion was about. I lowered my hands and hopped my ass onto the polished banister. If my childhood meant anything, all those rainy days sliding down the railing in my parent's home would still be with me like riding a bike.

I lifted my legs, and for one terrifying moment, when my jeans seemed to stick rather than slide, I imagined being tackled to the floor and thrown in society's blender, but I leaned back and willed myself an arrow. The tips of Broad-Clean's fingers just grazed the collar of my jacket before I zipped down the railing.

At the last moment, as if I were ten years old and made of rubber again, I hopped off the banister, landed on my good foot and carried forward on my momentum. The two guards at the main security checkpoint had happened on the same plan at the same moment and tripped over each other reaching for me. I skirted past, sounding the metal detector as I hobble-ran to the giant doors. Whoever it was that beckoned me to stop must've felt she had a uniquely persuasive voice. Needless to say, I gave her the bird, raised high overhead, with the hand that had been relieved of its nails.

Everything, though, depended on what awaited me when I threw open the doors. My fate was in the hands of an academic, odds you prefer never to have. I lowered my shoulder into the door, forgetting in the rush, the gunshot wound I'd taken. A checkerboard of deepest black and blinding white filled my vision. Inexplicably, my ears began to ring. I carried forward blind, and so it was my ears that first embraced my fate. "Say goodbye to Governor DeLonghi. We're done with her zoo, tell it to us true!" They weren't exactly rhyming couplets, but the chants sounded like poetry to me.

My sight slowly swam back to clarity, and with it, a swell of gratitude. There had to have been a thousand protestors marching on the Capitol lawn. I dragged my tired body into the throng. A part of me wondered if I should've taken that shot, but the deepest part of me knew I'd chosen wisely.

Only after I'd travelled well into the middle of the crowd did I turn to see if anyone had continued in pursuit. If they had, I couldn't see them. I asked a woman nearby if I could borrow her phone. She considered me skeptically. I was the wrong age and style to be a protestor in this particular crowd, and I wondered how many of the women knew Doctor Shulgin personally. He had charisma and charm.

When the lady decided I was safe enough, she reached into a fanny pack and snagged her phone. I accepted it, and dialed a number I'd written on the back of my wrist.

"Yeller?"

"Deb, it's Lu. Go ahead and send Doctor Shulgin the file." She replied that she already had, since in her estimation whether I made it out or not, the Doctor needed the info, and Marva had to pay. That was a sound agreement, but I gave her grief anyway. I asked her to call me a Lyft. She told me there was an Uber waiting on 13th and L Street.

"That's four blocks from here."

"Time to smoke."

I shook my head. It was almost like she thought about me or something. "They'll never wait."

"He will. I paid him to."

I didn't ask how she managed to do that, but thanked her and disconnected. I thanked the woman for letting me borrow her cell, and scanned the crowd one more time for any security people. My escape plan had come off better than I could have imagined.

By the time I'd walked the four blocks, my foot felt like diced cabbage over an open flame and my shoulder had a throb hotter than daytime soaps. But my blood nicotine serum was copesetic and I had one more oxy in my purse.

The Uber driver drove a Silver Malibu. I felt sorry for him, though it was tough to feel too bad for someone with hair like his. It flowed black and thick enough for two heads. I asked if he drove for Lyft too, and he said he'd given them up after the surge pricing had changed for the bajillionth time. Last I knew Uber was way underpaying drivers, but he said Lyft had been reducing their rates with all kinds of algorithm adjustments while Uber had hiked pay and made the fee schedule super transparent.

Was there ever a company that just wanted to do the right thing and not screw everyone over? He didn't answer but asked if I wanted music. I said I'd prefer not. He took that as a signal I wanted to chat, but I told him I was absolutely fine with friendly silence. He asked what I'd done to myself, and I was thinking perhaps his hearing needed checked.

"What do you mean?"

He pointed to his collar bone. "You're bleeding."

I glanced down. The stitches in my shoulder had broken open. The blood on my jacket was not so bad, but I'd bled a fair amount on my shirt. "Oh, it's nothing. Kinda had a bit of a scuffle with a guy."

He nodded slowly. "Do you need a bandage?"

I shrugged. "I think I'm going to rest." Closing my eyes, I let my mind wander. It was a hummingbird in winter, looking for a smear of vibrant color.

55

Debbie welcomed Dr. Shulgin into our office. She brought him a dish of almonds and two fingers of bourbon. He apologized that his wife couldn't accompany him. Debbie apologized that she had to run. We'd agreed, following the revelation of Marva's election fraud and the media circus circling us all, to spend at least a month working good-old-fashioned infidelity cases. I agreed it was time to rest. To that end, Debbie was meeting with a woman who'd called about her wife. Debbie decided she'd take the call since she'd had less to do with Dr. Shulgin's parts of what many were calling Marvagate. I told her to take the Savana since she was on official business. Who knows why she declined, saying she preferred the Supra, and didn't mind paying her own gas. Her loss.

I produced the cigar I'd bought in Lincoln, and scored it, asking the Doctor if he smoked. He said he'd had to quit, but loved the smell. After I had it lit and chuffing, I leaned back in my new office chair. Debbie had put some essentials on her credit card and said I could hit her back when the insurance claim came through. I felt a strange gratitude my desk lamp had survived the ransacking, though I wished the police had come up with anything conclusive on the burglars.

News still hadn't broken regarding the fates of Lieutenant Bilson and Officer Howard, though both had been reported missing and were the subjects of a citywide search.

I puffed on my cigar. "So, Dr. Shulgin, I've been dying to know. Why did you start the flash mobs?"

He crossed his legs. "You may call me Victor." He made a fist and tapped over his heart twice. "And today we were." He folded his hands atop his knee. "I'll admit, if your friend—"

"We were what?"

He chuckled. "Sorry. Bad pun. Victors. We were victors."

I nodded. "My old partner would've eaten that one up. Go ahead. Sorry. You were saying?"

He uncrossed his legs and shifted his weight. "Right. Where was I? If your friend hadn't sent me the file when she did, my wife and I had decided to stay out of your business, but when we saw how damning the details were, it seemed you'd gone to great troubles in getting them." Marva, Victor said, had been an antagonist to his charity from her days as a socialite when she still hid behind her hotshot husband and the drug research lab.

She called meetings with Victor's opponents to help them contest all of his legal attempts to prevent pollutants from drilling enterprises. He waved his hand in the air. "Nannie always tells me I get too detailed and people's eyes glaze over. The point is, Governor DeLonghi spent enough of her own money opposing good, sound ecological precedents that when she came out as running on an environmental platform, I smelled a rat. Oh, it was a smelly rat, indeed."

He said she hardly hid her disdain for wildlife and clean air and he never thought she'd get anywhere close to winning the Democratic party's nomination, but she had, and before he knew it, she was in office. Ashamed he'd failed to do more when he could've prevented Marva's election, he began working with others in the university and among the nonprofits with interests whom she'd harmed to grow his numbers, and they began the protests. He was appalled that Clean Air Commission of Lincoln and Heartland Game and Wildlife among others had seemingly been hoodwinked by Marva, but after seeing the documents I'd given him, it made sense. "I'm still not sure where this leaves our community, because if the very people you look to on firm environmental policy are the people who can be bought, who can we trust?"

I shaped my cigar ash in the glass ashtray. "There's always going to be people on the take. And there's always going to be people like you. I thought of Suzie. I thought of Fyre. I thought of Mike Shotz. "And some people get dragged in in ways they never expected." I thought of myself. "And some people are so jealous and lovesick they can't tell what's good and what's bad."

Victor cocked his head, narrowed one eye. "Lovesick?"

I told him about Lyle. "And the truth is, I'd've seen none of it if I hadn't been looking for a reason to crush that woman." You can't tell a stranger about the magic of many lives so I had to settle for expressing that I had seen a darkness in Marva very few others picked up on. I think I'd even said that line enough I'd started to believe it, but the day Marva first walked into my life, she had me hooked. I thought she was the victim of a bad turn. Fool me once.

Victor settled back into his chair. "Do you think he loves you?"

I'd expected we'd discuss the financial opportunities surrounding Marva's arrest. It's a strange world where breaking a high-level fraud case can lead to paid media appearances and speaking opportunities. I'd even netted a few offers to join corporate investigation firms. The kind of thing that would put me in the money for five lifetimes. "I doubt he'll ever talk to me again. The last I saw he was at Marva's side when she was cuffed and being taken into police custody."

"Doing his job."

"Exactly."

"Will he be implicated in any of it?"

I poured myself more bourbon. "He had no clue what she was up to." I offered Victor a refill.

"My liver says no." He sipped what he still had and mingled a few nuts with it. "Interesting choice of liquor, you have."

"It's cheap. Lights on fire. I'm a thirsty lady."

He nodded. "Some say Mary Magdalene was a whore. Others that she was Jesus's lover. According to the gospels, the only thing we know without debate is that she was one of a few people who appreciated Jesus enough to visit his tomb." Victor fell silent.

If he meant for me to make some connection between Mary and my stories, it was going over my head, and I said so. "I grew up around the Bible, but I don't really believe it, no offense."

"Imagine being the kind of person who chooses to believe in the resurrection. Not now. Not in these times. Calling yourself a Christian in the world today is no different than calling yourself a vegan. You'll get a few lopsided stares and a few cackles. But when Jesus was alive, if you were found supporting him, it was dangerous, and to claim he'd raised from the dead. Pardon me, but that was lunacy."

"It's still lunacy."

Victor smiled a sly smile. "Maybe so, but not dangerous."

"I'll give you that." I drank off my refill. "Remind me, what does this have to do with Marva?"

"Nothing!" Victor stood. He circled to the back of his chair. "We're talking about love. Love is the crazy thing that can lay dormant for a thousand years and never diminish."

I worried the little bourbon I'd given him was too much. "Oh, yeah. Sure."

He burrowed into me with eyes so intense I looked away. "Does this Lyle love you?"

I thought of him in the hospital bed, lifetimes ago, telling me it was all about me. Death had taken that from him, but I was left with the memory forever. "I think it's possible he could love me."

Victor stood. He turned so he stood in profile to me. "Wait until the dust settles with Marva DeLonghi. If I am astute, I think your friend has remained scarce because he chose her even though you wanted him not to. But if he loves you, and I see in your eyes you know he does, he will come back. Shame is more corrosive than water and we are no limestone to withstand it even a day."

"You have a poetic streak, don't you?"

He clapped. "Don't tell my colleagues in the Fine Arts Department. They'd have me shot before calling my words poetic."

I finished my cigar and butted it in the ashtray. We discussed our thoughts on media appearances, speaking opportunities, and the like. I wanted him to take it all. He accepted, saying he'd never thought of running for office before. "Strike, as they say, while the iron's hot."

There was more, much that bored me, and after a time, I showed him out. He lingered in the doorway. "I'm going to miss the mobs. It was a thrill. I never saw myself as the kind of person who stood against tyranny. And I suspect nothing I'll do will ever feel so...punk rock." He gave a slight bow and retreated down the hallway.

I glanced down the opposite side of the hall. A woman named Willow had been cleaning out Suzie Q.'s shop. They had been friends. I decided to peek in on her. She was packing crystals. "Knock, knock."

Willow looked up, eyes wide. "You startled me." She had a long face.

I raised my hands to signal no threat. "I'm sorry. Just wanted to see how things're going."

"Gosh." Willow wiped at her brow with the front of her wrist. "Suze had a lot of junk. No offense."

"None taken." I could feel in Willow's body language she wanted to work alone. Losing a friend, and in the way that Suzie had been murdered, that would shake a person. It shook me, and so I wanted to offer some words of comfort, but felt stupid trying. "I just...you that, um...to say I'm sorry. Suzie was a really special person." My face felt hot and my hands clammy. "And it was horrible what they...I'm sorry."

Willow nodded. "Thanks."

I wished I'd steered clear. "All right. Well listen, I'm just down the hall if you need any help. I tapped my walking boot. "Don't let this thing fool you. I'm still freakishly strong."

She smiled sadly. "I'll keep that in mind."

I returned to my office. As I heated a pan for eggs and bacon—the hankering had been on me heavy ever since Sandra left Leo's—I lit a cigarette and filled my glass with bourbon. I cracked two eggs into the pan with butter, salt, and pepper. You have to go slow if you want firm whites and runny yolks. Standing over the pan, I had the simplest of ideas. I hobble-jogged out to my desk and snagged my purse from the hook by the door. I dug the 8 Ball out and held it to my face. "Why didn't you tell me you belonged to Marva?"

You never asked. Tee-hee!!!

"Fine. I'm going to melt you down and make you into toothpicks, you smart ass S-O-B."

Stone don't melt, silly. Smirsh!

Something was burning. "Fucking eggs!"

56

I'D SENT SOMEWHERE IN THE NEIGHBORHOOD OF TWENTY texts to Debbie and she hadn't replied. The last had been a joke—*Don't make me hire a P.I. to find a lost P.I.*—a bad joke, but I was starting to feel a little nervous. It would be just our luck that Debbie would take a call from a creep-wad in her first official solo call. I made the rounds reaching out to the area emergency rooms from Bergan and Immanuel to Methodist and Veterans. Nobody had done an intake on her.

Without Shotz in the department, I didn't have a good line with the police. So I called Debbie's apartment manager. He sent someone up to her unit, but nobody answered. I texted Debbie again. *I'm starting to worry about you. If you don't get back to me within the hour, I'm calling the police.* Twenty-four hours wasn't much to stir concern where the cops were concerned, but I wasn't going to sit on my ass and wait around either. I'd file a report and hit the streets, turning over all the leaves.

My phone buzzed. I plucked it off the desk. My breathe caught: *Putch.* I think I'd accepted Lyle would never call again. Dramatic? Try being me, I guess. I went to answer when a text box appeared in my dropdown notifications from Debbie: *Knock knock*

I answered the phone just quick enough to say I'd call right back. "I need to chew Debbie a new one."

"Luke I—"

If I was honest, having a perfect reason to blow Lyle off gave me a thrill. I opened my texts and replied to Debbie. *Where the FUCK have you been?!?*

...

...?

...At the door, silly.

Debbie had a sense of humor, but completely blowing off my concern was out of character for her. I scooted my chair out and set my cigarette in the ashtray. Debbie was going to get a couple pieces of my mind. I'd hardly slid the chain back when the door jarred. "Hold your horses." I slid back the bolt and the door flew open, knocking me off my feet.

Marva DeLonghi, was supposed to be on house arrest, which meant she wasn't supposed to be in my office. I reached for the knife that wasn't at my hip. Marva closed the distance between us. I lifted a foot to deflect her kick.

She had a phone in her gloved hand and held it up to me. Centered on the screen, Debbie sat with her arms behind her back and her back to the wall. Directing me what to say to Debbie, Marva said, "Tell her it turns out my wife was never cheating on me." She wiggled the phone in a screwing motion. "What's that? I don't have a wife? Ransom's high-maintenance if that counts."

I sat up, bracing my weight on my bad hand. "Debbie, you're gonna be okay."

Marva snatched the phone away. "Don't make promises you can't keep." She pocketed the phone, reached into her back pocket and produced a plastic bag. I couldn't make out what was inside, and I wasn't looking too close on account of I figured if I could sweep her legs I could maybe climb on top and put her down for a little nap.

My left leg came in a little. I needed to distract her. "How are you going to explain being out of your house?"

"Don't you want to know what I've got in this bag?"

I had a brief glance. "Not really."

Marva stepped forward. "Look closer."

One good kick, and she'd go down. "I can't see."

She lobbed the bag at me, and out of instinct I made to catch it. I wasn't quick enough and the bag bounced off my chin and fell into my lap. When I saw what was in the bag, I swept it off me like a poisonous spider. It was full of teeth, and they clattered against each other as they dropped to the carpet. When I returned my gaze to Marva, I looked into the barrel of a gun.

She played smug like Beethoven played the Fifth. "See what it is now, honey-baby." I nodded, and she twitched the gun barrel at me. "Up with you." I stood. "Get against the wall."

"What are you planning to do here?"

She got the barrel of the gun so close to my nose the tang of mechanic's oil filled my nostrils. "I'm not going to do anything. See. This gun belongs to your beloved Lyle." She pointed to the bag of teeth. "Those belong to your partner Ms. Lenvil. Lyle's fingerprints're all over the bag and the gun. Imagine how people will talk about him. Such a sick, sadistic murderer." She reached into her front pocket. "It's a shame, really, for a kind man to be ruined because of your selfish, nosy, drunken shenanigan."

You don't expect someone holding a gun to your head to say a word like shenanigans. "Puh-lease! No one's going to believe your head of security just up and—"

"Defended his former boss." She tapped her toe on the carpet. "Got revenge on the two women who were so jealous they'd stop at nothing until they'd framed Governor DeLonghi for election fraud?" She tilted her head and closed one eye. "I think the police'll have this case open and shut before the week ends." She giggled, actually giggled like girls at play with dolls giggle. "Lyle must be halfway to Texas by now, I'd imagine. You should've seen him when I warned him he'd be in prison right along with me for voter fraud. I see why you're so taken by him. He's a kind man, a good man, but a fool. They don't come any more trusting. He made such a great head of security for me because he was so supportively naïve. He believes whatever you say and backs you without question." She took aim. "Now, I'd love to stay and chat, but I'm on a tight deadline. Haha. Dead. Line. Get it?" She looked around. "So here's the last thing, though. You've still got my Eight-Ball, and so what's going to happen is you're going to tell me where it is, and I'm going to let Lyle live. You're dead either way, but he doesn't have to be, if he's smart and lays low, well, he can have a fine life. You should have seen him when I sent him away. He was so grateful for the car and the money."

"There's nothing in it for me to tell you where the Eight-Ball is."

"Did I mention the car has tracking on it?"

"Won't it look kind of strange if you frame the guy and he winds up dead half a country away?"

"Murder-suicide, babe. Happens all the time these days. They'll call you a tragedy, and I'll be out of prison in a few years with a slap on the wrist."

I was about to vent a rush of bravado and anger when the office door swung open. It happened fast enough I thought nothing conscious, except I had a whole lifetime of thoughts in the space of a millisecond. Lyle had a gun and it was aimed at Marva's head. "Shit!" I kicked hard, connecting with Marva's shin. Her leg bent the wrong way, and the crack made my teeth clench and my stomach turn.

At the same time, Lyle's gun fired. The muzzle flash and puff of gunpowder filled the air with cordite fumes. That was followed by a nauseous odor of burnt hair. Marva collapsed to the ground. The side of her hair was smoking. Lyle's bullet had missed her by a literal hair's breadth. I lunged at her as her gun fired. The slug spun me around. It went through my hip, but I hardly felt it.

I fell on Marva and wrestled the gun from her, and I pinned her to the ground and told Lyle I was shot.

"Get off her." He had his gun aimed. I could see it in my mind's eye.

I raised one hand. "Call nine-one-one. I need an ambulance. Don't shoot her. Don't..." My consciousness was slipping..."Don't." I willed myself to focus. "Unless I've lied to you about something, anything, important before." I couldn't find the rest of the words.

57

I LOST A KIDNEY THAT DAY—NEARLY MY LAST LIFE. DEBBIE
had lost all her teeth in the hours prior, or lost is the wrong word. Her
teeth had been forcibly extracted. Marva gained bars, cinderblocks, and
an aluminum toilet. The first time I remember waking, Lyle and Debbie
were both in the room. I thought I was dreaming, because Debbie had a
bright, Hollywood smile. I must've made enough sense when I tried to
talk that she caught my meaning, because she drew her lips back and slid
her teeth out of her mouth. It nauseated me to see, and I coughed bile.

She sucked the teeth into her mouth, apologizing. Lyle said I was
going to be just fine. I wanted to tell him something, but I didn't know
what. Sleep came up around me from all sides, and it tugged, and it
pulled me under.

The next time I woke I felt young and beautiful the way all living
things are when they are grateful to be alive. I asked Lyle why he chose
me in the end. He said he'd tell me when I was better, the whole story.

Getting well from a bullet wound that puts your liver, colon, kidney
and stomach in a blender and stirs them all up is a bit of a journey, I'm
told. I'm told a lot of people don't make it back from that kind of
injury. One of my many doctors told me I must've had something really
important to live for to pull through the way I did.

There was about a month of nights in that hospital bed, and it was summer, full humid, sunset at ten PM, mosquitos in droves when they discharged me. Every doctor, nurse, physical therapist and Chaplin I spoke to told me I was either done with the smoking and drinking or I would waste my miracle recovery.

I lit a cigarette in the Savana from a pack in the glovebox. Debbie was in the driver's seat, Lyle in back. He leaned forward. "So you just want to throw it all away, huh?" He tossed the husk of a grilled corncob out the window and before I could get after him said, "Biodegradable."

"We'll compromise." I turned my head around and soaked Lyle's lanky frame into my soul. "From now on I'll drink Bourbon and water and smoke lights. How's that?"

He smirked, tore a hunk off a loaf of rye and chewed it contemplatively. "Hey. It's your funeral."

58

Marva thought Lyle too one-dimensional. Of that, I was equally guilty. She believed him too loyal. I believed him too blind. In the end, he'd been both and neither. His loyalty to me had never allowed him to settle into Marva's role for him, and he spent his year as head of security noting the different ways Marva acted in contradiction to her claims. Much of it, he said, came down to the "political tango," that thing all politicians do, the one we call lying or gerrymandering, or backroom dealing, the thing that for all its annoyances and eye-rolling really ain't so bad, but some of it was worse.

Regarding me, he was blind enough to believe I'd legitimately lost my way over my anger toward Marva, and blinder still to miss why I hated her—namely, my love for him (a condition I've still not remedied) —but he was perceptive enough to recognize the police never filed my intake report the night Lieutenant Bilson supposedly arrested me. I'm alive to tell this story because he followed up with the OPD the next morning.

Now, Debbie's due credit too, because we wouldn't have made it to the moment when Marva stormed into my office without her, but a lot of good it would've done if Lyle hadn't tried to drop my purse at the precinct the night Bilson took me. The police had no record of my arrest, but he figured that night he'd just beat them in, so he held onto the purse, meaning to take it back the following morning.

Sometime past midnight, he found himself curious about a few details and figured the police wouldn't notice if he had a look around my phone. I used the same password on everything, one Lyle knew. He unlocked my phone and in browsing found the pictures I'd snapped of Broad-Clean whom it turned out was a man named Rex Olister, and not just any man, but a police captain in Lincoln.

Lyle had seen a lot of Rex over the year, and Rex was synonymous with rough dealings. If something shady needed doing, Rex was the man for the job. It tended to be if he knew you, but you didn't know him it meant you were being carted away by paramedics, or sometimes worse. Though, on this note, my lawyer has made it clear I need to distinguish between a certain three law-breaking individuals, Officer Howard, Lieutenant Bilson, and Captain Olister and the Omaha and Lincoln police departments as a whole. The departments themselves have the citizens of their city's best interests firmly at heart. Feel free to message me on Twitter @LukeEMiaPI for a more nuanced perspective. But I think it's fair to say power has a way of empowering those who have it at the expense of those who don't.

I've gotten off track. The point here is, Lyle saw the picture of Rex on my phone, and it recolored a whole lot of claims Marva had made about me. Unfortunately, in regards to *my* claim—the one about having died ten times—that one Lyle considered a metaphorical hyperbole, and so I'd been forced to push Marva out of the path of Lyle's shot to save my life. If you feel a little confused on the whole action, join the club, I donated a kidney to the effort.

What else is there to say? Debbie now collects dentures. She bought a pair of Clark Gable's for seventy-five thousand dollars using the settlement money from Marva's conviction on attempted murder and a half dozen other crimes. My self-consciousness at the one and only tooth I'd loss made me feel guilty.

You couldn't call it reckless spending, not when she used several hundred thousand on my medical bills, and paid my lessons with a concert. Several hundred thousand more to defend Lyle in court against charges he'd aided and abetted a litany of Marva's illegal dealings. In fact, if anything Debbie had used her modest windfall of just under a million bucks to make herself indispensable to our agency. The day she bought our office building, which the former owner called cursed following the ransacking of my office and Suzie's murder, she assured Lyle and I we didn't owe her anything and if we felt she was a poor fit for the business, she understood. Lyle, assured her I would never consider her a bad fit again. Maybe he knew something I didn't. I had gobs of moods to deal with.

You could say I'm relatively assured Debbie is a good fit for our agency business though, since she and I now share Suzie's old shop and studio as a two-bedroom apartment. I sometimes dream of Suzie, as if her ghost lingers. Her murder is still unsolved, actually, as are the murders of Howard, Bilson, Keith Goodman—known to me as The Professional—and Michael Marlowe Shotz.

Realizing Philipe Ruskov had the organizational dexterity to shoot and kill three police officers and wipe the trail clear highlighted the kind of problem he could be to people on the wrong side of his favors. Lucky for us, he had said based on quality work bringing down Governor Marva DeLonghi, he had no sense he'd be calling in any favors, and he probably never would. Yeah, so he didn't put that in writing, but just him saying he figured we were even was a momentous occasion. I dwelled on the idea that we might actually be the first people to settle a favor with the Russian.

Lyle kept his old apartment, and he adopted Boaze kitty. A plumber found my old office cat living between floors while running copper lines for a new sink. He—the cat—had apparently been surviving on a colony of bats like his own personal buffet. Rabies tests came back negative, so all in all, we'd been restored to full strength: Lyle, Debbie, Boaze, Kitty, and me.

Marva DeLonghi was never getting out of jail, and the offices of M&K Detective Agency doing business as L.M.K.P.I had enough cases to keep us busy for all of eternity.

Perhaps the only dark cloud on the horizon was the closing of Leo's Diner. You might say Sandra was the secret heart and soul of the place, or perhaps the owners simply tired of waking so early, but it didn't last three months after she'd gone. Debbie tried to fill the void by cooking bacon and eggs with sourdough toast every morning but whether it was the dishwater coffee or the smell of moldy vinyl booths, the void remained.

It was a cold morning in November when we sat at our dining table with cups of coffee—mine splashed with bourbon—and plates of bacon and eggs, I held the 8 Ball. Lyle had miniature urn he'd bought off Amazon, and a white silk handkerchief. I'd wanted to use the 8 Ball occasionally for the real tough cases, but had been outvoted. Debbie and Lyle said the risk of negative outcomes spilling over onto them was too great, not to mention everyone who received "aid" from the 8 Ball had negative results of some kind. In good conscience we couldn't solve clients' mysteries knowing the solution would backfire on them in potentially life-threatening ways.

The urn was carved of wood with an image of a tree in leaf on its lid. We wrapped the 8 Ball in a silk handkerchief and interred it. Lyle, being the tallest of us, placed it on the top shelf of my walk-in closet, because it was our burden to keep it safe, and they could trust me not to use it, since I'd promised not to. I keep my promises.

ACKNOWLEDGMENTS

It is a pleasure to thank the people and organizations whose encouragement and kind assistance made this writing possible:

Robert Olen Butler whose comments helped me shape a funnier followup to 9Lives. Heather O'Brien for reading this book and offering keen early edits, and plot comments. Ashley, my bride, my first reader, the only person I frequently bark at, and yet...still she supports me. Without Ashley, I tremble to imagine and hope I never must.

Great big thanks for a late proofread by Dr. Shane Simonsen who refused payment. May the universe pay it forward to him. For any laughs, thank J.P. Valliéres, who demanded more humor of my stories. For teaching me the foundations of writing I am grateful to Margaret Lukas, Joseph Salvatore, Samuel Ligon, Gregory Spatz, and Frank Shimerdla. And a special thank you to Xe Sands for taking risk on my books and agreeing to perform the audiobooks in this series. If you love audio, you'll adore her voice. She is the voice of Luke so perfectly.

A handful of local establishments are mentioned throughout the book, but in many ways their existence is fictionalized to suit the needs of the author. For all errors of representation, I take full responsibility. I am saddened to report Leo's Diner did, in fact, close within the past year, may the Fantasy Island never be forgotten.

ABOUT THE AUTHOR

Jody J. Sperling is the author of numerous works of fiction including novels and short stories. He has also published nonfiction. When not writing or reading, Jody can be found recording his podcast, TRBM, a show to connect writers with readers and vise versa. He lives outside Omaha with Ashley and their three boys.

Please leave a rating and review of this book on Amazon or Goodreads, or Facebook whether you loved or hated the story. Reviews are our lifeblood. Click this direct link to the Amazon review form if you read the ebook.

ALSO BY JODY J. SPERLING

The Seven-Figure Marketing Mindset for Novelists

The 9 Lives of Marva DeLonghi

FORTHCOMING – PREORDER NOW

The 24/7 of A Russian Named Ruskov

The 6 Sorrows of Shohei Matsui